Sangu Mandanna is the author of *The Very Secret Society of Irregular Witches*, *Kiki Kallira Breaks a Kingdom*, and other novels about magic, monsters and myths. She lives in Norwich with her husband and kids.

Praise for *The Very Secret Society of Irregular Witches*

'A warm witchy hug of a book'
Tasha Suri, author of *The Jasmine Throne*

'A cozy tale about the powerful alchemy of believing we are worthy of the family we find'
Travis Baldree, author of *Legends and Lattes*

'Witty, witchy and wonderfully romantic . . . will warm your heart with its endearing characters and grumpy-sunshine love story'
India Holton, author of *The Wisteria Society of Lady Scoundrels*

'A perfect comfort read'
Stephanie Burgis, author of *Scales and Sensibility* and *Snowspelled*

'A lighthearted tale of a coven everyone will long to join'
Louisa Morgan, author of *A Secret History of Witches*

'This book is like a warm welcome home'
Library Journal

'This charming romantic fantasy is a gem'
Publishers Weekly

'Like the perfect cup of tea on a rainy day: cosy and comforting, with just the right amount of steam'
Natasha Ngan, *New York Times* bestselling author of *Girls of Paper and Fire*

'This book is as soft and unsubtle as a pile of golden retriever puppies drenched in glitter'
New York Times

'An absolute delight . . . uplifting and comforting'
My Weekly

'The warmest of hugs through a book'
The Fantasy Hive

'A delightful cocoon of magic and humor'
Shelf Awareness

'A delightful feel-good story . . . with the togetherness shared by the kindhearted characters'
Harlequin Junkie

'A magical tale about finding yourself and making a found family'
Kirkus Reviews

'Beautifully written with gentle humor and a lot of heart . . . sweet, heartwarming and whimsical'
The Nerd Daily

'Full of romance and chosen family . . . a healing experience'
Washington Post

'An excellent way to start off witchy season'
BookRiot

'A spellbinding story . . . a real joy to read'
MyWeekly.co.uk

THE VERY
Secret Society
OF
Irregular Witches

SANGU MANDANNA

HODDERSCAPE

First published in Great Britain in 2022 by Hodderscape
An imprint of Hodder & Stoughton
An Hachette UK company

This paperback edition published in 2023

3

A CIP catalogue record for this title is available from the British Library

Paperback ISBN 978 1 399 70989 7
eBook ISBN 978 1 399 70987 3

Printed and bound in Great Britain by Clays Ltd, Elcograf S.p.A.

Hodder & Stoughton policy is to use papers that are natural, renewable and
recyclable products and made from wood grown in sustainable forests. The logging
and manufacturing processes are expected to conform to the environmental
regulations of the country of origin.

Hodder & Stoughton Ltd
Carmelite House
50 Victoria Embankment
London EC4Y 0DZ

www.hodderscape.co.uk

To Steve,
because it's past time I dedicated one of these to you

CHAPTER ONE

The Very Secret Society of Witches met on the third Thursday of every third month, but that was just about the only thing that never changed. They never met in the same place twice; the last meeting, for instance, had been in Belinda Nkala's front room and had involved freshly baked scones, and the one before that had been in the glorious sunshine of Agatha Jones's garden. *This* meeting, on a cold, wet October afternoon, happened to be taking place on a tiny, abandoned pier in the Outer Hebrides.

A pier. In the Outer Hebrides. In *October*.

Of course, they weren't actually called the Very Secret Society of Witches. They weren't called anything at all, which was why Mika Moon had decided to come up with a name for them herself. She had cycled through several alternatives first, like the League of Extraordinary Witches and the Super Secret Society of Witchy Witches. She was still rather fond of the latter.

The ridiculous names were mostly to annoy Primrose, the ancient and very proper head of the group, a position Primrose had presumably bestowed upon herself at some point in the past hundred years or so. (This might have been something of an exaggeration on Mika's part, but it was impossible to tell how old Primrose really was. She wouldn't say.)

Now, huddled as deep into her coat as she could get, Mika rocked impatiently on the balls of her feet as twenty other witches joined her on the pier. This, she supposed, was another thing that almost never changed: their number. Mika was one of the newest additions to the thing-that-was-definitely-not-a-society, and *she'd* been part of it for almost ten years, which meant it had been a very long time since they'd welcomed anyone new. This was not to say that there were only twenty-one adult witches in all of Britain; witches were uncommon, certainly, but Mika knew that there were others out there. Primrose, who had appointed herself the duty of finding and inviting new witches to the not-society, had mentioned that some had turned her down over the years.

Mika found it difficult to believe anyone had been able to resist Primrose's persuasions (which an uncharitable person might say better resembled genteel bullying), but still, it was rather comforting to know that this small, soaked group on the pier wasn't all that was left of them.

Not that their numbers mattered. These meetings were the only time any of them were ever supposed to speak to one another. Primrose Beatrice Everly would never dream of telling anyone how to live their lives (so she said), but she was of the firm opinion that Rules would keep them all safe and so those Rules really ought to be followed. Too much magic left unchecked in one place, she said, would draw attention. For the sake of all of them, they had to lead separate lives. There could be no connection between any of them, no visits, no texts, no emails—nothing, in short, that could lead anybody from one witch to another.

(Primrose, of course, was an exception to the Rules. Mika supposed it was just one of the many privileges of being the oldest, most powerful, and most bossy.)

Consequently, any sense of community and kinship in the group had to be crammed into these short hours once every three months, which made it a very nebulous sense of community indeed.

As rain dripped steadily down from the cold, muddy-grey sky, Primrose cleared her throat. "How are we all, dears?"

"Wet," Mika couldn't resist pointing out.

"Your contribution is noted, thank you, poppet," said Primrose, unperturbed.

"We're pretending to be a book club, Primrose," Mika replied, exasperated. "We don't need to hide in the middle of nowhere! Why couldn't we just meet for a sodding coffee somewhere with central heating?"

"I, for one, think our safety is worth more than our comfort," Primrose said, and then went straight for the jugular. "But, considering the most irregular way you spend your time, dear, I am not in the least surprised that you don't seem to feel the same way."

Mika sighed. She'd walked right into that one.

At thirty-one, she was a rather young witch in a group that mostly skewed older. While she didn't exactly have a handy spreadsheet with each witch's age on it, she was quite sure that she, Hilda Kim, and Sophie Clarke were the only ones this side of forty, so she should perhaps have been a lot more intimidated by Primrose than she actually was. But the truth was, she knew Primrose a lot better than most of the other witches here, and she and Primrose had had a wobbly relationship since before Mika could remember.

The problem, really, was that witches were always orphans. According to Primrose, this was because of a spell that went wrong in some bygone era. Mika was certain this tale was a figment of Primrose's imagination, but she also had no better explanation because the fact remained: when a witch was born, she would find herself orphaned shortly thereafter. It didn't matter where in the world the witch was born, and the cause of death could be anything from innocuous illnesses to everyday accidents, but it was inevitable. Some witches were then raised by grandparents or other relatives and, in time, came to discover the existence of their own magic. All things considered, assuming that they weren't catastrophically reckless with their spellwork, they grew up to lead quite normal lives.

But some witches, like Mika, were the daughters of witches. And some of those witches, like Mika, were also the *granddaughters* of witches. It was unusual, certainly; most witches, only too mindful of the axe over their heads, chose not to have children of their own, but it did sometimes happen.

And so, when Mika Moon, the orphaned child of an orphaned child of an orphaned child, found herself left in the care of an overworked social worker in India in the early nineties, Primrose found her, brought her to England, and deposited her in a perfectly proper, comfortable home with perfectly proper, comfortable nannies.

Mika remembered none of this, of course, but she remembered growing up in the care of nannies and tutors of all genders, ethnicities, and temperaments, each of whom was only permitted to stay for as long as it took to catch a glimpse of something magical (which was not long) before they were replaced. So Mika remembered having plenty to eat, a warm bed, and all the books she could possibly read, but very little in the way of companionship or love.

And she remembered Primrose, who visited from time to time, usually to hire a new caregiver or to remind Mika of the Rules. Mika's feelings about Primrose were, thus, mixed. Primrose had kept her safe, for which she was grateful, but she also resented having such an inconsistent, autocratic figure in her life. Once she reached adulthood, the nannies and tutors went away and Mika declined Primrose's offer to stay. She moved out of the house and, for the past thirteen years, she had more or less only seen Primrose on the third Thursday of every third month.

While it seemed to Mika that she had never done anything Primrose approved of, she had not done anything Primrose especially *disapproved* of, either. At least, not until last year, when Mika had started uploading videos to her social media accounts.

Witchy videos.

Hence their present feud.

For the moment, Primrose seemed to have moved on. "Is anyone having any trouble?" she asked the gathering.

"I'm having a hard time not telling my fiancée the truth about my magic," Hilda Kim offered. "I feel like I'm hiding so much of myself from her, and I hate it."

"You could always try *not* getting married," said Primrose, who felt it was everyone's duty to make sacrifices for the greater good. "And while you ponder that, dear," she went on as Hilda opened her mouth and then shut it again as if she'd thought better of whatever she was about to say, "Is anyone having any *actual* trouble? Any inquisitive neighbours asking too many questions? Any uncontrollable magical outbursts?"

There was a round of shrugs and heads shaking. Primrose shifted her gimlet eyes from one witch to the next, lingering a little too long on Mika. She looked rather disappointed when no one spoke, like she'd been hoping to be able to chastise someone for being careless.

"Then," Primrose continued, an enormous spellbook materialising in her hands, "does anyone have any new spells to share?"

There were a few: a spell for more restful sleep, a potion that would temporarily turn cat fur pink (only cat fur, and only pink), a spell for the finding of a lost thing, and a spell to instantly vanish dark circles under the eyes. (Upon hearing this last one, Primrose, who hoarded her own spells like a dragon hoards gold, looked incredibly annoyed that she hadn't been able to figure it out first.)

When the spellwork part of the meeting was complete, Primrose cleared her throat. "Finally, does anyone have any news they'd like to share?"

"It's okay to say it's time to gossip, Primrose," Mika said merrily. "We all know that's what comes after the spellwork."

"Witches don't *gossip*," sniffed Primrose.

This was patently untrue, however, because gossiping was precisely what they proceeded to do.

"My ex-husband wanted to get back together last week," said Belinda Nkala, who was in her forties and never had time for anyone's nonsense. "When I turned him down, he informed me that I am apparently nothing without him. Then he left," she added

6

calmly, "but I fear he's going to be suffering from an inexplicable itch in his groin for a few weeks."

Several witches laughed, but Primrose set her lips in a thin line. "And have *you* been playing such petty tricks lately, Mika?"

"Oh, for the love of fucking god, Primrose, what does this have to do with me?"

"It's not an unreasonable question, precious. You do like to take risks."

"For the millionth time," Mika said, irked beyond belief, "I post videos online *pretending* to be a witch. It's just a performance." Primrose raised her eyebrows. Mika raised hers right back. "Hundreds of people do the same thing, you know. The whole witch aesthetic is very popular!"

"Witchcore," Hilda said, nodding wisely. "Not quite as popular as cottagecore or fairycore, but it's up there."

Everyone stared at her.

"I didn't know fairies were real!" shouted Agatha Jones, who was almost as old as Primrose and tended to believe all young people needed to be shouted at lest they miss the import of her pronouncements. "Whatever next!"

"You see, Primrose?" said Mika, ignoring this interruption. "People call themselves witches all the time. I'm not putting myself or you or anyone else at risk. Nobody who watches my videos thinks I'm *actually* a witch."

It was unfortunate for Mika, then, that at that precise moment, over five hundred miles away, in a big house in a quiet, windy corner of the Norfolk countryside, a skinny old man in a magnificent rainbow scarf and enormous fluffy slippers was saying exactly the opposite.

"Absolutely not!"

This came from Jamie, the scowling librarian, who was not in fact the skinny old man in the scarf and slippers. That was Ian. And the third person in the library was Lucie, the housekeeper, a chubby, round-cheeked woman in her fifties, who sighed as if she knew exactly how this argument was going to go. (She did know, and she was right.)

Ian smoothed down the tail of his scarf and replied, in the deep voice that had charmed audiences in many a small theatre over his eighty-odd years, "Don't be difficult, dear. It doesn't become you."

Jamie was unmoved by this criticism. "You can't seriously be considering bringing *that*"—and here he jabbed a finger at the dewy, sparkly face on the screen of Ian's phone—"into the house?"

"Why not?" Ian asked.

"Well, for one thing, there's no way she's a real witch," Jamie said irritably. This was not unusual. Most of the things Jamie said were said irritably. "What kind of witch would show off her magic on a platform with millions of viewers?"

Mika would have been immensely gratified to hear this, had she been there, but it looked like her double bluff had not hoodwinked Ian.

"She's a real witch," he insisted.

"How the hell can you possibly know that?"

"I have excellent observation skills. Just watch part of the video." Ian wiggled his phone like he was dangling a lollipop in front of a toddler. "A minute. That's all I ask."

Jamie's glare stayed firmly in place, but he crossed his arms over his chest and leaned back against his desk to look over Ian's shoulder. Gleeful, Ian tapped the screen and the video started to play.

The woman on the screen looked like she was in her late twenties or so, and was pretty in the way most people with bright eyes and merry smiles are pretty. Jamie narrowed his eyes, trying to figure out what had caught Ian's attention. Nothing about the woman seemed out of the ordinary. Her hair was a very dark brown, long and curling loosely around her bare shoulders. Brown eyes, large like a doe's and framed by thick black eyelashes, blinked cheerfully out at them from a dewy face that had been dusted with some sort of sort of shimmery powder, presumably to make her look more otherworldly. She obviously wasn't white, but it was hard to pinpoint her ethnicity beyond that: her skin was a peachy, browny, goldeny *something*, but maybe that was the glitter. The name at the top corner of the video, @MikaMoon, didn't offer any answers, either.

"The secret," she was saying, her smile full of mischief, "is to harvest the moonlight at exactly two minutes past midnight." Her accent was English, but he couldn't pin it down to any one part of the country. She held up a bowl of liquid silver. "Take a tiny spoonful of the harvested moonlight," she went on, stirring the silver substance with a glass spoon that tinkled pleasantly against the sides of the bowl, "and add it to your cauldron."

As she emptied a spoonful of the supposed moonlight into a cauldron, tiny sparkles drifted up from within, dancing in the air like fireflies before fading away.

"And there you have it!" she said triumphantly. "The perfect potion for a wounded heart."

Ian paused the video. Jamie looked at him in confusion. "Was I supposed to be impressed by the special effects she added to the cauldron? The nonsense about a wounded heart?"

Ian scoffed. "The cauldron? No, I'm not interested in the cauldron. *She's* what interests me. Don't you see it? She's practically *aglow* with magic."

At this, Lucie spoke for the first time. "You're using your stage voice, love," she said sensibly, patting Ian's hand. "It never works on Jamie. But," she added, this time to Jamie, "I reckon we should hear Ian out. You know he has a knack for this sort of thing. If he says she's a witch, he's probably right."

"See?" said Ian, looking rather pleased with himself. "She'd be perfect!"

"Ian!" Jamie was incredulous. "Even *if* she's a witch, her face is all over the fucking internet! The risk—"

Rolling his eyes so dramatically that they practically vanished into the back of his head, Ian said, "She has fourteen thousand followers. *I'm* more famous than that and you don't seem to mind *me* being here. Of course," he added quickly, lest Jamie take the opportunity to inform him otherwise, "we'll make it clear that if she does come to stay, neither Nowhere House nor the girls are to appear in her footage in any way."

"And what makes you think this woodland sprite will even *want* to be involved?"

"We won't know until we ask."

Lucie stood, obviously fed up. "A vote is the only way to settle this," she said.

Ian shrugged. "Then we'll need my husband, won't we?"

"Ken must have gotten the girls to bed by now," said Lucie. "I'll fetch him."

"I get the tiebreaker," Jamie reminded them.

"Which is only useful if there's a tie, dear," said Ian.

The library door clattered shut as Lucie left. Gritting his teeth, Jamie stormed up and down the rows of old wooden shelves, putting books back where they belonged. The library at Nowhere House had been built as an extension to the main house fifty or so years ago and it was beautiful, with big windows and a spiral staircase leading up to the second floor, and crammed full of books, manuscripts, and globes. On one side, the windows looked out at the sea below the dunes, and on the other, you could see the trees, swing set, and lavender in the front garden.

It was easily Jamie's favourite place in the world, but just at that moment, he couldn't appreciate it. He was too busy picturing all their secrets coming unburied and all their lives coming undone.

When he returned to the front of the library, Ian was exactly where he'd left him, watching the video again.

"I wish you could see what I see," Ian said a little wistfully. "There's so much magic around her, it's like she's on fire. Like the girls."

Jamie loved Ian dearly, but Christ, it was like the man had wandered straight out of a book of poetry and no one had had the good sense to send him back in.

"As none of the girls look like they're on fire to me, Ian," he replied somewhat acidly, "that's not much help. And like I said, it doesn't matter if she *is* a witch. It's too much of a risk to bring someone new into this."

11

Ian put a hand over Jamie's and held tight. "We have no other ideas, James. We're running out of time."

"Edward will—"

"It's not just Edward," Ian cut him off. "He's absolutely our biggest problem right now, but I'm also thinking about what comes later. After. This is about the rest of the girls' lives, too. Lillian, God love her, has well and truly cocked this up. Is this life really what we want for those beautiful, precious children? They can't go to school. They almost never leave Nowhere House. All they have is each other."

"And us."

"And us." For a moment, the ever-present twinkle in Ian's eyes was gone. He pointed at a photograph propped against a stack of books on Jamie's desk. "Look at us. Even with the best of intentions, we can't give the girls everything they need. I'm eighty-two years old. I know what it is to hide who I am. I know what it's like to live on the edges of society. The girls may always have to keep a part of themselves secret, but I still want them to be able to go out there and *live*. They need someone who knows what that's like, what it is to look like they do and feel like they do, and who can show them how to bravely and safely chart a course across the rest of their lives."

"I know that," Jamie said gruffly. "I *know*, Ian. But that can wait until *after* Edward. And trusting this hypothetical witch to help us is a massive gamble. I'm not so sure it's going to pay off."

"Unless you have a better idea, it's a chance we can't afford *not* to take."

By the time Lucie returned to the library with Ken in tow, the vote wasn't necessary. All that was left to decide was how to convince Mika Moon to come to Nowhere House. (Ian wanted to send her a message that would start with the words *WITCH WANTED*. It would, he felt, set exactly the right tone. The others did not agree.)

And all the way up in Scotland, Mika continued to shiver on a rainy pier, completely unaware of the wrecking ball headed her way.

CHAPTER TWO

W*ITCH WANTED.*

Two weeks later, those were the words that had Mika tapping her fingers nervously on the steering wheel of the Broomstick, her trusty butter-yellow hatchback. She had just driven past the sign that welcomed her to Norfolk, a part of the country she hadn't been to since she'd spent two years as a student at the University of East Anglia, and the satnav stuck to the bottom corner of her windscreen told her she still had about an hour to go.

WITCH WANTED. Live-in tutor wanted for three young witches. Must have nerves of steel. Previous teaching experience not necessary. Witchiness essential.

Fourteen thousand followers weren't very many, really, but it was enough to make sure Mika's social media accounts always had a collection of odd, intrusive, or downright offensive new messages on any given day. She could now tell just by looking at an overview of her inbox, with its previews of each new message, which ones would be worth reading and which ones would not.

A message that began with the words *WITCH WANTED*, presented just like that in all capitals like it was announcing the birth of a new royal baby, should have gone straight into the bin. Mika knew, even as she clicked on the message out of pure curiosity, that it would probably be some kind of invitation to partake in kinky witch sex with the sender.

Imagine her surprise, then, to discover it was, in fact, even weirder than that.

She had found herself reluctantly amused. In spite of her better judgement, she had sent a reply.

Full marks for creativity, but I'm afraid my nerves are made of marshmallow.

As it happens, came the response, almost instantly, **we're desperate enough to take your nerves in whatever state they're in.**

And then, before Mika could scoff or quit the app or do any of the other things she might have been tempted to, a new message appeared. It had a single word.

Please.

Which was how, after asking many more questions and getting very little in the way of actual answers, Mika found herself driving all the way from her flat in Brighton to a place that was, most ominously, named Nowhere House.

All because someone on the internet had good manners.

That, and the fact that her last job had ended in September, the six-month tenancy on her flat was almost up, and as unlikely as it seemed that this was a real, legitimate, not-at-all-hinky offer, she needed a new place to live and the paid work that came with it.

And also maybe, just maybe, because the magic, that song that never left her, had given her a little nudge.

"In a quarter of a mile, turn left," said the satnav.

She had left the big, busy roads behind by now and was on a

country lane, winding through small towns and villages dotted with pubs, schools, and old cottages, each place named something quaint and quintessentially English like Catfield or Hickling. Soon, even these dwindled away, leaving behind the streams and ponds of the Norfolk Broads, endless farmland dotted with sheep, cows, and horses, and, on the horizon, the heathery dunes that lined the coast. It was almost implausibly perfect, an idyllic world painted with the soft gold strokes of the November sun.

As the Broomstick inched closer and closer to the dot on the map that marked the mysterious Nowhere House, the farmland gave way gracefully to woods, with tall, mostly bare trees and blankets of yellow leaves lining each side of the narrow road.

"You have reached your destination."

Mika slowed the car, frowning. She couldn't see anything other than trees, leaves, and the road. Had she been tricked? Was she about to be murdered in the woods like every wide-eyed damsel in every horror movie ever? She tutted disapprovingly.

She double-checked the last texts her mysterious summoner had sent her.

You may have a hard time finding the house. Look very closely.

Okay, then.

After making sure there were no cars behind her, she reversed slowly, peering out of all the windows to make sure she hadn't missed anything along the road.

There. She *had* missed something: a pair of simple iron gates wedged between hedges that were half-hidden by trees. Through the gates, she could see a narrow, pebbled driveway that led past a barn and a cottage, coming to an end in front of a large, gabled house set against an endless pale sky.

Mika turned right and guided the Broomstick up the driveway at a crawl, mindful of the supposed existence of three children, any of whom could no doubt be counted on to run into the driveway with no warning at any given time. But as she passed through the gates, there was an unmistakable crackle in the air around her.

Magic.

It couldn't be. Could it?

Unsettled, Mika wondered if it was too late to turn the car around and flee. She glanced warily ahead at the house at the end of the driveway, but before she could make up her mind, she came level with the barn and cottage. Someone waved wildly at her through the latter's front window.

Pulling the Broomstick as far to the left side of the driveway as she could without actually knocking over the low stone wall that surrounded the cottage, she cut the engine and climbed nervously out of the car. The cottage was adorable: a tiny, storybook piece of perfection with a bright red door, an actual thatched roof, and a small, exquisitely tended front garden set on either side of a path of large flagstones. There was a tiny vegetable patch in one corner of the garden, with a handful of perfectly ripe squashes waiting to be harvested, and Mika spotted an old man kneeling among them.

He stood as Mika stepped on to the path, squinting against the sun. He was bald, Japanese, and in his seventies, dressed in jeans and a striped jumper with a gardening apron over the top, with broad shoulders slightly rounded by age and a warm smile that made it impossible not to smile back.

"You must be Mika," he said, pulling his apron off and wiping his hands on it before holding his right out to her. "Welcome."

"Thank you," said Mika, shaking his hand. It was calloused, very much the hand of a man who did a lot of gardening. "Are you Ian?"

At that, he laughed. Before he could answer, the front door of the cottage banged open and a hurricane in fluffy slippers whirled out.

"*That's* Ian," said the man, patting her on the shoulder with what she suspected might be sympathy. "Good luck."

The cyclone turned out to be an old white man who was so exuberantly energetic that Mika found herself exhausted just looking at him. He was tall and skinny, with a shock of white hair, twinkling blue eyes, and a striped rainbow scarf wrapped around his long neck. Between the scarf and the fluffy slippers were, rather unexpectedly, a very ordinary pair of black trousers and a black jumper.

"Ian Kubo-Hawthorn, at your service," said the cyclone, beaming as he seized Mika in a hug that almost crushed all her bones. His voice was deep and musical, with the kind of crispness that she associated with Shakespearean performers and BBC presenters. "Perhaps you've heard of me?"

"Ian," said the other man.

"You're right, of course, dear," said Ian at once, the words rocketing out at the speed of light. "Now is not the time. You've met Ken, I see," he went on to Mika, jabbing his thumb in the direction of the other man. "I'm his husband. Or he's my husband. I'm not sure which way it goes."

"Both, I think," said Mika.

"Ian and I live here in the cottage," said Ken, his calm, mellow voice an almost comical contrast to Ian's.

"It gives us a bit of privacy," said Ian, winking. "We'd get none of it at the main house, I promise you. But *you*," he added hastily, as if he had just remembered he was supposed to be making the house sound appealing to her, "will have plenty of privacy at the main house if you decide to stay with us."

Mika looked between them, tried valiantly to repress a smile, and said, very firmly, "I'm afraid I'm going to need some answers before I decide *anything*. You were extraordinarily mysterious in my inbox. Deliberately, I suspect."

"There are some things one doesn't want in writing," said Ian unapologetically. His eyes crinkled at the corners. "But we are so very grateful you came all this way just to have this conversation, my dear. You can't imagine how much we need you."

"Do you actually need a live-in tutor?"

"Yes." Ken answered the question before Ian could, possibly (and correctly) guessing that Mika was more likely to believe him. "Come with us to the main house and you'll see why." He draped his apron over the stone wall and started to lead the way up the rest of the driveway.

"Am I okay to park here while we're at the house?"

"Yes, of course," said Ian. "We normally leave our cars in the barn, which you're welcome to do if you move in, but you're fine where you are for now."

Mika glanced back once at the gates, at the spot where she'd felt that peculiar, unlikely crackle of magic. Was she imagining that glimmer of gold dust in the air?

"Mika?"

She looked away quickly, locked the Broomstick, and followed the two men across the smooth pebbles of the driveway.

Ian jabbed his thumb over his shoulder. "Something at the gates caught your eye?"

"Not at all," Mika said at once.

"Hmm," said Ian, sounding amused.

Ken turned to her as she drew up with them. "Do you know anything about Lillian Nowhere?" he asked.

Mika shook her head. "Should I?"

"No, probably not. Lillian is an archaeologist, and the owner of Nowhere House."

"Oh, am I supposed to be meeting her?"

"No, Lillian's away at the moment," Ian told her. "She usually is. She tends to be home for a few weeks, then away for a few months, then back here for a few weeks, and so on. This time, it's an excavation in South America. That's why the house and the children are in our care."

"Yours and Ken's care?" Mika frowned, struggling to believe that they were living in a cottage while three children lived alone in the big house.

"Ours, and Lucie and Jamie's," said Ken. "Lucie has been Lillian's housekeeper and friend for almost thirty years now. Jamie worked at the library when the children first arrived"—Ken gestured at the large extension on the right side of the house—"but now he's more or less the only parent they have. As for Ian and me, I've been Lillian's groundskeeper for over twenty years. Lillian and Ian met at a charity gala back when he was still acting. She hired me and sold us the cottage for almost nothing."

"All of which is relevant backstory to the tale we're about to tell you," Ian assured Mika.

An absent archaeologist, a housekeeper, a librarian, a gardener, a retired actor, and three unlikely witches. As backstories went, it was one of the weirdest Mika had ever heard.

"Who exactly *are* the children?" Mika asked. "I mean, how are they related to any of you?"

"Legally, they're Lillian's adopted wards," said Ian. He paused, and his mouth twisted ruefully as he added, "But she's away so often that Jamie and the rest of us have done the real raising of them."

They had stopped in front of the house while Ken had been speaking, and Mika looked up at it now. It was an old, two-storied structure, with gabled roofs and windows, walls built out of warm, brownish grey brick and covered in vines of flowering ivy, and a merrily smoking chimney. On either side of the faded white front door, which was tucked under eaves, were wide bay windows, both gabled like the windows of the second story. And in front of the house, stretching out on either side of the front path all the way out of sight around the house, were the gardens, which were just as lovely as the tiny garden outside the cottage: oak trees, lavender plants, freshly cut green grass, a swing set, and an entire fenced-off vegetable patch. It looked, frankly, like a small piece of heaven.

"It's beautiful," she said simply.

"Beautiful enough to move in at once?"

"Ian."

Mika bit back another smile and held firm. "I still need my answers. You haven't really explained why you need me."

"Let's go in," said Ken, pushing open the front door.

21

Mika lingered for a moment, her eyes on the garden. She hadn't imagined the magic at the gates. There *was* magic here, she could feel it, and it wasn't just because *she* was here, either.

There couldn't *really* be three young witches living here together, could there?

"Is something the matter?" Ian asked her, rocking excitedly on the balls of his feet.

Mika avoided answering that by asking a question of her own. "How are the lavender plants still in bloom?"

Ian looked a little disappointed, like he'd hoped she might say something else entirely, but Ken smiled. "That has nothing to do with me, I'm afraid. You'll notice a number of unseasonal oddities here."

It's because there's a lot of magic here.

But she couldn't say that. Maybe there really *were* witches here. Or maybe this was something else entirely, some sort of wicked, Gothic trap designed to ensnare reckless, naïve witches who didn't know how to keep their mouths shut. Was that unlikely? Yes. Impossible? No. Either way, this much she did know: she, Ian, and Ken were all dancing around the subject, each trying to figure out how much the other knew, and she couldn't be the one to crack first.

So she pretended to lose interest in the unseasonal lavender, smiled her sunniest smile, and said, "Shall we go in, then?"

Mika had had a number of doubts about the existence of the children, people on the internet not typically being known for their attachment to the truth, but the inside of the house put most of those doubts to rest. It was crammed full to bursting with cheerful armchairs, blankets, plants, and books. The walls were painted a creamy white that was occasionally interrupted by the squiggle of a crayon or a smudge of finger paint; the pairs of trainers, ballet flats, and wellies crammed into an untidy line in the front hallway varied in sizes from pre-schooler to adult; one of the windows had a distinctive smear on it that suggested a child's nose was frequently pressed up against it; and, of course, there were toys all over the place.

A lot of work had obviously been done on the house to keep it clean and warm. New radiators clanked merrily and there was a lit fireplace in the enormous front room. Bright cushions and cosy rugs added life to the soft sofas and armchairs. The stairways, tables, and floorboards were all made of polished, sturdy wood, and there were potted plants in every hallway and room they passed on their way to the very back of the house, where they stopped at last in a rustic, sunlit kitchen.

There were two people in the kitchen: a short, round white woman in her fifties, who Mika presumed was Lucie, and a scowling white man in his mid-thirties, who had to be Jamie. The woman, who was examining a tray of potted herbs with a critical eye, turned as they entered, but the man remained at the open French doors on the other end of the kitchen, his arms crossed over his chest and his scowl pointed out into the back garden.

"Perfect timing! You can start dinner," the woman said to Ian.

"Mika, meet Lucie," said Ian, bounding across the kitchen. "Won't someone put the kettle on while I preheat the oven?"

"Ian's the best cook in the house," Ken said to Mika in an undertone. "But don't tell him I said that. It'll go to his head."

Lucie had pink cheeks, wrinkles clustered almost exclusively around her eyes, brown hair with grey roots, and what looked like a sloppily made paper tiara sitting askew on top of her head. Flicking the switch that would turn the kettle on, she smiled warmly at Mika. "It's lovely to meet you, Mika," she said. "Goodness, your smile is even prettier than it is in your videos!"

"Isn't it just?" Ian said, so proudly that you would have thought he'd had a personal hand in the architecture of Mika's smile.

Mika laughed, then addressed the man by the French doors. "You must be Jamie. Hi."

He turned, his lean shoulders shifting almost grudgingly. He wasn't quite as tall as Ian, so Mika put him at about six feet or so, a full head taller than her. The mortifying phrase *devastatingly handsome* flashed across Mika's brain before she promptly banished it. His brows were dark and straight, his face all hard, angular planes, and he had short, untidy hair somewhere between dark blond and brown, a beard shadow of the same colour, and unsettlingly sharp grey eyes. Considering the scowl, she thought it was downright impolite of him to look as good as he did.

"Jamie Kelly," he said. He had a rough voice, like it had been sandpapered. And was there a bit of Irish in there? "Hello." A perfectly polite reply, but not friendly. Not even a *little* friendly. There was none of the easy warmth and enthusiasm that the others had offered.

Mika refused to take it personally, so she simply smiled at him. "Did you used to live in Belfast?"

"Yes." He didn't smile back.

Mika turned back to Ken, more than ready for the answers she'd been promised. "I should probably mention that the only experience I've ever had working with children is this one time I had to extract a pea out of a toddler's nostril on a train, but I assume that's not the kind of thing you asked me here to do."

"We have most of the children's education covered," Ken explained. "They're homeschooled. They have a few online lessons, but for the most part, we educate them ourselves. Jamie teaches them English and history, Ian teaches them theatre, cooking, and unwise things like how to climb trees, Lucie teaches them maths, and I teach them Japanese, science, gardening, and whatever else I can come up with."

Mika looked from one face to the next, bewildered. It all sounded extraordinarily normal. "It doesn't sound like there's anything left. What do you need a live-in tutor for?"

There was a pause, as if a collective breath was taken, and then Ian said: "To teach them *magic*, of course."

She supposed she shouldn't have been surprised, considering his first communication had very specifically expressed a desire for a witch. "Magic," she said slowly. "You want me to teach them magic."

"Well, you *are* a witch, aren't you?" said Ian, like nothing could be more obvious. "So are they. Ergo, they need you."

"Is this some kind of extracurricular activity where you let the girls decide what they want to be and then teach that?" Mika asked. "So they've decided they want to be witches and you've found someone who posts witchy videos online to humour them?"

Another silence. Lucie and Ken looked uncertain, while Jamie narrowed his eyes. Only Ian remained unfazed. He tsked. "Mika Moon," he said in a grandfatherly tone that left her in no doubt that she was being gently, kindly, told off. "Yours is one of hundreds of accounts that posts witchy videos. I don't want any of those undoubtedly lovely people. I want *you*. Why do you think that is?"

"Proximity?"

"@SilverSpoons lives in Suffolk," said Ian. "*Much* closer than Brighton. She has fifty-three thousand followers to your fourteen thousand. And yet, as you may have observed, she's not here."

A small tremor of unease passed through Mika, but she had spent the best part of thirty-one years learning how to deftly manage exactly this sort of situation, and so she held her ground. "Just to be clear," she said, opening her eyes very wide like she was incredulous, "you've watched my videos and now you think I'm an *actual* witch? With *actual* magic?"

Good God, let it not be so. Primrose would murder her dead.

"Yes," said Ian simply. He stepped up to her, tipping her face up to look him in the eye. His eyes were earnest and kind as they searched hers, begging her to trust him. "Mika. Please."

That *please* again. Fuck's sake.

"Okay," said Mika, taking a step back and switching strategies. "Let's say, hypothetically, that real witches exist. Are you saying the three children living in this house are witches?"

"That is *exactly* what we're telling you."

"Not possible," said Mika.

For one thing, witches were uncommon. It wasn't every day you stumbled upon one, let alone *three*. And for another, three witches living together was absolutely *not* allowed. Primrose was, admittedly, not lord and master of every witch there ever was, but she was old, powerful, and, most importantly, *persuasive*. There was no way she would have permitted three young witches to be raised together in one house.

Unless she didn't know about them.

"Ian," Lucie said uncertainly, "I don't think—"

"Oh, I give up!" Ian interrupted, throwing his hands up in the air. "Skirting around this is excessively exasperating. Mika, I gather you don't want to tell us the truth until *we* tell *you* the truth. Very well. You win."

"Ian—"

"There are three children living in this house," Ian said firmly, looking Mika straight in the eye. "All three of those children are witches. Jamie, Ken, Lucie, and I know they're witches. We know about witches. Lillian told us. Because *she's* a witch."

"*Ian*," Lucie protested.

"Hold on," Mika said, well and truly taken aback. "*Lillian* is a witch? The woman who owns this house? The archaeologist who's never home?"

"The very same."

"And *she* told you about witches?"

Ian nodded enthusiastically. "So you see?"

Mika's thoughts tumbled over each other as she tried to make sense of what she'd stumbled into. It added up, didn't it? There was so much magic here that it *had* to be the home of a witch, or in this case, a number of witches. And what about the magic she'd felt at the gates? What if what she'd really felt was the presence of wards, a set of protective enchantments placed around the house and gardens, hiding the children inside? Mika herself had grown up in Primrose's warded house, a place where spellwork and accidents would go unnoticed by neighbours, passers-by, and even other witches. What if Nowhere House's wards were the reason Primrose didn't know these particular children existed?

Did Primrose know *Lillian* existed? She must. Lillian was very likely one of the witches who had, at some point, declined Primrose's invitation to join the group that was absolutely *not* called the Very Secret Society of Witches.

"You don't believe me," Ian guessed when Mika stayed quiet.

"I don't *not* believe you," Mika replied cautiously.

Brusquely, Jamie said, "Come here."

Unfazed by his tone, Mika crossed the kitchen to the open French doors and stood beside him. Jamie was looking outside again. Mika followed his line of sight into a large, beautiful back garden with a thick hedge around the border and undulating heathery dunes beyond it. A vivid patch of giant sunflowers interrupted the line of the hedge, beside which was a small wooden gate that led, presumably, over the dunes and down the other side to the sea.

Jamie wasn't looking at the gate; he was looking at three girls playing in a tree house at the far end of the garden. Mika squinted to see them better. The oldest, a Black child with long limbs, very dark brown skin, and thick coils of dark hair pulled back into a ponytail, couldn't have been more than ten or eleven years old. She sat with a book on her lap. The other girls looked younger, one with peachy skin and straight, shiny black hair to her shoulders and the other with a messy light brown braid and brownish gold skin more or less the same colour as Mika's.

Mika's heart thumped a little faster. When Ken had told her

that Lillian had adopted the children, she'd assumed that they'd been adopted at the same time from the same family, which would have made it impossible for them to be witches. Unless she was a twin, which was uncommon, a witch almost never had biological sisters who were also witches. It was an inevitable consequence of the whole orphan situation.

But these girls *weren't* related to each other, and, moreover, even from all the way over here, Mika could see the unmistakable gold dust motes of magic around them. The power sang to her, like calling to like, and she had to hold herself very still to resist.

Oh, goodness. They really *were*—

"The oldest is Rosetta," Jamie cut into the tumult of her thoughts, his tone still sharp and suspicious. "She's ten. Lillian found her in London when she was about three months old, after a fire killed her parents. The one with straight black hair is Terracotta. She's eight. Lillian found her in a tiny Vietnamese town when she was a year old. Her parents had died of a fever that decimated half their town, the same fever that was killing her grandmother when Lillian arrived. And the youngest, Altamira, is seven. Lillian found her in the rubble of a Palestinian hospital when she was a few days old."

Mika had mixed feelings about this, not least because it sounded so much like what Primrose had done to her, but now was not the time to have that particular conversation.

"Unusual names," she commented.

The others had come up to the doors, too, so it was Lucie who replied: "Lillian named them all after great archaeological discoveries."

"At least one of them must have already had a name when she found them," Mika pointed out. She had. She didn't know what it was, just that she hadn't been born with the last name Moon. "You said Terracotta was a whole year old when Lillian found her."

"She didn't want anyone to be able to track them down, considering what they are."

"How are you so sure they're witches? It is just because Lillian said so?"

But there was no need for anyone to answer her, for at that exact moment, as Mika watched the three girls in their tree house, she saw the youngest trot over to the rope ladder. The moment the child's foot touched the ladder, it burst into bright green flames.

CHAPTER THREE

esus fucking Christ," said Mika.

"No need to worry," said Ian cheerfully. "This happens at least twice a day. No one ever gets hurt. Not even the ladder."

"That's because it's witchfire," said Mika, who had been swearing because she couldn't believe there really were three small witches hiding in bloody Norfolk, of all places, not because she was afraid for any of those three small witches' lives. "Witchfire only works on cauldrons. It's completely harmless to everything else, though it does burn indefinitely if it isn't properly extinguished. Didn't Lillian tell you this?"

Ken sighed. "I'm afraid Lillian told us very little."

As they watched, the child climbed down the ladder, unaffected by the green flames, her messy braid bouncing in time with each rung. She got to the bottom, picked up a tattered stuffed rabbit that had been lying at the foot of the tall oak tree, and then promptly climbed back up the burning ladder again.

"We have to smother the fire with blankets to put it out," Ian went on, practically quivering with excitement. "It's terribly tedious. I don't suppose you know of a better way?"

As there was very little point in trying to hide her secret now, Mika raised one hand and flicked her fingers like she was trying to snatch a leaf out of the air. The witchfire, recognising the summons of a stronger and bossier entity than itself, came meekly, detaching itself from the rope ladder and vanishing into Mika's closed hand like a puff of smoke.

"Good God," Lucie murmured.

"Hah!" said Ian, triumphantly. "You see why we need you?"

"How did you know?" Mika asked. "Nothing in my videos should have given me away."

Ian lifted his bony shoulders in a shrug. "You had a certain sparkle about you. Like the girls do."

"For what it's worth," Jamie interrupted, as if he could see the dismay in Mika's face, "no one else here noticed a thing."

Still. Maybe it was time to make a graceful exit from the internet.

Mika looked back out at the tree house, where the children were still deeply absorbed in their activities, uninterested in the fact that the witchfire had gone out without any blankets involved. Primrose would have conniptions if she ever found out. She would come here with only the best of intentions and a lifelong commitment to the Rules (or, as she put it, the Greater Good), mow down every objection anyone might offer, and find these children safe, comfortable homes.

Far, far away from one another.

"Too much magic in one place attracts attention," she would say. "Even wards can only hide so much. And attracting attention, as witches have discovered time and time again over the centuries, is dangerous. Alone is how we survive."

But Primrose *didn't* know about the children, and Lillian obviously had matters in hand, so it was a moot point.

"Tea?" Lucie asked Mika, holding out a cup, her face wreathed in a smile. "Come sit down."

"So," Ian said, bouncing eagerly on his own chair. "Will you stay?"

Mika held her cup between her hands, letting the heat seep into her fingers. "I still don't understand. Why do you need *me* to teach the children how to use magic? Hasn't Lillian been teaching them?"

"Lillian has never been home long enough to teach them," Ian said with a snort. Lucie made a protesting sound. "No, Lucie, it has to be said. The fact is, Lillian has always been obsessed with whatever discovery she's chasing. Her passion for her work is wonderful, but it has come at the children's expense. They see her so infrequently that they don't even know her. Moreover, she has a terrible habit of only telling us what she thinks is necessary, so we don't often have the answers the girls need. Believe me when I say you *are* needed, Mika."

"Lillian put warding spells around the house and grounds," Lucie added, sounding torn, like she agreed with Ian but felt disloyal saying so. "Ian paints a one-sided picture of her, but it's important you know that she didn't just abandon us to our own devices. She put protections in place. No one can come to Nowhere House unless they've been invited, and even then the wards make it difficult to find the house. All our post goes in the big mailbox by the front gates. Spells and accidents stay hidden. The girls are safe here."

"Safe, but limited," said Ian.

"The children need to learn how to control the wild, enormous power they possess, Mika," Ken said quietly. "They need someone in their life who understands what they're experiencing."

Mika chose her words with care. "I obviously don't know Lillian, but it's possible that part of the reason she's never here is because she knows it's risky."

"Risky? How?"

"Witches don't— Witches aren't supposed to—" Mika hesitated, somewhat unnerved by the unprecedented experience of not having to lie, and tried again. "Witches don't spend time with other witches."

"Why not?"

"Magic is attracted to the people who can use it. It can also be mischievous. When there's so much of it in one place, it takes a very, very strong will to keep it in line. Accidents are much more likely."

"Surely that's even more of a reason why we need you," Lucie said, her eyes widening in alarm. "Isn't *yours* the strong will that can keep the girls' magic in line? You saw what just happened when Altamira touched the ladder. The girls often have accidents like that."

"She's not saying their magic is out of control because they have no one to keep them in line," Jamie said sharply, his hard, angry eyes on Mika. "She's saying their magic is out of control because they're together."

The others turned anxious eyes to Mika. She didn't flinch. "He's right," she said. "Every witch struggles to control magic as a child, but very few of us lose control as dramatically as Altamira just did. The reason the girls lose control like that so often is because they're together."

"Then it sounds like we found you just in time," said Ian, with admirable bullheadedness. "The girls *are* together, so it seems to me that we can either let things go on as they have been, or we can have a strong adult witch teach them the control they need."

"But I'd be yet another witch in the same place. I'd attract even more magic to this house, and it would be even more difficult to keep it all in check. Lillian's wards might not be able to contain that much power. None of us would be any safer with me here."

"On the contrary, my dear," said Ian. "What isn't safe is three young girls who are afraid of what they are and who don't have any idea how to coexist with their power. It's all very well to make a ladder burst into green flames here in their own back garden, but can you imagine what would happen if they lost control anywhere else? You are able to go where you like and live more or less how you wish, but those three girls can't go anywhere lest they accidentally set something on fire or turn a lamppost into a toad!"

"Lampposts can't be turned into toads," said Mika.

"Which is something none of us knew," Ian promptly replied, "because we are not witches."

"I know it's not ideal," Mika said gently, "but almost all of us grow up in isolation, sequestered from the rest of the world until we come to grips with our magic. And we *do* all come to grips with it, by ourselves, by the time we reach adulthood. Rosetta, Terracotta, and Altamira won't be any different."

Lucie's face was soft with something like pity as she said, "That doesn't sound like any way to spend the most innocent and joyous years of one's life."

"Besides, the girls don't have that kind of time," said Ken. "Edward's our most pressing problem."

Mika put her cup down and looked at the four faces around the table, bewildered. "Who?"

There was a surprised pause. Then, with an expression on his face that may have been guilt, Ian said, "I, er, may not have mentioned one teeny, *tiny* little thing."

Jamie sighed. "For fuck's sake, Ian."

"You didn't tell her about Edward?" Lucie asked Ian accusingly.

"Mika may not have come if I'd told her about Edward!"

"*Ian,*" Ken said. Mika had a feeling that that was a common refrain in this house.

"Who exactly *is* Edward?" she demanded.

Jamie glowered at his teacup. Lucie and Ken seemed just as unhappy with the turn the conversation had taken, and didn't appear to know what to say. Mika's confusion grew. After a moment's pause, Ian let out a mournful sigh. "Edward Foxhaven is Lillian's solicitor. He thinks the sun shines out of her arse, but he loathes the rest of us."

"Why?"

Ian raised an eyebrow. "We're an unconventional household."

"Which part troubles him the most?" Mika asked. "You and Ken? Or the foreign children?"

"It's difficult to say," said Ian, considering. "Jamie's in the running, too, on account of his Northern Irish roots."

"Why hasn't Lillian replaced him?"

"She doesn't see it. He frames it all so politely, so *nicely*. I'm sure you've experienced that kind of thing yourself." She had. "Still, Edward's bigotry hasn't mattered until now. He's only ever been to the house a couple of times, and the children were much littler the last time. But now we're in a pickle because he'll be coming here in December. He has to collect some sensitive documents from Lillian's study."

Mika grimaced. "And you're afraid that when he's here, he'll see the children set a rope ladder on fire."

"Or something of that ilk," said Ian. "If it were a different solicitor, we'd take our chances and hope that if something *did* go wrong, they would behave reasonably. But Edward detests us. If he finds out the girls are witches, he'll be vicious."

"*You* can't collect these documents yourself? And take them to his office?"

"We wouldn't know what we're looking for." Ian made a grumbly noise. "Like I said, Lillian tells us as little as possible. Edward handles her will, her investments, and her stocks. She says these documents are in her study, and that only she and Edward know what they are, so I'm afraid we have no choice but to take her word for it. What this amounts to is, like it or not, Edward is coming here."

"Can't she just come home and sort out these documents herself?" Mika asked, completely flummoxed by Lillian's cavalier attitude. "Then Edward wouldn't need to come here at all."

"That *would* solve the problem, wouldn't it? Unfortunately, Lillian doesn't see it that way. She says she can't possibly leave the excavation at such a delicate time."

"We can't take the girls out for the day, either," Lucie said, correctly guessing Mika's next question. "It's been two years since they last left Nowhere House. Two years since their magic became too unpredictable to risk taking them beyond the wards."

"But all is not lost!" Ian said brightly, abruptly disrupting the sombre mood. "Because *you're* here!"

Mika shook her head. "You're hoping I can teach the girls how to control their magic before Edward's visit, but that's a *big* ask."

"Big, but essential."

"When exactly is he coming?"

"The twenty-sixth of December," said Lucie. "We gave him a number of excuses and insisted we couldn't make it any sooner, but he refused to put it off any later than that."

"Trust him not to have anything better to do on a holiday," Ian grumbled.

The twenty-sixth was five days after the Winter Solstice. "I don't know if that's possible," Mika said bluntly. "That's, what? Six or seven weeks away? They could make a decent start in six weeks, but most of the important stuff will take *years* to master. Altamira's only seven. I was fifteen before I could trust myself not to lose control."

"But if you were here," said Ken, "couldn't you help them stay in control while Edward's in the house? Or keep their power in check if they *do* lose control?"

Mika grimaced. "I've never been in a situation like this before. I don't know anyone who has. I can't make you any promises. I *might* be able to keep all the power in Nowhere House on a leash, but if I can't, the magical outburst will be worse than anything you've seen before. It's a risk to all of us."

There was a moment of quiet. Mika heard a shriek of laughter from a child outside.

Her tea had gone cold.

"I need to think about it," she said, standing up. The whole afternoon had been an enormous shock and she couldn't quite think straight.

"Do you want to meet the girls before you go?" Ken asked gently.

"No," Mika said at once. "It wouldn't be fair to meet them if I decide not to come back."

But when she got back into the Broomstick, she didn't drive away immediately. Hands gripping the wheel very tightly, she found herself thinking not of Primrose's wrath (which would be mighty) or how very dangerous it was to put herself in a position where exposure was so probable (and it was *far* too probable), but of a little girl in a safe, comfortable house with a string of safe, comfortable nannies.

Sometimes, when she looked back on her childhood, Mika had trouble remembering all her nannies and tutors. There had been so very many of them that she would sometimes catch herself forgetting names or struggling to conjure up a face or attaching a memory to the wrong person.

What she *did* remember, in perfect, crystalline detail, was the loneliness. She remembered how much she'd longed for company. A parent, a sister, a friend. Someone who was there because they *wanted* to be and not because they were paid handsomely to be. She remembered how terrifying and exhilarating it had been to turn eighteen, to make her own way into the world, and to do Normal Stuff. She'd gone to university (like a lot of other people), had had sex for the first time after a rowdy night out (like a lot of other people), had lived in eleven different cities (this was maybe less like a lot of other people), had made friends (only briefly, which was probably not like a lot of other people), and had, in short, kept herself busy. And yet, somehow, the loneliness had never gone away.

Maybe that was because the loneliest part of growing up, the part she remembered most vividly, was the one thing that had never changed. Magic. As a child, she had discovered the existence of her magic alone, had been afraid of it and then fallen in love with it alone, and had learned to use and control it alone. Even now, thirteen years into adulthood, she continued to experience the joy and wonder of magic alone.

Apart from when she posted her witchy videos online, of course. *That* was the closest she'd ever gotten to sharing who she really was with anyone.

What wouldn't she have given to have grown up with more?

Before Mika knew what she was doing, she was out of the car and back at the front door of Nowhere House. Ian must have been spying on her (frankly, she'd have been disappointed in him if he hadn't) because the door opened before she could knock on it.

"I'm supposed to be moving out of my flat in a month," she said. "If I come to stay *here*, I'll need to bring all my things."

He squealed like a toddler at a birthday party. "Of course! Anything at all. Everything. All of it!"

"Like my plants."

"We have plenty of space."

"And my dog."

"We love dogs."

"And my koi. With their pond."

Ian cocked his head. "An actual pond?"

Mika waited.

"Of course you can bring your koi and their pond," Ian said. "You can bring a whole bloody lake if you need to!"

"Okay," said Mika, wondering what she'd gotten herself into. "Then I'll be back on Friday."

"You're a gift from the gods, Mika Moon."

"Don't get soppy yet, Ian Kubo-Hawthorn," she replied. "This is either going to be the miracle you hoped for or it's going to be an absolute fucking disaster."

CHAPTER FOUR

Of all the places Mika had ever lived since she'd left Primrose's house (and as she never, ever lived in one place for more than six months, there had been an awful lot of places), the one thing that they all had in common was the sea. From the tiny shed she'd rented from a lovely old couple in Cornwall to the crumbling cottage she'd found in Lancashire, she had let herself be led by what she could see out of the window. If there had been so much as a glimpse of ocean, she'd said yes.

In short, she loved the sea.

(Well, within reason. A bitterly cold, rainy pier in the furthest reaches of the country? No, of that she was decidedly less fond.)

It was the sea she was looking at now, through the window of her flat, as she waited for her kettle to whistle. Nowhere House was in Norfolk and this was Brighton, and yet the sea here was just as it had been there when she'd seen it yesterday: wild, foamy, and a perfect, sparkling, silvery blue.

It didn't matter if she was looking across a garden with a tree house or through the shutters of a tiny shed or out of the window of a slightly grotty flat—the sea was the sea. It frothed and frolicked and had a beastly temper, but Mika would never wake up one day and find it gone. It knew all her secrets. It knew her. And it stayed.

The kettle whistled, but she didn't notice. Instead, she considered the peculiarities of Nowhere House.

By the time she'd gotten back to the flat the previous night and checked her phone, there had been an email from Ian waiting in her inbox. It had included a contract, one that had informed her that she had been hired for a two-week trial period followed by at least six further weeks of unspecified tutoring, would be paid a *very* decent wage, and that her employer was one Ian Kubo-Hawthorn.

Had they told Lillian about her? Would she even care? It seemed unlikely, considering she appeared to be so unconcerned about the home, friends, and children she'd left behind that she couldn't be bothered to fly back from her excavation for a few days and sort out some paperwork.

There were still a number of unanswered questions looming over this whole thing, but none of those questions had stopped Mika from signing the contract and emailing it back. She didn't understand all the peculiarities of Nowhere House, but she did know that there were three young, untrained, uncertain witches there and her doubts could not be allowed to get in the way of her giving them whatever help she could.

Someone knocked at the front door, tugging Mika's attention back to the present, the kettle, and the distressing lack of clean teacups.

"It's open!" she called, embarking on a quest to find *something* one could drink tea out of.

At the sound of her voice, there was a joyous bark from the hallway outside the flat. Then her front door swung open and a big, beautiful golden retriever bounded in. Tail going a mile a minute, the dog made a beeline for the tiny kitchen area and butted her head lovingly against Mika's legs, demanding immediate attention. Mika obliged, crouching to ruffle, nuzzle, kiss, and squish her much-loved companion.

"I missed you, too, Circe," she said. She straightened, grinning at the young man who'd trotted into the flat on Circe's overexcited heels. "How was she?"

"The best pup in all of Brighton, as usual," said Noah, who lived next door. "And as someone who sees just about every ball of fluff in this city on the daily, you know I don't say that lightly."

The day Mika had moved in just five months ago, she'd bumped into Noah in the hallway. He was quite possibly the most beautiful man Mika had ever laid eyes on, all glowy dark skin and laughing brown eyes, and he had seemed so instantly enraptured with her that she had spent five idyllic minutes lost in scandalous fantasies... before discovering that Noah had been admiring Circe, not her. They'd laughed about it and she'd invited him in for tea and now here they were. Noah, a veterinary nurse, was easily Circe's favourite dog-sitter.

"Down, Circe," Mika said now, returning to her doomed quest for a clean cup. Was she going to have to wash one up? She was, wasn't she? Sigh. "Are you staying for tea, Noah?"

"As if I'd ever turn down a cup of your tea," he said, but he sounded distracted. Mika glanced up and saw that he was looking around the flat, his brow furrowed. "Where's all your stuff?"

Mika hated this part, but she'd done it so many times now that the words came easily. "Packed. I'm moving."

Noah blinked. "You what? When?"

"Friday."

"*This* Friday? Why?"

"I have to be somewhere else, so I didn't see any point in putting it off," said Mika. "The flat came furnished, just like yours did, so it hasn't taken me long to pack."

"You have to be somewhere else?" Noah repeated. "Where?"

She stuck as close to the truth as she dared. "I got a job, but it's not in Brighton."

Noah knew she'd been looking for work since her waitressing job at a local café had ended in September. They'd sat together over a number of cups of tea, swapping stories about rejected job applications and rapidly dwindling savings accounts. Mika had even warned him that she probably wouldn't be able to afford to renew her tenancy next month. (It was the truth, but she had decided not to mention the fact that she had never intended to stay on in the first place.)

Poor Noah. He was looking at her in such bewilderment. And why wouldn't he? In his world, people didn't just up and move house with barely any warning. They had employers to give at least a month's notice to, family members popping in to help them pack, and scores of friends to throw them tearful going-away parties. They didn't pack up their possessions in a single morning, say "I'll be off, then," and just *go*.

Noah flung himself into one of the chairs at the chipped, wobbly monstrosity that passed for a table and scratched Circe behind the ears, a rather mournful look on his face. "I'm going to miss this most excellent of dogs," he said. "And you, of course," he added, as something of an afterthought.

Unoffended, because Circe really *was* the most excellent of dogs and absolutely deserved the lion's share of Noah's sorrow, Mika put two freshly washed teacups down on the table and scooped up her jars of tea leaves. "What'll it be today?"

Noah perked up. He studied the labels on the jars, considering the question as if it was of the utmost importance. "Luck," he said after a moment, nodding decisively. "If I'm going to have to deal with a new neighbour, one who may or may not own a clown costume like the man who lived here before you did, I'll need all the luck I can get."

"Good choice," said Mika, who felt that she, too, could use a little luck.

She unscrewed the lid of the jar labelled LUCK, shook a handful of small, dried tea leaves into a teapot, and returned the jar to its place between SLEEPY and WHEN YOUR UTERUS IS UP TO ITS USUAL TRICKS.

Steaming water from the kettle went in over the leaves. As Mika popped the teapot's lid back on with a clink of ceramic, she wondered, like she had a hundred times before, what Noah would say if she told him why he was so fond of her tea. *There's more than just tea in those leaves*, she imagined herself saying. *When you drink it, you take a bit of magic with you for a little while.* Noah, like every neighbour and almost-friend Mika had had before him, didn't believe the jar labelled LUCK would *actually* bring him luck. And if he happened to be particularly lucky after drinking it (which he would be), he would brush that off as a coincidence.

She'd never told him or anyone else the truth. Noah didn't know she was a witch. He didn't know that she slept on her sofa because there was a greenhouse and *pond* in her bedroom, which took up so much space that she'd had to get rid of the bed frame the flat had come with. He didn't know that she moved house every few months, never went back to the same place twice, and had never found somewhere she truly felt at home. She didn't keep these secrets just because of Primrose's Rules, either. After a lifetime of going out of her way to fit in with the people around her, after years of perfecting a nice, normal mask to hide who she really was, she couldn't fathom taking it off.

Pretending to be a witch on the internet? Easy-peasy. Telling someone she was a real witch in real life? Unthinkable.

Noah clinked his teacup against hers. "To your new job," he said. "What will you be doing?"

"Tutoring kids."

"As in teaching?" He looked dubious. "I didn't know you had any teaching experience."

"I don't," Mika admitted.

"You don't sound very sure about this."

"I'm a little nervous," she said truthfully, "but it'll be okay. I can deal with *my* doubts. It's the kids' that might be trickier."

As it happened, *doubt* was not an adequate word for the way Terracotta Nowhere was feeling. And, as Jamie found out that night, she was more than happy to say so.

"Over my dead body," she said.

Jamie raised his eyebrows at the apparition standing over him, unimpressed. "And how do you plan to manifest that grisly outcome?"

"Okay," she said, crossing her arms over her chest and sticking her nose in the air. "We can make it *her* dead body, then. I actually prefer that option. I can murder her in her sleep on her very first night."

"We've talked about this," said Jamie mildly. "Murder can't be your first choice every time you don't like something."

"*You've* talked about it," Terracotta replied. "*I* still think it's a good first choice."

Jamie dropped his head back against the armchair and put an arm over his eyes. Would it do any good to point out to her that it was one o'clock in the morning, he'd been asleep less than an hour, and he was decidedly *not* up to discussing whether or not to violently dispose of the new tutor? No, probably not. Just as it would probably be useless to remind Terracotta that nobody liked being woken in the dead of night by a murderous child in a ghost-white nightgown.

"Jamie," Terracotta persisted. She perched on the arm of his chair, shoving his elbow unceremoniously out of the way.

Resigned, Jamie opened his eyes. He'd fallen asleep reading in the library, like he did quite often, and he'd turned off all the lights except for the wall sconce above him. It was a soft, golden light, but it illuminated the stubborn expression on Terracotta's face perfectly. Even perched precariously as she was, her back was straight and her arms were still tightly crossed. She had a direct, unwavering stare, one that she tended to deploy masterfully to get her way, but Jamie had gotten wise to her tricks a long time ago.

"Give it up, brat," he said, tugging on one of her bare toes. "She's coming, whether you like it or not."

Terracotta scowled, which he had no doubt was supposed to be intimidating but instead had the unfortunate effect of making her face even cuter. Which was something Jamie would never tell her, of course. "Why? We don't need her! *You* don't want her here, either."

He didn't deny it. "Where's this coming from?"

"I don't trust her," she said.

Jamie winced. She sounded so much like him. Had *he* taught her to be mistrustful of everyone and everything? An eight-year-old?

"You don't know her, Terracotta," he said. "Neither do I."

"But you met her, didn't you? When she came here the other day? What was she like?"

He thought somewhat wistfully of Altamira, who asked things like, "Why is the sky blue, Jamie?" and of Rosetta, who was all "But why didn't either Romeo or Juliet even check for a pulse?" and wondered why Terracotta never asked him easy questions.

Mika hadn't been what he'd expected. He'd expected the dewy, glittery, otherworldly sprite from the video, but the woman who had walked into the kitchen had been entirely ordinary. She'd been unmistakably recognisable, with the same tousled dark hair, sunny smile, and long-lashed brown eyes he'd remembered, but there'd been no dew, no glitter, and no soft, soothing chatter about moonlight. She'd been wearing a very ordinary pair of jeans and a very ordinary yellow jumper with a frayed cuff that she'd repeatedly picked at. Really, it had all been so ordinary it had taken Jamie too long to clock the fact that it had been *aggres-*

sively ordinary. So uncompromisingly ordinary that the truth had to be anything but.

Then Ian had blurted out their story and Altamira had set the tree house ladder on fire and the illusion had shattered. In her surprise, Mika had inadvertently given them a glimpse at a braver, more powerful, and less certain version of herself. He still didn't *want* her in their lives, no matter what Ian said, but that had been the moment he'd admitted (silently, and only to himself) that maybe, just maybe, they *needed* her.

"It's complicated," he said out loud.

Terracotta wrinkled her nose. "Grown-ups never say that about *good* things."

Well, she wasn't exactly wrong.

"Here's something I *do* know," Jamie said. "She's coming here to help you, Rosetta, and Altamira, and she's risking just as much in doing that as we are in letting her into our lives. And she's gaining far less than we will. So we don't have to trust her, but I reckon we owe her the benefit of the doubt."

"I'm not making any promises," came the ominous reply.

CHAPTER FIVE

Friday morning saw Mika driving right past the warded gates of Nowhere House once more. Backtracking, she wondered if this was going to happen *every* time.

She guided the Broomstick up the pebbled driveway. This time, she drove past Ian and Ken's cottage, past the barn, and stopped at the bottom of the little path in front of the actual house. Circe, who had spent most of the trip blissfully asleep on the back seat, now stuck her head between the two front seats, licked Mika's ear, and proceeded to give the ivy and gables of Nowhere House a thorough once-over.

"What d'you reckon?" Mika asked her softly. "Does it seem like an okay place to live for a couple of months?"

And after that, she'd do what she always did. She'd go somewhere else, and then somewhere else, and then somewhere else after *that*.

Mika had barely had a chance to turn the ignition off before the front door opened and Ian flung himself down the path, with Lucie, Ken, and two young girls right behind him. Mika's eyes went straight to the children: Rosetta and Altamira, the oldest and the youngest of the three girls. They hung back behind the adults a little, like they were either shy or unsure, but their faces were bright with interest and Altamira couldn't stop bouncing up and down on the balls of her bare feet.

Mika was struck once more by the friendly, welcoming energy of the magic around them and the way it called to her. She could hear its song and she could see the gold dust in their hair, settling on the tips of their noses and curling around their ankles.

But where was the last of the girls? There was no sign of Terracotta, or of prickly, scowling Jamie, either.

"You're early, my dear!" Ian said happily, beaming at her through her open window. "We weren't expecting you until this afternoon. When did you leave Brighton?"

"An hour ago," said Mika.

Lucie and Ken glanced at each other in confusion. Ian screwed his forehead up like he was trying to make the math make sense. "I beg your pardon?"

"The Broomstick can get me places pretty quick," Mika explained. "It's a bit of a risk, so I don't do it very often, but I didn't want Circe and the fish to be stuck in a car for four hours."

"Where," Ian demanded, looking around, "is this broomstick?"

"I call the car the Broomstick."

"Extraordinary," Ken said from behind Ian, patting the bonnet of the yellow hatchback.

"I *am* a witch," Mika reminded them, amused by their astonishment. Had Lillian never showed them the kinds of things witches could do? "Isn't that why I'm here?"

Lucie tutted at Ian. "Let the poor girl out of the car," she said. "You're in the way."

Ian grinned at her as he backed away from her door. "Ready?"

No, Mika was *not* ready. She'd almost hoped Ian would stand by her door and keep her talking until next year.

As she got out of the car, her palms started to sweat and she was abruptly seized by the total conviction that this was, frankly, madness. What was she thinking? These girls were *children*. Meanwhile, she was a barely functioning adult. Was *she* really going to be one of the first grown witches to enter their orbit?

Christ, what if she became their Primrose?

The thought was so horrifying that Mika almost got right back into the Broomstick and bolted, but it was much too late for that.

Then, with impeccable timing, Circe nosed her way past Mika and bounded straight for the two girls. Their faces lit up.

"She's very gentle," Mika assured them. "And she loves a fuss. You're more than welcome to play with her."

Altamira squealed and flung her arms around Circe immediately, and Rosetta knelt on the path to stroke Circe's back with a big, surprised smile on her serious face. Circe let out a contended bark, basking in the attention, and the ice was well and truly broken.

Really, people didn't deserve dogs.

"Her name is Circe," Mika said, and remembered, somewhat belatedly, to add, "and I'm Mika."

Rosetta tore herself away from Circe and politely introduced herself. "And this is Altamira," she went on. "Terracotta is, um, not feeling very well."

"That's a shame," said Mika, privately wondering if Jamie had also been afflicted with this mysterious illness. "I hope she feels better soon."

Satisfied that Mika had conveyed them to a place with excellent new friends, Circe trotted back to Mika's side, tail wagging. Both Rosetta and Altamira took this as an indication that it was safe to come closer.

Mika glanced uncertainly at Ian, Lucie, and Ken, none of whom made the slightest attempt to intervene. She assumed this meant they wanted to let *her* decide how she wanted to handle her relationship with the girls, which was very nice and everything, but she hadn't the faintest idea of what to *do* with children.

Okay, then. Maybe it was best to treat them like they were simply very small adults.

"Do you think you could help me move my stuff into the house?" she asked the girls. "There's a *lot*, I'm afraid."

The girls agreed to this with enthusiasm, possibly because they were just very kind girls or possibly because they were very curious about Mika's possessions. Either suited her just fine.

"Let me get everything out of the car," she went on, "and then you can show me where it all needs to go."

Ian, who was peeking nosily through the car's rear windscreen, ventured an opinion. "It doesn't look like there's much in here, my dear. Where, for instance, is the pond we were promised?"

"Pfft," said Mika, which made Rosetta and Altamira giggle. "I'm a witch! How long do you think my secret would stay secret if anyone could just peek into my car and see all my witchy possessions?"

At which point Mika proceeded to reach into the car and retrieve, in order: two quaint white wheelie suitcases made out of rattan; a scuffed trunk with the words CIRCE'S FAVOURITE THINGS embossed on the leather strap that buckled it shut; a collection of sturdy twigs; a cauldron made out of solid gold; her collection of tea jars; a box of teacups, teapots, homemade jams, dried herbs, and other kitchen bits; a smaller cauldron; thirteen wooden crates packed to the brim with books and potions; a spellbook bursting at the seams; a picnic basket filled with silver spoons, glass droppers, and tiny Pyrex measuring cups; a collapsible greenhouse that *un-*collapsed right there in the middle of the driveway and became an actual, full-size greenhouse crammed with pots, plants, and herbs; a stray sock; and, finally, a pond.

More precisely, a rocky, mossy pond that was a good six feet across on its shortest side, that seemed to be *floating* in the air, and that appeared to have somehow arrived, intact, with water, lily pads, and four koi fish swimming around in it.

Satisfied with a job well done, Mika dusted off her dress and closed the driver's side door of the yellow hatchback with a final click.

"I . . ." This was about as much as Lucie could come up with. "Well, I . . ."

Her eyes very round, seven-year-old Altamira said, with perfect gravity, "That was some excellent Mary Poppins shit right there."

Rosetta gasped. Lucie and Ken turned as one to Ian, who looked more than a little guilty.

And Mika, well, Mika just about died laughing.

"Thank you, Altamira," she said, wiping tears from the corners of her eyes. "It *was* rather impressive, if I do say so myself. Now do you think you could show me where I'm going to be staying?"

Taking one of the wheelie suitcases by the handle, Altamira

turned and trotted cheerfully to the open front door. Mika followed her, two crates of books stacked on top of each other in her arms, with Circe at her heels and Rosetta right behind them with the other suitcase in tow.

Inside, she left her shoes by the front door and let the girls lead her to the stairs, past the big, colourful front room, two closed doors, and the open door to the kitchen. The house was bright and airy and just a tad untidy, just as she remembered it from earlier in the week, and despite its enormous size, she was struck by how snug it felt. How *cosy*. Mika moved house so frequently that she'd never lived anywhere that felt well and truly lived in. She'd lived in Primrose's house for eighteen years, of course, but that didn't count because it had always felt like Primrose's house and, in any case, no one would have ever called it *cosy*.

But Nowhere House, for all that its name conjured up a place that was lonely and rootless, was anything but. It was, in fact, *very* lived in.

Giving the house a closer look than she'd had the opportunity to on her previous visit, Mika noticed that there were dozens of framed photographs on the walls of the girls at various ages from infancy to the present, the girls with one or more of the adults, and even a couple of lovely, chaotic, unstaged pictures of all three girls with all four adults.

Lillian, on the other hand, was barely present. Of the few photographs she *was* in (at least, Mika assumed it was her), she was on the edges, in motion and unclear, as if she hadn't wanted to be included and had tried to get out of the shot at the last minute. Mika, who had not had any luck finding a decent picture of Lillian when she'd Googled her the night before, got the sense of a woman past middle age, with white skin, fair hair, and a slim figure, but that was about it.

"She doesn't like having pictures taken of her," Rosetta explained, correctly interpreting Mika's confusion as they both examined the walls. "She says it's because of what she is."

Mika nodded; she knew of at least two witches in the Society who point-blank refused to allow themselves to be photographed. She didn't understand it, precisely, because it wasn't like witches were ageless, immortal creatures who were afraid someone might dig up an old picture of them from two hundred years ago and expose everything, but it wasn't up to her to quibble with how other witches preserved their secrets.

At the top of the stairs, a large landing branched off into several rooms. There was a single bay window set into the wall opposite the stairs, letting more light in, and Mika looked outside to orient herself. She choked back a giggle when she spotted Ian below, waving his arms slowly over the floating koi pond like he was determined to find the invisible strings holding it up.

"This is my room," Altamira announced proudly, jabbing a finger through the open doorway of one of the rooms leading off the landing. Mika caught a glimpse of a rainbow-patterned play tent, a handheld game console, and an absurd number of stuffed animals before she was swept along to the doorway of the next room, a much more muted, calming room with piles of books everywhere. "This is Rosetta's room. And this one is Terracotta's."

Mika noticed that Terracotta's bold, bright room had Pokémon plushies, an intricate model train, and absolutely no Terracotta. She also noticed the mortified look on Rosetta's face.

"She's not ill at all, is she?" Mika asked.

Cheeks very red, Rosetta shook her head. "She didn't want to come meet you," she admitted. "She told me I could tell you as much, but I didn't want to."

"You were afraid it might upset me," Mika guessed. "That was very kind of you, Rosetta. I promise I'm not upset. Terracotta can meet me whenever she's ready."

"Ahem," Altamira cut in impatiently, her free hand scratching Circe's golden head. "I still haven't shown you the other rooms!"

"Woof," Circe agreed.

"I'm so sorry," said Mika at once. "Go ahead."

"Well, that one is Lucie's room, and that one is Jamie's," Altamira went on importantly. The doors of both rooms were only slightly ajar, so Mika couldn't really see what was inside. "That's the door to the upstairs bathroom. There's another one downstairs. And this," she added, bouncing on the balls of her feet again, "is where you'll be staying!"

The source of Altamira's excitement was a white door at the end of the hallway. She opened it to show them a short flight of stairs, which presumably led up to a loft or attic.

"I'll be in the attic?" Mika asked, thrilled with this turn of events. "I've never lived in an attic before! How *romantic*. A witch in an attic!"

"It doesn't sound romantic to me," said Altamira doubtfully.

But there was a tiny smile on Rosetta's serious face. "I was afraid you might think you'd been relegated to playing the part of the madwoman in the attic," she said to Mika.

"It didn't even cross my mind," said Mika, grinning. "I do appreciate a child with a literary turn of mind, Rosetta!"

With an enthusiastic bark, Circe decided *she* would be the

first to examine their new room and vanished up the stairs. Mika let the girls go next, trailing her suitcases behind them, and she followed with the boxes.

The attic was a big space, *enormous* compared to the spaces she was used to living in. It spanned what must have been half the house, with the ceiling starting high at the peak of the roof and sloping down to the opposite wall. It was spotlessly clean, with polished wooden beams, hardwood floorboards, and walls painted a warm, sunny yellow. A fluffy cream rug covered part of the floor. Whatever had been stored up here before had obviously been moved because there wasn't a single box, cobweb, or dusty treadmill to be seen. Instead, there was a desk, a rocking chair, a chest of drawers, a nightstand, and a double bed made up neatly with crisp white sheets, four pillows, and a duvet printed with a garden of large, clustered white daisies on a yellow background. It was simple, with all the essentials, leaving her plenty of space for her own possessions and the opportunity to decorate however she wanted. The faint scents of paint, new furniture, and citrus cleaning spray lingered, which meant the room must have only been sorted out the previous day, and Mika was touched by how much trouble they'd gone to.

But the real beauty of the attic was the balcony. It was beyond a pair of double-glazed glass doors set into the back wall of the room, both of which had been left wide open to let in the cold and the sharp, sea-salt air. As soon as she saw it, Mika dashed across the attic to get a better look. The balcony was small, with a busy little hive of bees thriving in the gables above and a simple white iron railing around the floorboards. The view was incredible. If she looked left or right, she could see over the trees and along the coast, where the occasional house and boat broke up a landscape of yellowish heathery dunes. Ahead, she could see the back garden, with the glorious sunflowers and the girls' tree house, and then, over the hedge, the wild dunes, the shrubs of vivid blue sea holly, the trail down to the empty white beach, and the sea itself.

"This is perfect," she breathed, turning back to the waiting girls and stopping in her tracks.

Altamira was hovering about a foot off the ground. The gold dust of magic around her was brighter than it had been before. She'd obviously sat down at some point in the past few minutes because she was now floating in a cross-legged position, her chin propped on her hand as she waited impatiently for Mika to finish looking around the room. She didn't seem to have noticed that she'd left the floor behind. Rosetta, also watching Mika, hadn't noticed it, either.

Well, this wasn't good. Mika had been five years old the first time she'd floated off the ground by accident. The next day, she'd had a new nanny and a rare unscheduled visit from Primrose.

It hadn't happened much after that. She'd learned to quickly control *that* particular bit of magical mischief.

She'd also been alone. There had been much less magic around. Altamira, just seven years old, in a house with two other young witches and more magic than Mika had ever seen in one place, didn't stand a chance.

But that was why *she* was here, wasn't it?

"Can you get yourself back down to the floor, Altamira?" Mika asked.

Rosetta turned, surprised. Altamira blinked, looked around, and burst into delighted laughter. "I'm floating! Look, Rosetta!"

"I'm afraid I'm going to have to be very boring and grown-up for a minute," Mika said apologetically. "I know you're having fun, but levitation isn't safe if you can't control it."

Altamira gave her a puzzled look. "You mean because I might fall? But I'm only a little bit off the floor anyway. It won't hurt."

"It's more about whether or not you can get yourself back down. Can you?"

Altamira uncrossed her legs and wiggled them. Nothing. She closed her eyes and screwed her face up, concentrating. Nothing.

"Have you ever cast a spell before?" Mika asked her. "On purpose, I mean?"

"I think so," Altamira replied. "There've been a couple of times, haven't there, Rosetta? Like that time I really wanted a plum off the tree, but it was too high for me to reach, so I just concentrated on it for a minute and wiggled my fingers and *asked* it to fall into my hand. And it did!"

Mika smiled. "That's good! That means you already know that the first thing any good spell needs is intent. You want something, so you figure out a way to make it happen. In your case, you wanted the plum, but it wouldn't have been enough to just look at the plum and think *I want it.* A spell needs the *how* as well as the *what.* You had to figure out *how* you might get the plum. Which is what you did. You asked for it to fall into your hand." Mika was quite certain she was explaining this very badly, not least because her own understanding of witchiness was nebulous, but she knew she had to try or there was simply no point in her being here. "Sometimes, for simple spells, that's all you need. *How* and *what.* And all the magical energy that's inside you and around you will do what you asked."

"So you're saying that when we cast a spell, it's pretty much just us talking to magic?" Rosetta asked.

"More or less," said Mika. "The tricky part is getting magic to listen."

Altamira was now upside down, her braid dangling about an inch off the floor. She looked like she was having the time of her life. "So how come I can't get myself back down?"

"Have you tried asking again, like you did with the plum? Instead of thinking, *I want to get back down*, try something like, *I'd like to be gently lowered back to the floor, please*."

Once again, Altamira closed her eyes, screwed her face up, and tried to cast the spell. Mika had been using magic so long now that casting simple spells was second nature to her, but it hadn't always been. Learning how to use magic was unwieldy and unpredictable, with no easy incantations or shortcuts. The spells jotted down in a witch's spellbook weren't *spells* so much as snippets of conversation the witch had either figured out for herself or had learned from another witch. Spells weren't tidy, clear commands to wave your wand and say "Abracadabra!" so much as they were friendly tips like, *If you want the spider vanished from the corner of your bedroom, make sure you ask the magic to put it somewhere specific or else you may find that it's been deposited under your pillow instead*.

Mika had discovered *that* the hard way.

"I can't do it," Altamira said at last, not sounding particularly bothered by this. She was still upside down.

"That's okay," said Mika.

She narrowed her eyes at the glimmers of gold around Altamira. The child was returned to the floor at once.

"The thing about magic," Mika explained as Altamira bounced to her feet, "is that it really likes us. There's a little inside all witches, which is what makes us just a bit different from other people, but most of the magic we use exists as energy outside us. You can actually see it if you pay attention. It looks like gold dust. And it's attracted to us because we can use it. It *wants* to be used. But it's also mischievous, like a naughty puppy," she added. "And if we forget to be very firm and bossy with it, it has a tendency to run wild."

Altamira found the puppy comparison hilarious, but Rosetta's face brightened with the interest of someone eager to learn more. "Is that why we keep losing control and accidentally casting spells?" she asked. "Because we haven't been bossy with the magic?"

"It's mostly because there's so much here that it's a lot harder for young witches like the three of you to control it," Mika said. "Ever since I arrived, I've been keeping the magic in check. I'm so used to doing it for myself that at first I didn't even notice I'd started doing it here, too, but I can feel it when I stop to think about it. It's like I'm keeping one hand on the puppy's leash at all times."

"But it can still slip away," said Rosetta, gesturing to Altamira. "So you have to grab the leash before it goes too far."

"Exactly."

Altamira had flopped down on the rug to stroke Circe, like she'd lost interest in Mika's explanations and dubious metaphors, so Mika decided to cut the unexpected lesson short. Circe, she noticed, had wasted no time in making herself at home; she was stretched out on the rug and looked ready to doze off.

"I figured out a lot of this on my own," she said to the girls, "but hopefully you won't have to. You can ask me anything you like, any time."

"You never did say why it wasn't safe for me to be floating," Altamira said, surprising her. So she *was* paying attention. Her bright eyes looked up to meet Mika's. "It was fun."

"I know," said Mika, "and you would probably have been okay because we're indoors. But if we'd been outside and you'd started to levitate and couldn't get yourself back down to the ground, you could have floated too high, past the wards, and someone could have seen you. Or, worse, the wind could have gotten hold of you and tossed you who knows where."

"Well, shit," said Altamira.

Mika bit her lip to squash a smile. Why were rude words always so unfailingly funny when they came out of a child's mouth? It was so terribly hard to look disapproving! Rosetta sighed. "You *have* to stop saying that," she said to her sister.

"I'll stop when Ian and Jamie stop," Altamira said cheerfully, which seemed fair as far as Mika was concerned. She scrambled to her feet. Like Ian, she seemed to have the inexhaustible energy of a bouncy ball. "Let's go get the rest of your stuff!"

"Are you sure you don't mind that this is the attic?" Rosetta asked Mika, a little anxiously. "Jamie and Lucie wanted you to use one of their rooms, but I told them you might actually prefer it up here." Her eyes dropped shyly to the floor and she added, hesitantly, "Because of balcony. And the view."

Mika looked at her in surprise. "I *do* prefer it up here. How did you know?"

"None of us like it when we're closed in," said Rosetta. "I mean, I love being tucked up in my bed with a book, but I always have the window open. Even in the winter. And Altamira likes the outside so much she doesn't even wear *shoes* unless someone makes her."

"I like to feel the dirt between my toes," Altamira explained, halfway down the stairs already.

"Ian says it's probably a witch thing," said Rosetta.

It probably was. The natural world was where magic thrived, after all. Casting her mind over the rest of the Very Secret Society of Witches, Mika could see the pattern there, too. She knew Belinda refused to live in big, industrial cities, for instance, while Primrose gave her rose garden more attention and affection than Mika had ever seen her give another person. Like Rosetta, Mika loved curling up in her warm bed, and she also always had a window open. Even in the winter.

But right then, as she followed the girls down the ladder, the thing that Mika found most interesting was not Altamira's fondness for the feel of dirt between her toes. It was what they'd said:

Ian says it's probably a witch thing.

It sounded like Ian knew a lot more about witches than he should.

CHAPTER SIX

On their way back out to the car, the girls paused to show Mika the rest of the house. The two closed doors downstairs, between the front door and the kitchen at the back, led to Lillian's master bedroom and her study. The bedroom was spare and uninteresting, like a hotel room, and it was clear that the study was the place Lillian spent her time.

Someone had obviously made an effort to dust the room, but they'd been up against the insurmountable obstacle of Lillian's scattered, untidy papers, reference books, and fossils. Indeed, as the girls pointed out to Mika, they were allowed to stand in the doorway and look inside, but they weren't allowed to touch anything in the room because "there's a lot of important stuff in there, and Lillian likes it to be just *so*, and she could be back any day."

Mika resisted the temptation to point out that if Lillian would only be a *little* less controlling, her solicitor wouldn't need to come here and put three children's secret witchiness at risk.

"Come on," she said cheerfully. "Let's go make sure Ian hasn't fallen into the pond."

Altamira had already run outside ahead of them. Ian, it turned out, had *not* fallen into the pond, but he seemed to have befriended the koi.

"You were gone a while," Lucie said, beaming down at the girls. "Everything okay?"

"I started floating," Altamira informed them, "so Mika had to rescue me."

"Well, I wouldn't go so far as to say I *rescued* you—"

Ian patted Mika on the shoulder, looking enormously pleased with himself. "Best idea I ever had," he said proudly.

"Thank you," Ken said to Mika, his eyes twinkling. "He'll be insufferable now."

"Why don't you tell us about some of the other spells you can do?" Ian asked enthusiastically. Ken and Lucie looked slightly pained, like they were afraid Ian was too nosy, but Mika didn't mind. "What, say, is your most *spectacular* spell? Can you make yourself breathe underwater? Can you transform yourself into a fish, or a bird, or another person? Can you—"

"Where's the pond going to live?" Altamira interrupted, peering so closely at the koi that her nose practically touched the surface of the water. "Are you going to put it in the attic?"

"I was thinking it could stay outside," said Mika, looking over at Ken. "If that's okay with you?"

"Of course," he said at once. "We can put it in the back garden. The greenhouse, too. There's a lovely sunny spot by the back wall, and the pond could go in the shade by the sunflowers."

"But—" Ian started to protest.

"We can talk about spells later," Lucie said firmly, taking him by the elbow. "Let the poor girl settle in first."

So Mika floated the pond and the greenhouse around the

house to the back where, just as Ken had promised, they found the perfect spot for each. As soon as Mika settled both into the ground and broke the spell that had kept them suspended in the air, she felt an almost physical weight lift off her. She rolled her shoulders, easing out the muscles.

After that, it only took a couple more trips to ferry the rest of Mika's possessions up to the attic. Then she went back outside to move the Broomstick into the barn while Ken and the girls stayed upstairs to unpack Mika's books (or so they said; Mika knew the girls, at least, just wanted to play with Circe), and Lucie and Ian went to start on lunch.

By the time Mika returned to the attic, her arms full of half a dozen potted plants she'd decided to bring in from the greenhouse, Ken had departed and the girls were rolling a ball across the attic floor for Circe to fetch.

Mika worked around them. She found homes for the plants by her bed, desk, and on the balcony, set her cauldrons and her tools on the desk, and unpacked her clothes. Just as she finished, Circe wandered off to explore the house and garden. The children stayed behind.

"While you're here," Mika said, "Would you like to see me cast one of my favourite spells?"

The girls' faces lit up. "Yes, please!".

Feeling an unfamiliar thrill (had she *ever* been able to show her magic off like this before? She couldn't think of a single time, not even with Primrose. *Especially* not with Primrose), Mika reached for a roll of sunflower-patterned fabric on the desk.

"Isn't that for paintbrushes?" Rosetta asked curiously.

"Usually," said Mika, unrolling the fabric to reveal eight small glass vials tucked into the elastic slots inside. "But I use it for what I call my Can't-Do-Withouts."

Each vial was labelled, of course, and Mika watched the girls read the labels with avid interest: the relatively mundane LAVENDER, PEPPERMINT, and CEDAR; the more curious MUSHROOM DUST, POPPY POLLEN, and CRUSHED PEARL; and finally, the downright exciting MOONLIGHT and STAR SHAVINGS.

"I'll tell you all about each of these another time," Mika promised them, taking the vial of pure peppermint essence out of its slot. "For now, I want to show you a different way to cast a spell. You've probably figured out by now that using magic is like running or climbing trees or painting. It uses energy."

They nodded. "I always need a nap after I accidentally set something on fire," Altamira admitted.

"I used to, too," said Mika. "If we were to try to do a spell that needs to be left in place for hours, maybe even days, it would be impossible for us to have the energy to keep that up. But something I wish someone had told me years before I finally worked it out for myself is that you can use tools to keep a spell in place for you. Like the wards around Nowhere House. Lillian's thousands of miles away, but the spells she cast are still in place. That's because she tied the wards to something that has its own magical energy. If I had to guess, I'd say she probably used the biggest, oldest trees as anchors."

"Is *that* why she goes out into the woods every spring?" Rosetta asked. "Is she recasting the warding spell?"

"She probably is, yes. All spells wear off sooner or later, no matter how powerful the witch or anchor is. Getting a whole year out of a spell is really good."

"It's more like a year and a month," Rosetta clarified conscientiously. "We know that because one year, Lillian didn't come back from a trip in time and the wards were down for a whole week."

"I thought *you* were going to cast a spell," said Altamira, uninterested in this tangent.

"I am." Mika held up the vial in her hand. "This is peppermint essence. Like the trees outside, it has its own magical energy. Watch."

Kneeling in the balcony doorway, on the threshold, Mika let three drops of the essence fall to the floor, right into the corners. They looked completely ordinary, like drops of water, but then she squiggled the familiar lines of a rune in the air and cast her spell.

At once, the drops of essence started to sparkle. Altamira gasped. The essence shone brightly, almost pure gold, and then subsided to a faint, scarcely noticeable glow.

"I just tied my spell to those drops of peppermint essence," Mika explained. "So now it'll stay in place until the magic in the essence wears off. It doesn't have as much power as a living tree does, so I usually add a new drop and top the spell off before bed every night."

"What does it do?" Rosetta asked curiously. "What's the spell for?"

"To keep spiders and bugs out of the room."

The girls burst out laughing. "We're witches," Altamira cried, practically rolling on the floor in her mirth. "We're supposed to *embrace* nature!"

"I embrace nature," said Mika, shuddering. "*Outside*. But I draw the line at creepy-crawlies in my bedroom."

This seemed to tickle them no end. Mika grinned, not in the least surprised. There'd been a time when she, too, had been unbothered by spiders and had chased frogs around the garden like she had absolutely no doubt Altamira did. Ick.

"Lunch!" Ian's voice boomed from two floors below them. Mika was frankly amazed it had reached them all the way across the house, but she supposed that was one of the perks of stage training.

Downstairs in the kitchen, the girls went to work getting plates out of the dishwasher while Mika was sent across the room to the table.

Mika had only just sat down when Terracotta, the last of the girls, entered the room. She came straight to the table and, somewhat to Mika's surprise, smiled at her. "Hello," she said, her voice high and young and sweet.

"Hi," said Mika, smiling back.

Unlike Altamira, who looked like she hadn't bothered to change out of her pyjamas this morning, and Rosetta, who was wearing a pair of jeans and an old pink T-shirt, Terracotta had dressed up. Her straight black hair had been scraped into a high, rather severe ponytail and her outfit was a formal, knee-length black dress with ruffles at the ends of the cap sleeves.

She continued to regard Mika with a steady, unwavering pair of brown eyes, but didn't say anything more. Mika wondered if she was waiting for someone to notice her outfit.

"That's a lovely dress," Mika offered.

Terracotta beamed. "Thank you. I'm wearing it because I might be going to a funeral later."

"You *might* be?"

She slipped nimbly into her chair, apparently satisfied that her outfit had been duly noted. "Yes. It depends."

"On what?"

"On you," Terracotta said, smiling angelically.

Mika supposed she really ought to have seen this coming, considering everything Rosetta had told her earlier. She considered the child across the table from her. "How would you do it?" she asked curiously.

"I was thinking it would be best to do it in your sleep," Terracotta replied without batting an eye. "Then you wouldn't even notice. I'm competent, but I'm not cruel."

"That's very considerate of you," Mika remarked, wondering if the rest of the household knew that there was a tiny psychopath in their midst.

Before the conversation could go any further, the sandpapery voice of Jamie, the librarian, interrupted them. "Cool outfit," he said, sounding amused. He tugged on the end of Terracotta's ponytail and Mika watched in fascination as the unnervingly intense expression on the child's face transformed instantly into a childish scowl.

"Jamie!" she complained, tilting her head back to glower up at him. "You're ruining it!"

"Ruining what? Your diabolical plot to scare the new tutor away, thereby saving you the trouble of having to murder her?"

Terracotta shot Jamie a betrayed, outraged look. "I told you," she hissed, making no effort to keep her voice down, "I don't want her here!"

Jamie's face, which had been fixed in a permanent scowl the

last time Mika had seen him, was remarkably patient and un-scowly as he looked down at Terracotta, but Mika could tell from the way his jaw tightened that he had no intention of letting her get away with such a poor display of manners.

Mika surprised everyone, including herself, by cutting in with: "Suck it up, buttercup."

"What did you say?" Terracotta demanded incredulously.

"Suck it up, buttercup," Mika repeated, perfectly cheerfully. "It's okay that you don't want me here, but I'm afraid you'll have to get used to it because I signed a contract. I'm staying put. And I wouldn't recommend sneaking up on me when I'm asleep, either," she added, giving the matter a moment's serious consideration. "I have a *very* protective dog, you see."

Terracotta crossed her arms over her chest and transferred her scowl to Mika, but didn't seem to have anything more to say.

"Oh, she absolutely got that scowl from you," Mika said to Jamie, marvelling at the resemblance. "It's uncanny."

Now they were both scowling at her. She smiled back.

Then Lucie bustled over, closely followed by the others, so there was no more time to discuss Mika's hypothetical demise.

Lunch came in the form of a large jug of iced tea, bowls of creamy mushroom soup, and buttered hunks of warm, crusty homemade bread. Mika, who'd been too nervous to eat any breakfast before leaving Brighton, discovered she was absolutely starving and was content to eat in happy silence while the others kept up an easy, steady stream of chatter.

Eventually, the conversation turned to the girls' tutoring. "While you're here," Lucie said to Mika, "we decided we'd cut back on the girls' usual lessons so that they'll have the mornings free to work with you. As long as that suits you."

"Of course," said Mika. She wondered if Terracotta, who was glaring absolute daggers at her, would even turn up to the lessons. "We'll start after breakfast tomorrow."

But *where* would they start? Mika had no idea. She'd been thinking about it almost constantly for days and still wasn't sure how she was going to tackle these lessons. She wasn't a teacher, and she certainly wasn't a teacher of *magic*, and it wasn't like there were handy lesson plans available to download online. Yes, she'd already done a bit of teaching today, but that had been out of necessity.

She was out of her depth. She would do her best, but she knew she was out of her depth. Had she made a mistake in not telling Primrose?

Fortunately, before she could get too lost in self-doubt, Ken had a question for her. "Do you know what you'd like to do this afternoon? You're more than welcome to come to the cottage for tea if you find yourself at a loose end."

"I'd love that," Mika said. "I could pop over after I've taken Circe for a walk." She smiled at the girls. "I thought I might let her have a run on the beach. Would the three of you like to come along?"

She expected Terracotta to reject this proposition instantly, but it came as a surprise when it was Jamie who said, quickly and a little too sharply, "No."

Mika blinked. The others fell silent.

Jamie looked like he regretted speaking, but he cleared his throat and went on, without looking at anybody. "I need the kids' help in the library this afternoon."

"Next time, then," Mika said to the girls, her smile pinned in place so that they wouldn't pick up on the chill in the air.

It was obvious to her, and quite possibly to everyone except the children themselves, that Jamie didn't need the girls' help in the library.

He just didn't want them going anywhere with her.

CHAPTER SEVEN

Mika went down to the sea as planned that afternoon. She went in her wellies (because thorns were thorns even if you *were* a witch), with her phone and tiny, sharp herb shears in the pockets of her dress. *All* of her clothes had pockets, even if she'd had to sew them in herself.

Circe bounded ahead over the dunes and down to the empty beach, heading straight for the water, while Mika paused to snip a handful of sea holly heads off a shrub, right above the node so that they'd grow back. She was surprised they were still flowering; like the riotously golden sunflowers in the back garden, the sea holly was blooming well out of season. It had to be because of the sheer amount of magic gathered around Nowhere House.

By the time she got to the beach and kicked her wellies off, Circe was frolicking in the water, barking in tandem with a pair of seals farther out. A cold wind blew in from the water, with a fine spray of salt, and Mika stuck her tongue out to taste it.

She marvelled at how empty the world seemed from here. There was a fishing boat far out on the water, but the only other person Mika could see was just a speck a long, long way down the beach. It was lovely, but unexpected. November was certainly not the season of ice lollies and families slathered in sun cream, but where were the elderly dog walkers in their tweed coats and the artists with their canvases and windblown hair?

The only explanation she could think of was that Lillian's wards extended all the way out here. If that was the case, she was *very* powerful.

Circe ran over, barking joyfully. She leapt up to put muddy, salty paws on Mika's shoulders and give her a very wet kiss. Then she was gone again, off to befriend the seals once more, and Mika laughed and let her.

Once Circe was well and truly tired out, they trotted back up to the house together. Circe shook herself dry (or dryish, anyway) and went to a warm, sunny spot in the front room for a nap. Mika was tempted by the possibility of a nap herself, but she went upstairs to the attic instead.

There, she plucked the sea holly heads out of her pocket and carefully stripped them into their separate parts. Petals, pollen, the sap from inside the stems—these were usually the most useful parts of any plant, and she stored each of these safely in tiny glass vials retrieved from her potion kit.

Sitting cross-legged on the floor with everything laid out around her, she reached out for the fine gold threads of magic in the air and set a small witchfire going under the smaller of her cauldrons. Then she opened her spellbook to a blank page, bit the end of her pencil, and brainstormed ideas. Finally, after a few false starts, she was satisfied with the short list she'd come up with:

2 sea holly petals
1 drop of sea holly sap
½ teaspoon of crushed pearl
1 drop of moonlight

Mika carefully measured each of the ingredients and dropped them into the cauldron. As the witchfire warmed the cauldron up, she watched the mixture combine and simmer down to a sparkling, bluish syrup. Potion-making was more of an art than a science, and it relied on a witch's instincts, but Mika had been experimenting and practicing for so long now that her instincts were good.

She transferred the syrup to a vial and examined it in delight. The syrup had a scent, faint but unmistakable, and the only word Mika could think of to describe it was *harmony*. She knew, in that bone-deep way of witches, that if this syrup was added to tea, it would cool tempers and smooth the jagged edges of raw feelings.

It had been an experiment, a tiny burst of inspiration that had sparked inside her head when she'd seen the sea holly. Such a spiky-looking flower shouldn't have conjured up a vision of peace and harmony and other fuzzy feelings, but Mika had had a hunch and she'd run with it. The already calming crushed pearl and the bottomless well of enchantment in the moonlight had helped, of course.

She sighed happily. In moments like this, she really and truly loved being a witch. She loved losing herself for hours in the hum of magic, the sparkle of gold dust in the air, the soft warmth of witchfire, the ideas and the creativity and the *fun*. Why would anyone ever want to do anything else?

The only thing that could make it better was not having to do it alone.

Remembering that she was expected at Ian and Ken's cottage for tea, she packed up her kit, put out the witchfire, and popped down to the kitchen to collect a jar of her tea leaves before going out the front door.

Ken let her into the cottage, looking genuinely pleased to see her. Lucie was already there, tutting over Ian's chronic aversion to dusting and doing said dusting herself. Ian, meanwhile, was in an armchair knitting what looked like a scarf in an alarming shade of flamingo pink.

"It's for Ken," he said brightly to Mika, gesturing with his needles.

Mika glanced at Ken, who could not possibly have looked less like a man willing to wear a colour so bright it was practically neon, and he gave her a slightly helpless shrug in response. "The things we do for the ones we love."

"Ian, put away the knitting and make Mika a nice cup of tea," Lucie ordered, now balancing precariously on the arm of a chair so she could dust the lampshade above them.

"Oh, I can do that," said Mika. "If you point me to the kettle, I'll make a cup for all of us."

She held up the jar of tea leaves she'd brought with her. Ian let out a shriek. "Is that *magical* tea?"

"Sort of," Mika laughed. "It's good for achy bones."

"In that case, I'll need a whole pot," said Lucie.

"What do you know about achy bones?" Ian asked Mika, eyebrows shooting up to his hairline. "Bright and youthful as you are?"

Mika let out a hoot of mirth. "You'd be surprised! I swear, it was like the instant I turned thirty, my body said, *That's it, I'm done putting up with your nonsense. Look after me properly or I'm going to break down like an old engine.* I've been taking the threat very seriously."

She left the room to the sound of their laughter and promptly tripped over a pile of partially assembled wooden planks in the hallway.

"I'm building a beehive!" Ian shouted apologetically. "I'm thinking of taking up beekeeping."

Ken, who followed her to the kitchen to help, said somewhat drily, "Yes, he's building a beehive. Just like he was building an amphitheatre last summer. Half the stage is still sitting in the barn!"

Mika smothered a giggle. "Sounds like he likes having a project."

"He's never without a project," said Ken. "He never finishes them, either. And God help anyone he ropes in to be part of it."

Balancing four cups of tea on a tray, Mika returned to the living room. Lucie had apparently decided the room was sufficiently dust-free for her because she was now holding a ball of yarn for Ian while he knitted. Mika handed over the tea and found a spot beside Ken on the sofa. She stayed for an hour, listening to Ian's tales from the stage (from the fond but long-suffering expressions on Ken's and Lucie's faces, these were tales they had heard too many times already), and then she and Lucie returned to the main house together.

"Do you think the girls have finished helping Jamie in the library?" Mika asked, straight-faced.

Lucie gave her a rueful smile. "It was too much to hope you'd believe him, wasn't it?"

"He wasn't subtle."

"Jamie can be difficult," Lucie said, but her voice was soft with motherly love. "It's not easy earning his trust. He's been the only parent those children have had since they arrived, and he guards them like a lion. There's a heart of gold in there, once you get past all the scowling."

"How did *he* end up in that position?" Mika asked curiously. "He must have been in his mid-twenties when Rosetta first came here, mustn't he? I wouldn't have thought him the obvious choice to care for three toddlers."

There was a pause as Lucie hesitated, like she was deciding how much to say. "I owe Lillian a debt I can never repay," she said at last. "It doesn't sit well with me to speak badly of her, but the truth is, she has an iron will, pays no attention to anything she doesn't want to hear, and she . . ." Lucie trailed off, hesitating again. She sighed. "I suppose I should just come out with it. Ken and I have been here so long that we're family, and Lillian always said as much, but she still . . . well . . ."

"Oh," Mika said gently, understanding. "She still treats you and Ken like the help."

"We *are* paid to work for her, so she's not wrong to treat us as such. But we've always felt like we have to stay in our place. It's just how she is. Imperious to a fault. So when it became obvious back then that she had no intention of actually parenting the infants she'd brought home, we didn't know how to step in." Lucie's eyes crinkled in a smile. "But Jamie, well, she couldn't put *him* in his place. He was the only one who could take her on in battle and actually win. We've all raised those girls, but Jamie's the one they imprinted on."

"And he doesn't want me here," Mika guessed.

"Give him time. He'll come around."

That night, tucked under the warm duvet with Circe stretched out by her feet, Mika was on the cusp of sleep when she became aware of the sound of footsteps crunching in the leaves below her balcony. Curious, she reluctantly left the warmth of her bed, plucked an old, soft, oversized hoodie off the back of a chair, and stepped out into the cold.

"Hello?"

"Jesus," Jamie's raspy, startled voice came from somewhere below. "Where the hell are you?"

"Oh, it's you." Mika stood on her toes and leaned over the balcony railing. Jamie was in the back garden two stories beneath her, illuminated by a wedge of light from the kitchen. "I'm on the balcony." She paused. Lucie had said Jamie could be difficult, but maybe this would be a good moment to ease the way a little. "Hang on, I'll be down in half a second."

She levered herself over the railing, and then floated herself to the ground. It was all very graceful and elegant, like a superhero descending grandly from the sky—until the very end, when one bare foot landed on a spiky pinecone, and she ruined the grandeur of her entrance with undignified yelps of pain.

Jamie's hand shot out, catching her by the sleeve before she could topple over. "You okay?" His face was perfectly serious, but there was a suspicious tremor in his voice.

"You can laugh, you know," Mika said, her yelps already giving way to somewhat hysterical giggles.

"I'll resist."

"Is that because you don't know how?"

That made the corner of his mouth twitch, which she found

rather charming. He gestured up to the balcony, his breath foggy and white in the air between them. "So you're like the kids, then. You've got your windows open in the dead of night in November."

"It's not that I don't *feel* the cold. I just don't mind it. Within reason." Mika tucked her hands into the pockets of her hoodie. "What are *you* doing out here?"

"Altamira left her penguin outside." He fished a stuffed animal out of his own pocket, its colours so faded and its fabric so chewed that there was no universe in which Mika would have guessed that it was a penguin if he hadn't said as much. "I convinced her to go to sleep without it, but only by promising that I'd find and restore it to her before she wakes up."

"Seems fair to me."

"So"—the shift in his tone took her by surprise, and she watched him warily—"Lucie mentioned she talked to you."

"I kind of thought *I'd* be the one to bring it up first," Mika said ruefully.

"You weren't getting round to it, and I haven't got all night," was the brusque reply.

Mika laughed. She could see what Lucie had meant when she'd said Lillian had found it impossible to put him in his place: this was not a man who had the slightest interest in social niceties. She liked it. She had spent all her life colossally afraid of fucking up those very same social niceties and giving away just how *not* normal she was, so it was both novel and nice to not have to worry about it for a few minutes.

"I didn't want *anyone* coming here," Jamie explained. "It's not you. It's anyone. There's too much at stake."

"Which is extremely reasonable," said Mika, nodding. "That's the thing. I get it. I understand what it's like to not trust people. I understand what it's like to be afraid that one mistake will destroy the life you've built. So I don't resent your mistrust in the slightest."

He cocked his head at her. "But?"

"But I think this is doomed to fail if you don't keep that mistrust to yourself. I'm here to teach *magic*, of all things, and that's tricky on a good day. It'll be downright impossible if the girls pick up on the way you feel. *They* need to trust me, even if you don't."

She was only too conscious of his intent, searching gaze. After a moment, he nodded. "Okay."

Oh. Well, that could have gone worse.

"Okay," she echoed. "Good. I guess I'll go back to bed, then . . ."

"Why the videos?"

Mika blinked at the unexpected question. "*My* videos?"

"I've gathered that you thought it would be safe to create them because you assumed, rightly, that most people would think of them as theatre. I just don't understand why you *wanted* to create them in the first place."

"Oh." She smiled. "See, outside of a few hours every few months, I've never been able to talk to anyone about magic. There's no one I can text or call or shout to in the next room when I crack a difficult spell or figure out a new potion. Then, a couple of years ago, I joined an online group dedicated to my favourite book series, and I discovered I love talking to people who are just as excited about the thing *I'm* excited about."

"You'd never had that before?" Jamie's voice sounded odd.

"No, but it got me thinking that maybe I could find a way to re-create it with witchy stuff. So I created an alter ego, a witch who brews potions in an enchanted tea shop." Pausing, Mika shrugged a little sheepishly. "I don't know. It felt like a way to talk about the thing I was excited about without *actually* talking about the thing I was excited about."

He didn't respond, and as the silence stretched between them, she wondered if she'd said too much.

"It probably sounds silly—"

"No." He said it at once, his voice all jagged edges. "No, it doesn't. It sounds like you've been alone for a long time."

"Oh, I'm used to that," Mika said, her voice just a little *too* bright. "That's the way it is."

"Not here, it's not," was all she got in reply.

CHAPTER EIGHT

The next morning, Mika waited outside for the children. She'd found the perfect place for their first proper magic class, in the back garden by the koi pond, where they could be out in the open while still sheltered from the blustery November wind.

She'd been watching Circe gambol around the garden in pursuit of a butterfly, but at the sound of the girls' voices, she turned. Altamira shot towards Mika like a bullet, all flailing golden limbs and bouncing ponytail, while Rosetta and Terracotta followed at a more sensible pace, their heads bent together over a comic book in Rosetta's hands. There was an easy affection between the girls as they argued good-naturedly.

Mika scarcely had a moment to marvel at this friendlier, softer side of Terracotta before her spirits took a nosedive at the sight of someone else following the girls down to the pond.

She and Jamie had come to something of an understanding the previous night, but that didn't mean she wanted to teach her first proper lesson with *his* intent, stormy eyes on her.

But she included him in her smile because she had no good reason to object to his presence. She was in her two-week trial period, after all, and she had known this first lesson at least would be supervised. It was perfectly reasonable. You didn't hire someone to look after and teach children without at least making sure they were safe, responsible, and capable of doing their job. And truthfully, Mika was fine with that.

She just wished it were someone *else* doing the supervising. Couldn't it have been Lucie or Ian or Ken, any of whom she suspected would have been kind and understanding if she messed up?

But no, she'd gotten Jamie, who loomed and scowled and who, truce or no truce, reminded her of nothing so much as a grim spectre waiting for Satan to summon him home.

She waited for the girls to get settled on the grass with her. Jamie took the comic book from Rosetta and found himself a spot beneath the nearest tree, his back against the trunk and his hands tucked deep into the pockets of his coat.

Mika tried to pretend he wasn't there. "There's a couple of things I want to talk about today," she said to the children, hoping her voice didn't sound as unsure and awkward as she felt, "but first, I wanted to find out if any of you have any questions about me or magic or anything else. I gather Lillian hasn't had the time to teach you, so I'm guessing there's a lot of stuff you've wondered about and—"

"How many other witches do you know?" Rosetta asked shyly, her eyes bright and eager.

"Are there any boy witches?" Altamira asked, sounding rather disgusted.

And Terracotta, her tone downright belligerent, asked, "Do you *really* think you can teach us how to control our magic by Christmas?"

Mika knew she had to tackle *that* first. "Absolutely not," she said. "I've already told your grown-ups that there's no way any of you will be able to completely control your magic in just a few weeks. That's not why I'm here. I'm here to help you *start*. I'll teach you how to use your power, show you how to begin controlling it, and protect you from any magical blowback."

Terracotta scoffed. "We don't need you to protect us."

Mika considered her. "Big magical outbursts can be extremely unsafe. Especially for people like Ian, Ken, Lucie, and Jamie, who don't have the power we do."

Terracotta blinked, taken aback. She'd never considered that before, Mika realised, watching the little girl dart a surreptitious and worried look at Jamie. Maybe Terracotta's hostility wasn't coming from a place of unkindness. Maybe it was, in fact, just the opposite. Maybe it was coming from a place of love.

"This is because of Edward, too, isn't it?" Rosetta asked Mika.

Mika glanced uncertainly at Jamie, her question obvious. He gave her a short nod. "It's fine, they know Edward's coming. You can talk about him."

"Okay, then," Mika said. "Yes, Lillian's solicitor will be coming to visit in December and it's very important that we make sure he doesn't find out the truth about the three of you."

"Would it be so bad?" There was a wistful note in Rosetta's voice that arrowed directly into Mika's heart. "I mean, would it really be the end of the world if more people found out about us?"

"I've often wondered that," Mika said. "It would be nice, wouldn't it? To not have to keep secrets anymore? To have friends?" Rosetta nodded, and Mika nodded, too, wishing with all her heart that she could give her a different answer. "But we can never know for sure how someone will react to finding out the truth, so it's just too much of a risk."

It was exactly the kind of thing Primrose would have said. The thought brought Mika no comfort.

Mika tried to soften the blow with the one thing that usually made her feel better. "Of course, you have to remember that more people know about witches than we think. Look at your own care-takers. They're not witches, but they know about us. And I know for a fact that plenty of witches have grandparents, aunts, uncles, cousins, and a whole lot of other relatives who raised them." She smiled. "The way I see it, there must be quite a few people out there who already know our secret and accept us. That could be a good place to start looking for new friends."

She didn't mention the one thing that made this almost impossible: the Rules. How was a witch to find a community of witches and non-witches who would embrace her when she was supposed to stay away from other witches, keep her life completely disconnected from theirs, and only see those other witches a few times a year?

"Anyway," Mika went on, injecting some cheer back into her voice, "to answer your earlier question, Altamira, I don't know if there are any boy witches. I've never met one. And, Rosetta, I know a few other witches. Twenty, to be exact."

"Twenty?" Altamira squeaked. "How do you know them? Are they your friends?"

"Um, not exactly," said Mika. "We meet once every three months. I call us the Very Secret Society of Witches. Primrose, the head of our group, doesn't like it when I call us that." Mika grinned. "Which may or may not be why I keep doing it."

Rosetta and Altamira laughed. Even Terracotta looked like she wanted to. "How come Primrose is the head of the Society?"

"Because she's the oldest, most powerful, and, most importantly, the bossiest."

"Then why isn't *she* here instead of you?" Terracotta, of course. "Ian said he found you, but why didn't you tell him to speak to Primrose instead?"

Mika hesitated. She glanced at Jamie, who was looking back at her with a furrow between his eyebrows. She decided to be honest.

"Primrose isn't here because she doesn't know about you," Mika said to the children. "I don't know how you've escaped her notice, but for now, at least, it would be best to keep it that way."

"Why?" Rosetta asked, her little face solemn.

"Because Primrose believes keeping all witches safe and secret is more important than anything else," said Mika. "She'll think all this magic in one place is too dangerous to you, to your caretakers, *and* to the safety of all witches, so she'll want to separate you."

"But she can't, can she?" Altamira sounded horrified. Mika noticed the way she tucked her hand into Terracotta's. "We don't belong to her!"

"She'll *want* to separate you, but that doesn't mean she *can*," Mika clarified. "As far as I know, Lillian is the only one who gets to make those decisions. But Primrose can be very persuasive, and"— She hesitated, glancing once again at Jamie, whose expression had darkened—"Well, the thing is, I don't know whether Lillian would give in. I don't know her."

"Primrose sounds dreadful," Altamira said emphatically.

"Her heart's in the right place. She just believes she has to do whatever is necessary to protect us all."

"Hmm," Terracotta said, almost admiring.

"In any case, Primrose *isn't* going to find out about the three of you, so it's a moot point," Mika added.

"You sound like you know Primrose pretty well," Jamie remarked, his rough voice scraping away the layers of her history.

Mika avoided his steady gaze and kept her eyes on Circe, who had draped herself under the tree beside Jamie and had put her head on his knee. "I grew up in Primrose's house. One of her houses. She visited quite often, so I've known her all my life. I know her as well anyone does."

"If she wasn't there all the time, who looked after you?" Rosetta asked.

"I had nannies."

"They knew you were a witch?"

Mika felt twitchy. Her past felt too raw and exposed, but she didn't have the heart to shut down the girls' questions, especially not after specifically telling them they could ask her anything. And not when she knew only too well what it was like to have questions that never got answered.

"No," she said after a moment. "They didn't know. Not to start with. When I was very young, I lost control of my power just like you do, so they always found out sooner or later. Primrose would replace them as soon as they saw anything they weren't supposed to."

"But didn't they ever tell people what they saw?" Altamira asked, wide-eyed.

Mika shook her head. "Primrose took away their memories when they left. It's a very powerful and difficult spell, one she's never shared with the rest of us."

What she didn't say was that Primrose had not just taken away the nannies' memories of magic. She'd taken away their memories of *Mika*. She had seamlessly replaced every memory of Mika with false memories of another, perfectly normal girl. "Better they move on to their next position with nothing about you in their heads, poppet," Primrose had said when Mika had protested. "Better safe than sorry."

And so all those nannies had gone on with their lives and none of them, not one, remembered a little girl named Mika Moon.

Mika could feel that Jamie's eyes were still on her, but she didn't dare look up at him. She conjured a smile. "It's probably for the best that the rest of us don't know how to mess about with memories anyway," she said to the girls. "I don't know about you, but the idea of breaking into someone's mind and stealing away their memories feels a bit icky to me."

Terracotta did not look convinced. "Sometimes you have to do icky things to protect the people you care about," she said, arms crossed tightly over her chest. "It sounds like Primrose understands that even if *you* don't."

Rosetta blushed a deep red, obviously embarrassed, but Mika smiled at her. "It's okay. I don't mind you saying stuff you think I might not like. I'd rather you did that than lied to me."

"Ken says lies are okay if you're saying them to be kind," said Altamira.

"Those are called white lies and, yes, I suppose Ken's right. If you have to choose between being kind or being truthful, it's usually better to be kind. That said," she added firmly, "I think I would prefer the truth from the three of you."

Goodness, this lesson had gotten *way* too existential. Maybe a small explosion would be a good diversion?

Then, with the blessedly short attention span of a child, Altamira interrupted Mika's decidedly irresponsible plans.

"Do the fish have names?" she asked, lying on her belly with her chin propped on one of the smooth stones of the pond. One little hand trailed in the cold water, waiting for the koi to come give her a friendly nibble.

"Of course," said Mika, relieved. She pointed to each fish in turn. "Hecate's the one with two black splotches on her back. Medusa's over there. She has one misshapen fin. The golden one is Ceridwen, and Freyja's tail is all white."

From under the tree, Jamie said, with what almost sounded like a smile in his voice: "Hecate, Medusa, Ceridwen, Freyja. And Circe. All witches."

"I've never pretended to be subtle," said Mika cheerfully.

She let Altamira have another minute to play with the fish before clearing her throat, deciding it was time to do some actual spellwork. "For now, I think the best way to start these lessons is for me to get an idea of how much power and control you already have." She reached into the koi pond and retrieved three smooth pebbles, placing one in front of each child. "An animation spell is one of the simplest there is, and it doesn't require the use of runes, so it's a good one for you to try."

"Animation?" Altamira asked.

"Making something move," Rosetta said to her sister, her eyes shining with enthusiasm. "Something that doesn't *already* move, I mean. Like stones. Is that right?"

"That's exactly it," said Mika. "What I want you to do is use your magic to make the pebble in front of you move. Make it rise a few inches into the air or make it stand on its end and spin, whatever you like. Magic is so keen to be used that it's always right at your fingertips, waiting, so you should be able to feel it as soon as you reach for it. Once you can feel it, ask it to do what you want it to. Just keep it simple, and be specific."

She watched their faces. Rosetta's enthusiasm had given way to uncertainty, like she wasn't sure of her own abilities. Altamira was clearly excited, but as the youngest, she glanced at her sisters to take her lead from them. Terracotta, on the other hand, took one look at the others' faces and lifted her chin.

"I'll go first," she said.

She was stepping up so that the others wouldn't have to, Mika thought. She couldn't help admiring the marshmallow heart hiding beneath Terracotta's porcupine prickles. She knew she would probably fight a lot of battles with the little girl in the next few weeks, but now she was pretty sure that Terracotta wouldn't be fighting them just because she wanted to be difficult. She'd be fighting them because she was ferociously protective of her sisters, the grown-ups who looked after them, and this safe haven they'd built together.

It made Mika ache in a way that was as joyful as it was painful. She couldn't fathom what it must be like to be so loved and to be so sure of that love that you would fight tooth and nail to protect it, but she was incredibly glad that these girls had that.

And if it was just a little heartbreaking to be reminded of what she'd never had and likely never would, well, she could live with that.

She smiled at Terracotta, who did not return it, and said, "Take your time. Close your eyes if it helps. Rosetta, Altamira, if you'd like to try with your own pebbles at the same time, that's fine. You don't have to take it in turns. And if you make a mistake or get it wrong, you can just try again."

"What if we cause a big burst of power?" Rosetta asked quietly.

"I'll be here to keep it in check," Mika promised her.

Quiet fell as the girls concentrated on the stones gleaming in the sunlight in front of them. Jamie stood and approached them, blowing on his hands to stay warm, his brows drawn together as he watched. Circe, having lost the use of his leg as a pillow, came to sit beside Mika and cocked her head as if she, too, was interested in the children's progress.

Beads of sweat popped up on Altamira's brow. "It's *heavy*," she complained. "It's like it doesn't want to move."

"The pebble has weight," Mika said gently. "You don't notice it when you pick it up in your hand because you've developed those muscles, but spellwork uses a different kind of power."

None of the pebbles moved, but Mika could feel the ripples of the girls' spellwork in the air. They were *so* close. When they stopped and turned back to her with slightly crestfallen expressions on their faces, she told them as much.

"You did really well," she said. "You held your focus for much longer than I expected you to be able to, and I think you were all really close to getting it right."

"I'm no expert, but I could have sworn I saw the pebbles twitch," Jamie added, tousling Terracotta's hair. His voice was warmer than she'd ever heard it, and his eyes were fond and twinkly, and she was rather distressed to discover that this meant his Annoyingly Handsome score was now even higher than it had been before.

"Why didn't it work?" Rosetta asked Mika.

"I think you just need time and practice," she replied. "I could see how hard you were all working just then, and putting the work in is the most important part. Instead of growing up having fun with your power and befriending magic, you've been taught to be afraid of it, to be afraid of mistakes and accidents, so right now, your power is in control of you rather than the other way round."

No one spoke. Mika could see they were doubtful.

"The thing is, being a witch is *extraordinary*," she said. "It might seem sometimes that all we are is odd and different, but the truth is, we're amazing. We're part of the earth below us and the sky above us. Our veins echo the patterns of rivers and roots. There's sunlight and moonlight in our bones." Heartened by the smiles that had started to light Rosetta's and Altamira's faces, she went on: "It's always a good idea to be cautious and respectful when you use a powerful force like magic, but you don't have to be afraid of it. That's why you practice. With practice, you'll lose your fear and gain the confidence you need."

"You can't know that," Terracotta said.

"I do know that," Mika said simply. "Because the three of you have something incredible to help you. You have each other."

As he watched part of the children's first lesson from the kitchen window, Ian was positively quivering with delight. As he watched *Ian*, Ken sighed. He was only too familiar with the warning signs.

"Ian," he said, calmly and sensibly and, he knew, entirely pointlessly. "Do *not*."

"What can you possibly mean, my darling?" Ian asked, turning wide, innocent eyes on his husband.

Ken scoffed. "I know what you're thinking."

Ian cracked. "It would be *perfect*," he gushed.

"*Ian*," Ken groaned. "You don't know if poor Mika even *likes* men."

At this, Lucie, who was seated at the table with her laptop and entering the latest household budget figures into a spreadsheet, looked up in alarm. "Don't you dare," she said. "Mika didn't come here to be roped into one of your ridiculous attempts to play matchmaker! Jamie will skin you alive. Don't you remember what happened last time?"

Ken grimaced. *He* remembered. Vividly. Four years ago, Ken had injured his knee and Ian had persuaded him to hire a sweet, enthusiastic girl as a temporary gardening assistant. Lizzie had only been with them for a week before Ian, the world's worst matchmaker, had locked her in the barn with Jamie and hoped sparks would fly. Jamie had promptly broken the skylight, gotten them both out, and politely (well, politely for Jamie, anyway) asked Lizzie to leave, with a month's pay. He hadn't spoken to Ian for days after that.

"But the thing is," Ian said now, using his serious voice, which was even more worrying than his mischief-making voice, "we all love Jamie too much to see him spend the rest of his life with only three decrepit old bags of bones for company."

"I'm fifty-six," said Lucie indignantly. "I'm closer to Jamie's age than yours! Watch who you're calling a decrepit bag of bones."

"More to the point," said Ken, "we haven't exactly told Mika everything, have we? How well do you think it'll go over if you push them into a romantic relationship and she finds out he has secrets? Jamie doesn't need to lose anyone else."

There was a pause as Ken remembered, with a sudden, piercing pain, the very first time he'd met Jamie. He knew from the looks on Ian's and Lucie's faces that they were remembering it, too.

Lucie diverted them quickly. "Why is it you're never concerned about *my* romantic life, or lack thereof?"

"Darling, you said it yourself, you're fifty-six," Ian said soothingly. "You're an established spin—"

"If you say the word *spinster*, I'll skewer you on a spit."

"You're an established spinner of stability and comfort," Ian finished quickly, his eyes full of merriment. "We would all fall apart without you! For my own selfish reasons, I *can't* have you going off on romantic adventures."

Lucie rolled her eyes, clearly trying not to laugh. "Nicely saved."

Outside, the girls were scrambling to their feet. They'd be in for a break and a snack any minute.

"Ian," Ken said firmly, before the others could get within earshot. "I mean it. Don't stick your nose in this."

"Of course not, my love," Ian said brightly.

Ken didn't believe him.

CHAPTER NINE

Jamie stacked books with unwonted ferocity, hoping the satisfying thump of heavy, dusty volumes colliding would work out some of his ill temper.

Had it only been three days since she'd arrived? He felt like it had been *months* since he'd known peace.

(Now, admittedly, it *had* been months since he'd known peace. He hadn't had a proper night's sleep since that night in June. But that wasn't what this was about. This was about her.)

For one thing, there was the dog hair. Hadn't anyone considered the fact that dogs shed their fur all the goddamned time? What had possessed them to invite a dog into the house? No matter where he went, a collection of golden hairs seemed to follow him. They were on his clothes. They were on the chairs. They were on the carpets. They were even in his *car* (How? The dog had never been in there!). The only refuge he had from the hair was his own bedroom and he didn't think that would last much longer because, for some unfathomable reason, the dog had decided she *liked* him.

Jamie returned to his desk to find Circe sitting upright beside it, tongue out and tail wagging, waiting eagerly for him.

"You know you're not supposed to be in here," he said, and even his own voice was intolerable. Where was the bite? Christ, he sounded almost *fond*.

Most irritatingly, Circe was a *very* well-behaved dog, which made it hard to resent her presence. While she refused to stay out of the library altogether, choosing instead to sit with her head on his knee while he worked at his desk, she never went near the bookcases, never tried to chew a shoe, pen, or valuable book, and never distracted him when he was busy. So, fine, maybe he was almost fond of her. Fond-adjacent.

On the other hand, he was absolutely *not* fond of Circe's owner.

Also irritatingly, it was difficult to say exactly why Mika bothered him so much. There were secrets in this house he didn't want unburied, and he didn't trust her not to somehow destroy the life they'd built, but those were things that would have troubled him no matter who Ian had invited into their lives.

Why did *she* specifically get under his skin? He couldn't exactly object to her interactions with the others. She was friendly, she treated the children with kindness and humour, and Ian, Ken, and Lucie had obviously taken to her. And he couldn't object to her tutoring, either. In just an hour of watching her work with the children, it had been obvious that she was a little green, but she was a talented witch *and* she seemed to genuinely care.

Her tutoring was working, too. It'd only been a few days, but all three girls could now make their pebbles move. Rosetta had even gotten *her* pebble to do backflips.

Maybe the problem was Mika's perpetual good humour, which was alien to him and even worse than Ian's boundless energy. That had to be it. She was so aggravatingly, relentlessly *sunshiney*.

And, like the actual sun, she seemed determined to nurture every green or living thing in sight. It was absurd. In fact, just yesterday, he'd gone outside to speak to Ken and had found her kneeling on the front path, spoon-feeding a bee. A *bee*. It wasn't that he didn't want to save the bees. Of course he did! Yet for some reason, Mika naming her pets after folkloric witches, Mika spoon-feeding a bee, Mika's eyes dancing with mischief? Made him want to move to a flat with glass walls and a city skyline view and exactly zero woodland sprites. Zero.

Yes, he was aware that this was unreasonable.

He hadn't always been this glass-half-empty. As a rule, he didn't like to look back into his history, but he cast his mind there now, dodging the thorniest, brambliest parts of his memories. He was After-Jamie, but there had been a Before-Jamie once and that was where he went, to that little boy in Belfast. Before-Jamie had had a beloved goldfish, and a brown school satchel that his mother had lovingly embroidered with quotes from his favourite books, and a father who'd pick him up after school and put him straight on his broad shoulders.

Before-Jamie's glass had been *more* than half-full. He hadn't looked for the worst in people. He'd trusted that even when things went to hell in a fucking handbasket, everything would turn out okay in the end.

After-Jamie knew better.

Even so, it was possible that resenting someone for having a staggeringly lovely smile was a *tad* over the top.

Almost as if he'd summoned her just by thinking of her, the library door creaked open a little further and Mika poked her head around it.

"There she is," she said, shaking her head at Circe, who barked lovingly in response. "I'm sorry, is she bothering you?"

"No, she's fine," Jamie heard himself say.

What—and he could not overstate this—the fuck? He'd just had the perfect opportunity to politely rid himself of the dog, the dog's owner, *and* the dog's persistent fur. Why hadn't he taken it?

Mika stepped farther into the room, obviously interested in the library. Brilliant. That was all he needed. He watched her with what he hoped was a polite but forbidding expression.

It didn't have its intended effect.

"How does the library work?" she asked curiously, craning her neck to look up at the second floor of old, crinkly books. "No one browses in person, obviously, so do you have to post a parcel every time a kid requests a copy of Peppa Pig's latest adventure?"

That startled a laugh out of him, which made her spin around and stare at him with a look that was just as startled.

"It's not that kind of library," he said, looking away quickly. "It's a private collection. Less Peppa Pig and more old, academic texts and reference materials. There are books here you can't get anywhere else in the country. Everything is listed on the library's website and I usually get requests for books from professors and academics. They used to come here, but once the girls arrived, that stopped. So yes, I do have to send the books in the post each time."

"What if they get lost?" she asked, looking slightly horrified at the possibility.

"Part of my job is to digitize every book in the library so that there's no risk of permanently losing anything. Ideally, we'd loan out *that* copy rather than send the actual, physical book, but legally speaking, we're not allowed to circulate unauthorized versions." He pointed to the three books stacked neatly beside his laptop. "And if a request comes in for a book I haven't yet had a chance to digitize, I pause whatever I was doing before, scan the book in, and then send it off. It's not a perfect system, but . . ." He shrugged, trailing off.

She nodded, approaching one of the bookshelves. He stood up, walked around his desk, and leaned back against it so that he could keep a wary eye on her, but she touched the books with a careful, light hand.

"You should do that more often, by the way," she said, her eyes on the spine of the book in front of her. "It's nice."

"Do what?"

"Laugh."

Jamie blinked, taken aback. He crossed his arms over his chest, suddenly not quite sure what to do with them.

But Mika didn't seem to expect a response, and an instant later, she had vanished behind a row of bookshelves. He didn't follow her. Instead, he looked down at Circe, who looked back at him as if to say *Yes, that* did *just happen.*

His phone chimed with a text alert, and he tugged it out of the front pocket of his jeans.

Ian had sent him a screenshot, followed by a text: **He's not budging. Dick.**

Jamie, the reigning king of the school of glass half-empty, had expected no less. He pinched the bridge of his nose, blowing out an exhausted breath.

That was, of course, the moment Mika chose to reappear from between the shelves. She looked at him with a small crease between her eyebrows and said, quite gently, "Are you okay?"

He surprised himself by telling her the truth. "Some days, I think I'm too tired to keep keeping secrets."

Jesus, what the hell was wrong with him? Why didn't he just tell her all about his childhood while he was at it?

"Just some days?" Mika asked, eyebrows raised.

He almost smiled. "Lots of days."

"Me too," she said simply. She knelt on the floor to give Circe a bit of attention, her pale bronze hands vanishing into the depths of the dog's soft golden fur, and tipped her head up to look at him. "Is it a general sense of weariness or did something specific happen?"

He chose his words carefully. "Lucie emailed Edward to try to push his visit back a few weeks, to give us more time. She's the only one of us he *doesn't* detest, so she hoped he might agree if she asked."

"But he didn't," she guessed.

"He did not."

This is not something that can wait indefinitely, Edward's email had said, according to the screenshot Ian had sent Jamie. I know you agree.

Jamie could state with absolute certainty that nobody agreed.

"At the risk of flogging a dead horse, has anyone tried speaking to Lillian again?" Mika asked. "I know the odds aren't good, but if you can convince her to come back . . ."

Jamie wanted to laugh, wholly without mirth, but he only said, "There'd be no point trying."

"I'm sorry," she said. "It's obviously not my place to say it, but no matter what her reasons are for being away so often, she should be here *now*. She left the rest of you with a ticking bomb and the very least she could do is fix the—"

"The girls are *not* a ticking bomb," Jamie interrupted sharply.

"I was talking about the solicitor, not the girls," she said.

He exhaled. "Sorry."

"But," she went on, watching him carefully, "I expect it would be normal to struggle with looking after three children who are different from—"

He cut her off for the second time, his jaw clenched with anger. "They're kids," he snapped. "Some days, they're the funniest, sweetest humans on the planet. Other days, I'm tempted to throw them out the window. Because they're kids. Not because they're different. Looking after them is difficult because, again, they're *kids*."

Jamie stopped abruptly, knocked off balance by something intensely vulnerable in her eyes. Regret replaced his anger.

"Mika," he said quietly, "if your battalion of nannies and caregivers ever made you feel like a burden because you were different, *they* were wrong. Not you. You do know that, don't you?"

"They didn't know I was a witch," she said, a little too quickly. "Not until they saw something they shouldn't, and then they were gone, so they never had a chance to treat me any differently."

"They may not have known you were a witch, but they knew you were different," he guessed. "They must have known from the start that you weren't like most of the other kids they'd known. And I assume they made sure you knew they knew that."

She blinked quickly and swiped an unsteady hand across her eyes. Jamie was furious to discover that, after days of wishing Mika's sunshine good humour into oblivion, it turned out he did *not* like the total absence of it.

"Yes," she admitted, addressing his shoes. "They always knew I was different. It took me years to work out how to behave like I was expected to."

His voice was shot through with anger again, but this time it wasn't directed at her. "You shouldn't have had to do that."

"Thank you for saying that."

She turned to go. Circe followed her.

At the door, Mika paused to look back at him. Her gaze was steady as she said, "If the girls want lives outside of this house, they'll have to learn to fit in, too. I wish they didn't, but the world isn't as kind as we'd all like it to be."

"It could be," he said, and couldn't quite believe those words had come out of his mouth. When had *he* become the optimist?

Mika smiled then. "Maybe."

CHAPTER TEN

W here's your family?"

Mika glanced up at Altamira, sitting on the other side of the cauldron between them. She'd been lucky, she supposed, that it had taken a whole week for someone to ask that question. Given she'd already had to field questions like, "Do witches' reproductive organs work the same way as other people's?" (Rosetta), "Why do some people call a penis a willy?" (Altamira), and "Would you prefer poison or decapitation?" (Terracotta), *this* should not have been the question that threw her.

"Keep stirring," Mika reminded Altamira, partly because the mixture in the cauldron *did* need stirring and partly to buy herself a few more seconds.

"You didn't answer the question," said Altamira, who felt it was her duty to point out any failings in others.

Mika added a drop of lavender essence to the cauldron. "I don't have any family," she said. Amazing that she could be so used to that fact and yet find it so hard to say out loud every single time. "I grew up in Primrose's house, remember? My mother and grandmother were both witches, so I was pretty much on my own from the start."

"If you never knew your family, how do you know your mum and grandma were witches?" Altamira pointed out reasonably.

"Primrose told me, and I have no reason not to believe her."

"And the reason all our parents died when we were little is because of the spell that went wrong?"

Mika hadn't been the one to tell the children about the fact that witches were always orphaned young. They'd already known; it was one of the few things Lillian *had* told them. Mika, who had always suspected that Primrose had made up the spell-that-went-wrong story, had been astonished to discover that this mysterious spell was apparently talked of elsewhere, too.

"Like I said before, I have no idea if a spell really did go wrong," Mika said now. "But yes, whatever the reason, that's why our parents died."

Rosetta, who was working at the other, bigger cauldron, spoke up. "If you're a witch," she said quietly, "does that mean you're more likely to give birth to a witch?"

"Based on what we know, yes," said Mika. "Anyone's child can be a witch, but a witch's child is far more likely to be one, too."

"Wait!" Altamira cried. "Does that mean I mustn't ever have babies? But I like babies!"

"First of all, you're seven," said Mika. "You've got a while to go before you need to worry about that. Second of all, witches *do* have babies. I exist, don't I? We don't *always* give birth to witches. We're just more *likely* to. Many witches choose not to have biological children because of the risk of, you know—"

"Dying soon after?" Rosetta asked.

"I was going for a euphemism, but that works," said Mika. She hesitated, wondering how much she could appropriately explain to them. "And yes, some witches choose to take the risk because they want children very much, but sometimes the choice is taken out of their hands altogether. Now can we get back to our potion-making?"

Terracotta had not come to this lesson. Mika knew she was practicing the simple spells she'd taught the girls so far, because Rosetta had told her so, but Terracotta had missed about a third of their lessons. She typically turned up to a session or two, became reluctantly captivated, and promptly decided not to come to the next lesson just to make sure Mika never forgot that she didn't like her one bit. When they were thrown together outside of lessons—at mealtimes, in the firelit front room in the evenings, or when it was Mika's turn to keep an eye on the children playing outside—Terracotta either ignored Mika entirely or, alternatively, discussed methods of murder in the most matter-of-fact voice. Mika had decided to be amused because the alternative was to be extremely, extraordinarily frustrated.

Other than this, and it was admittedly a small thing, her first week at Nowhere House had gone very well. Over the course of their lessons, she'd watched the children's confidence and control grow; she'd taught them the properties of her eight Can't-Do-Withouts; they'd foraged for ingredients and brewed potions together; the girls had stayed up late one night so she could show them how to harvest moonlight; and Mika was quite certain she had Nowhere House's reserves of power well in hand.

There'd been a few other hiccups. Altamira needed constant rescuing from the well-meaning but overenthusiastic magic that tended to gather around her; Jamie seemed to be going out of his way to avoid being in the same room as Mika; and Mika had had to firmly quash Ian's and Lucie's hope that she would be able to teach How to Be a Woman of Colour as well as Witch 101.

The latter had taken her by surprise, and she'd had to point out the obvious: that just because she was a witch and just because she had brown skin, it did *not* mean she had answers to all the questions the girls would inevitably have about their own identities. But she'd said so kindly because she knew that, mistaken as Ian and Lucie had been in assuming she could be everything to everyone, all they really wanted was for the kids to have the opportunity to know others like them.

Which was far from easy, of course. Like Mika, the girls had an intersection of identities that put them smack dab in the middle of a small minority in Britain. They were witches, they weren't white, and they'd been born far away. Much as they might all wish otherwise, there would always be people who would question whether they were British enough, normal enough, *anything* enough. And the one place they might have all found something close to acceptance and kinship, in a community of diverse witches, was a place that didn't exist outside of a measly couple of hours every third month.

"Damn it, Primrose," Mika said under her breath. Since their first lesson, this had become Altamira's go-to response to any inconvenience, and it had only been a matter of time before Mika had found herself saying it, too.

Now Mika left Altamira to her stirring and went to check on Rosetta's cauldron. She'd handed Rosetta her spellbook at the start of their lesson, opened it to a relatively simple energizing infusion, and had set her the task of brewing her first potion entirely by herself. Rosetta, whose skill far outstripped her confidence, had been terribly nervous at first, but the moment she'd started work, her nerves had been forgotten.

"This looks good," Mika said, peering at the gently frothing mixture inside the cauldron. Eyeing Rosetta's stirring hand, she added gently, "It helps to stir in the same direction the whole time. Potions like consistency, so maybe you could decide at the start whether you're going to go clockwise or anticlockwise and then stick to it. Your wrist won't thank you, but you'll get a better potion out of it."

"That makes sense," Rosetta said, her cloud of black curls bobbing as her serious brown face brightened in a smile.

Mika's heart constricted. Rosetta reminded her so much of her younger self. There had been a time when Mika, too, had been shy and serious. She had been *desperate* to please, and had tried in vain to contort herself into a shape that her nannies and tutors would deem lovable. It was obvious that Rosetta had absolutely no doubt whatsoever that she was loved, but there was still something there, something painfully familiar in this child that made Mika want to reach out and wrap her arms around her.

Rosetta was lonely. It was obvious she loved her sisters and adored her caretakers, and was for the most part an extremely happy young girl, but Mika knew loneliness. She'd seen it in the way Rosetta had latched on to her the minute she'd arrived, and in the way she'd asked wistfully if it would be such a bad thing if more people knew about witches, and in her endless questions about what life was like as an adult witch. Rosetta spent time online. She watched TV and played video games. She knew there was a whole world outside Nowhere House. Unlike Altamira, who was still young and content, and Terracotta, who wanted their small, closed circle to stay that way, Rosetta, the shyest of the three, was also the one most interested in what was outside the gates.

On impulse, Mika said, "I was thinking of going into Norwich to see this bookshop I've heard about. Would you like to come with me?"

Mika regretted it as soon as she said it. The bookshop was in the very heart of Norwich, a good forty-five minutes away. It was *miles* outside Lillian's wards. And Norwich was a small city, but it was still a city and cities were full of people. She had no business inviting Rosetta to leave Nowhere House for the first time in years, let alone to go into a city almost an hour away, and she certainly had no business getting her hopes up before checking with one of the other adults.

Rosetta's eyes widened. "Can I? Am I allowed?"

"We can ask, can't we?" said Mika. "I reckon Ian would go for it, especially if he gets to come along! And, you know, part of the reason I'm here is to help the three of you open up your world a little, so this seems like a good way to give it a go."

"Okay," said Rosetta. Her excitement was tentative, but it was there.

There was no way Mika was going to dash her hopes now. She would get Rosetta to that bookshop if it killed her.

"No."

Everyone looked at Jamie, unsurprised. Well, they *shouldn't* be surprised. No one who knew him could possibly have expected him to agree to this particular piece of reckless, irresponsible lunacy.

"You'll have to forgive him," Ian said to Mika. "Jamie doesn't mean to be rude, but he can't help picturing the apocalypse round every corner."

"I *do* mean to be rude," Jamie snapped. "I always mean to be rude when someone suggests putting one of those kids in a stressful, unprecedented situation and expecting fuck all to go wrong. It's not safe to take them past the wards."

"It *wasn't* safe," Mika countered. "There's still a risk, I admit that, but it's a much, much smaller risk now that I'm here. *I* can keep a lid on the magic. That's my job."

"What if you can't? Lillian never even tried."

"Lillian never tried because she was never here," Ken said mildly.

Jamie scowled at him. Had they *all* lost their minds?

"Jamie—"

"Let's say, hypothetically, that Mika *can't* keep the magic in check," Jamie said flatly. "Let's say the worst happens. Then what? Are we supposed to assume Mika will be able to protect Rosetta from the pitchforks and police?"

"You would have been a natural on the stage, dear," said Ian, patting him affectionately on the arm. "In the real world, however—"

To Jamie's surprise, it was Mika who interrupted. "Jamie's not wrong. I don't know about pitchforks, but it's always possible that someone will call the police. *But,*" she went on, and the tension in his shoulders ratcheted right back up, "in my experience, most people who witness an unintended burst of magic tend to think it's a cool trick. They *ooh* and *ahh* a bit and then move on."

Okay, that was a good point. He tried not to scowl. "What if someone records it on their phone?"

"A video is even easier to dismiss as fake," said Mika. "And all of this assumes something will go wrong, which is very unlikely."

"It's a risk—"

"You asked me to come here to help prepare the girls for the world outside Nowhere House," Mika reminded him.

"*I* didn't ask you to come here," Jamie reminded *her*.

Ian, most bafflingly, had stopped injecting himself into the argument and now had his chin propped in his hand, watching them with a dreamy smile on his face. Jamie gave him a narrow look, decidedly mistrustful.

So far, as was typical, Ken and Lucie hadn't said anything, but now Lucie offered, "I've no doubt I'll spend the whole time you're gone counting the seconds until Rosetta's back safe and sound under this roof again, but I also have no doubt that this very short, ordinary trip will make that child very, very happy. And Mika's right about the fact that we have to do this sooner or later, or what's the point in doing any of this? So if we're putting this to a vote, I vote yes."

Jamie was furious, both with Mika for suggesting this and with himself for standing in the way of something he *knew* would make Rosetta happy. "I vote no," he said brusquely. "It's too soon."

"I vote yes, obviously," said Ian.

Everyone looked at Ken. "I think it's an excellent idea, Mika," he said gently. "I know you know what you're doing, and Rosetta will love it, but as a first step, it feels too big. It would be safer to take Rosetta ten minutes down the coast for fish and chips."

Mika nodded like she understood. "We could do that instead.

I don't mind where we go. I just thought she'd like the book-shop."

"Ken's always so sensible," Ian said fondly.

"Seriously?" Jamie demanded. "*Ken's* sensible, but *I* get ac-cused of picturing the apocalypse?"

Ian beamed at him. "I have to keep Ken happy. For sexual reasons."

"Ian," Jamie groaned. "No one wants to picture their great-grandparents having sex."

"Of all the nerve! I'm not that old!"

When the laughter subsided, Jamie rather reluctantly steered them back to the problem at hand. "So that was two votes no and two votes yes. And with my tiebreaker, that—"

"Your tiebreaker is a pain in my arse," said Ian sulkily. "Mika, my dear, couldn't you have had a little forethought and suggested this *next* week, at which point you would have been out of your two-week trial period and we could have given *you* a vote?"

"*I'm* getting a vote next week?" Mika looked astonished.

"Of course," Ken replied. "You'll be well and truly one of us then."

Mika continued to look stunned, like it had never occurred to her that she might be considered part of something, and Jamie found he violently hated it. He was *livid* that she was so surprised by such a simple gesture. Hadn't she *ever* been treated as any-thing but an outsider?

"So shall we suggest Ken's fish and chips idea to Rosetta?" Lucie asked.

"No," Jamie said abruptly, only too conscious of the fact that he'd lost his fucking mind. "Do the bookshop thing."

Four astounded faces swung round to him.

"Excuse me?" Ian spluttered.

"I'm not repeating myself, Ian."

"Well," said Lucie. Her voice wobbled with laughter. "*Well*."

God, they were all the worst.

"You could come, too," Mika said to him, her brown eyes so bright they reminded him of looking directly into the sun. "To the bookshop. If it'll make you feel better about it."

That was *not* what he'd had in mind.

He looked away. "Okay."

"I could not possibly have come up with a better idea myself," Ian said gleefully. "I, for one, cannot *wait*."

CHAPTER ELEVEN

Mika had just finished watering the plants in the greenhouse when Jamie came to find her. She set the empty metal watering can on the shelf, checked on the rosemary and shallots she'd planted just last week, and turned back to where she'd left her coat.

And bumped straight into someone's chest.

She let out a startled yelp and rocked back on her heels, off balance. Jamie's hands closed around her upper arms at once, steadying her, and the sudden scent of pine needles made her dizzy. Warmth bloomed out from the places where his hands touched her bare skin. She blinked up at him. He let her go very quickly.

"Sorry." He backed up a couple of steps, into the narrow doorway of the greenhouse. The sun was behind him, making it difficult to see the expression on his face. "I just came to tell you we're good to go."

"Wait," she said, closing the gap between them again and seizing the lapels of his shirt. She inhaled. "Definitely pine needles. And the ocean? What *is* that?"

He cleared his throat. "My aftershave, I guess?"

"But you don't shave. Do you? I mean, there's always that short, bristly shadow on your—" Mika stopped and took two hasty steps back. Her love of all sensory joys had gotten her in awkward situations before, notably that time on a train when she'd reached out to stroke an old lady's beautiful pashmina without remembering to ask permission first, but this took the cake! Her cheeks grew hot, and she smiled sheepishly. Really, it was impossible not to see the humour in her own mortification. "Um. Sorry. Even after a lifetime of reminding myself, I still forget what is and isn't socially acceptable behaviour."

"You've met me, haven't you? I'm not exactly a bastion of socially acceptable behaviour."

"Well, for what it's worth, I'm now done sniffing you." She ran an eye over the greenhouse again, just to give the hummingbird flutter of her heart a minute to calm the hell down.

He watched her. "You have an insect in your hair."

"Yes, that's intentional," said Mika affably. "I find they make wonderful ornaments."

His eyes lit with unexpected laughter. "I was going to get rid of it, but if it's there on *purpose*—"

"No! Take it out, please?"

He plucked a ladybug out of her hair. His hand brushed the shell of her ear and she backed away quickly, tucking her hair behind it and pretending to be very interested in the ladybug he'd rescued.

Jamie's voice was brusque as he said, "They're waiting for us," and walked out of the greenhouse.

Mika blew out a slow breath and followed him around to the front of the house, where the Broomstick was waiting. Ian had insisted they take it today because, he said, he and Rosetta were not about to pass up the opportunity to travel in a witch's enchanted car. They were both in the back seat already, bouncing up and down like a pair of toddlers on their first roller coaster.

Mika got in the driver's seat, retrieved her keys from Ian, and waited for Jamie to fold himself into the little hatchback beside her. As he buckled his seatbelt, she marvelled at the fact that she'd had a golden retriever, a greenhouse, and an entire koi pond in this car, yet it had never felt as small as it did right now, with Jamie Kelly's elbow just an inch away from hers.

Oh. Oh, no. He'd pushed the sleeves of his white buttondown shirt up past his elbows. She could see his forearms.

Forearms were invariably her ruin.

She sighed, started the car, and peeled away from the house before she did something that would well and truly put the cherry on top of her mortification sundae.

"Wheeeeeee!" Ian squealed behind her, as if he didn't drive his own car faster than this. (He did. Ken had told her.) "When does the speed spell kick in?"

"When I need it to," said Mika. "Emphasis on the word *need* there. I'm not using it today."

"Spoilsport."

"I don't mind," Rosetta said happily. She'd twisted as much as her seatbelt would allow and had her arms propped on the bottom frame of her open window, her eyes glued to the woods and rolling fields zipping past. "I don't want to miss anything!"

Mika looked at Rosetta in the rear-view mirror. When they'd told her about this trip, she'd allowed herself only a heartbeat of unabashed delight before she'd cast worried looks at Terracotta and Altamira because she hadn't wanted them to be left out. They had both immediately informed her that they didn't want to go to a bookshop, thanks, and were more excited about getting to spend the afternoon swimming in the sea under Ken's watchful eye. (Privately, Mika thought this sounded like a ghastly way to spend an afternoon. There was no force in the universe that would have persuaded her to dip more than a *toe* in the North Sea in November, but Terracotta and Altamira seemed to positively delight in the cold.)

Reassured, Rosetta's excitement had been boundless. She'd dug out the clothes she only ever wore on birthdays, had insisted on washing her hair this morning, and had sat patiently for an hour while Ken had dried, untangled, combed, and styled it until it was a perfect halo of thick, beautiful curls around her face. It was heartbreaking to Mika that Rosetta thought a trip to a bookshop justified all this effort, but it was also wonderful to see how happy she was.

As if he'd been thinking the same thing, Jamie turned his head now to look Rosetta in the eye and smiled the warm, twinkly smile that he only ever gave the children. "You okay, kid?"

"I'm whatever okay is when you multiply it by a million," Rosetta said, still gazing raptly out the window.

"And Mika obviously has everything well in hand," Ian said, "so we're off to a splendid start." There was a pause, and then, his tone shifting, he went on: "If something *should* go wrong, Mika, how do you propose to handle it?"

"By leaving straight away and trusting that whatever's happened is dismissed as a trick."

"Perhaps you and Rosetta could preserve your anonymity by disguising yourselves," Ian suggested.

"What, like with hats and moustaches?"

"Or with *magic*," Ian said meaningfully. "On account of you being a witch and all."

Mika noticed Jamie's whole body had tensed. She had no idea why he'd agreed to this outing after how adamant he'd been that it was madness, but the last thing she needed was for Ian's apocalyptic hypotheticals to put him off before they even got there.

"Ian, nothing's going to go wrong," she insisted.

"Hmm," Ian said noncommittally. "But *could* you disguise yourself if you needed to?"

"Ian." Jamie's voice was clipped.

"I've heard of glamour spells," Mika said, considering the question with academic interest. "They project an illusion, so you could make yourself look however you wanted, but they're very difficult and I don't know the right runes. If I *had* to cover my tracks and I knew as much in advance, I'd probably stick with something less complicated, like a tea to confuddle the senses of anyone who drinks it."

"Is there such a thing?"

"I've never tried to brew one, but I don't think it would be difficult to figure out. But again," she emphasised, "extreme measures are *not* going to be necessary today."

Ian dropped it after that, and looked out of the window with a slightly troubled expression on his face. Mika wondered if she'd misjudged him and he was, in fact, a lot more worried about this trip than he'd let on.

But then, as they drove past a pretty country church, Ian piped up again. "So, my dear. Do you have anyone special in your life?"

While the endearment could have been addressed to anyone, the question made it obvious that it was Mika he was asking. She rolled her eyes. So he wasn't *that* worried, then.

"I live with *you*," she said. "When exactly do you think I see this hypothetical special someone?"

"So it's been a while then," said Ian, rubbing his skinny chin like a cartoon villain.

"A while since what?"

"He means since you had sex," said Rosetta, without taking her eyes off the window.

Jamie choked. Ian shrugged as if to say, "Yes, that *is* what I meant."

"Inappropriate," Mika said to Ian. Her stern tone was somewhat undercut by the fact that she was trying very hard not to laugh. "It is categorically *not* your business, Ian Kubo-Hawthorn, but if you must know, it's been a few months."

"Was it serious?"

"It's never serious," said Mika. "I haven't done serious since I was at university, and that was a huge, colossal, fuck-off *ginormous* mistake."

Out of the corner of her eye, she saw Jamie look curiously at her.

"Is it the secrets that stop you?" Ian asked.

"It's always the secrets," Mika said. She flicked the indicator, turned left, and followed a sign for the A47. She thought suddenly of Hilda Kim, sweet, extroverted Hilda who had told the Very Secret Society that she was struggling with hiding a big part of herself from her fiancée. "I couldn't fall in love with someone who didn't know I was a witch. I think it would hurt too much. It's why I never stay long in any one place, and never stay in touch with anyone I happen to meet while I'm there. If I get close to people, I'll want to tell them the truth. And if I tell them the truth, I'll probably lose them."

"You don't know that," Rosetta objected. "You're awesome. I refuse to believe anyone who knew you would turn on you."

Mika's heart became a puddle of goo. "You're too pure for this world, Rosetta."

"To be clear," said Jamie, ruining the moment with his usual flair, "you're saying you won't live in one place for more than a few months because you don't want to get close to people you might later lose, but you're happy to bond with a dog and four fish?"

"First of all, I don't want to get close to people I can't ever be myself with," Mika reminded him. "The secrecy is kind of the key point. Even if I choose not to tell the truth, if I stay too long in one place, anyone who gets to know me might figure out I'm different. And second of all," she went on, "Circe is only four years old. I'm not going to lose her for a good long while. As for the fish, they're koi. They can live for over thirty years if they're properly cared for. I'm not exactly risking my heart by letting them have a piece of it."

"Look!" Rosetta interrupted them to goggle at the cars and lorries rumbling beside them on the wide, busy A47. "I've never seen so many cars in real life!"

Mika seized on this interruption. In the rear-view mirror, she could see that Ian had a look on his face that suggested he was not yet done with the subject of her romantic escapades, and she was determined to divert him. "Does Lillian have any family at all?" she asked, wondering if anyone else out there knew about the girls. "Have you ever met them?"

"Oh." Ian shrugged, his eyes pointed out the window. "She told us once that she and her sister were raised by relatives who despised them. She left them as soon as she was able and never looked back, so no, we've never met any of them. Mind you," he went on, "that's *her* version of it, but as you might have noticed by now, Lillian is not exactly forthcoming."

"I don't think she's ever outright *lied* to us," Jamie objected.

"Withholding information is just as bad as a lie," Ian replied petulantly. "And you needn't give me that look, James. I know you feel like you have to defend her when I get going, but I'm not saying anything that isn't true."

Mika cast a doubtful sideways look at Jamie. "Why do you feel like you have to defend her?"

Jamie turned his head around so that he could scowl at Ian in the back, clearly irritated that he was now going to have to explain something he didn't want to, and said, shortly, "I left home at sixteen. Lillian took me in."

"So you lived at Nowhere House *before* you started working at the library? And you were still just a child when you left home?"

"He took the ferry from Belfast to Liverpool, then got on the first train from Liverpool going anywhere," Ian said. "All by himself, this wee lad. He didn't care where he was going so long as it was away from home. The first train turned out to be a train to Norwich. He got off at this end, bumped into Lillian outside the station, and she took one look at him and brought him back to the house with her."

"Where Lucie, Ken, and Ian proceeded to take great pleasure in fussing over me," said Jamie with a faint smile.

"He needed fussing over," Ian insisted.

"How old are you now?" Mika asked.

"Thirty-six."

Twenty years. Nowhere House had been his home for more than half his life. It was no wonder he was so territorial.

"We made him finish school a little way up the coast," Ian went on, as proud as an indulgent grandparent, "and then we packed him off to Cambridge for a few years. He stayed on after he got his degree to lecture at the university, then went to Amsterdam for a year to teach *there*, then moved back to Nowhere House for good when Lillian turned up with Rosetta."

"Are you quite finished narrating the entirely uninteresting documentary of my life?" Jamie asked irritably.

"For now," Ian chirped.

Mika was desperately curious to know what had made Jamie leave his childhood home so dramatically, but she was quite certain asking him wouldn't go down well. Instead, she said, "What about the rest of you?"

"Lucie was the housekeeper, just like we told you," Ian said. "She didn't always live at the house. You'll have to ask her to tell you the whole story, but the long and short of it is, she had a violent husband. When she left him, she came to Lillian, who insisted she stay."

Nowhere House was shifting in Mika's mind. The new Nowhere House was messier than the first, a place made up of fractured pieces that, somehow, had come together to make something whole and wonderful.

As for Lillian herself, well, Mika had a lot of bones to pick with her, but Ian's stories had given her a bit of a boost in Mika's estimation.

"And you and Ken?" she asked Ian.

"Ours is an unexciting tale, I'm afraid," said Ian. "We came to Nowhere House because Ken turns gardens into works of art."

Mika watched him narrowly in the mirror. "And that's all it was?" she prodded. "It didn't have anything to do with you and the way you seem to be able to spot a witch just by looking at her?"

Their eyes met. Ian's twinkled. He gave her a too-innocent shrug.

Mika let it go for the moment. Instead, she said, diplomatically, "It sounds like Lillian's rescued a lot of people in trouble."

"Lillian likes her strays," said Rosetta.

Ouch. Mika felt Jamie go very still beside her. Even Ian had been silenced.

Rosetta looked around at them. Her cheeks flushed guiltily, but she held her ground. "We talk about it, Terracotta, Altamira, and I," she said. "I know Lillian's given us a lot and she's always been nice to us, but it kind of feels like she thinks of us as stray puppies she picked up from the shelter rather than as actual people. If she cared about any of us as much as she cares about whatever point she was trying to make when she took us in, she'd have stuck around more. *Mika's* taught us more in a week than Lillian has in all the time we've known her."

"It's okay to feel that way," Jamie said, his voice low. "She *does* care, in her own way, but her way is . . ."

"Not right for us," Ian finished for him, which was a more polite assessment than Mika had expected from him. "Let's just get it out there: she has done a lot of good, and she has enjoyed the warm fuzzies of doing a lot of good, and she has also stuck around for absolutely none of the real work."

Out of the corner of her eye, Mika saw that Jamie's jaw was tight and he was clearly conflicted, but he didn't contradict Ian.

"I don't pretend to know much about people," she offered, fixing her eyes on the road ahead, "but one thing I've noticed over the years is that some people are nice and some people are kind. Lillian sounds like she's more nice than she is kind. Does that make sense? Niceness is good manners, and stopping to give someone directions, and smiling at the overworked cashier at the supermarket. These are all good things, but they have nothing to do with what's underneath. Niceness is all about what we do when other people are looking. Kindness, on the other hand, runs deep. Kindness is what happens when no one's looking."

"You know, my dear," said Ian, sounding much struck, "I do believe you're right."

Mika cut Jamie a look. "*You*, for example, are not nice."

He made a sound that could have been a laugh. "Thanks?"

"Meanwhile, Ken is both nice *and* kind."

Rosetta and Ian nodded vigorously at this. "It's true," said Ian. "The man has no flaws! Not one! That is, apart from his refusal to partake in my many madcap schemes."

"That's not a flaw," said Jamie wryly. "That's having a spine, and a whole lot more common sense than you do."

Mika laughed. "See? Not nice at all."

"Did you see that?" Rosetta interrupted, bolting ramrod straight. "That sign back there? We're close!"

As they reached the edge of the city, Mika grew quiet, her eyes flicking to the map on the screen of her satnav. Norwich had evolved in ten years, she could see that already, but she still wanted to stay well clear of the University of East Anglia, with its familiar misty green fields and glass walls and all the memories it came with.

Luckily, they approached the city from the opposite side, avoiding the university entirely as they wove through a network of crisscrossing streets lined with trees, pubs, and old-fashioned terraced houses. Rosetta had gone silent, too, her eyes wide with awe as she tracked an enormous cathedral.

Mika found a space in a multistorey carpark that seemed to have been built underneath Norwich Castle—or near enough to *feel* like they could have been in a castle's dungeon anyway—and they made their way out into the bright, cold sunshine on foot.

Instantly, the city seized them in what felt like a friendly and slightly daunting hug. Someone was already playing Christmas music in a nearby shop, loud enough to spill out into the narrow, cobbled street. People trotted past, this way and that, checking their phones and gesturing animatedly to their companions. Pigeons dodged passers-by, darting between their legs to snatch up dropped bits of sandwiches and scones.

There was a quaint timelessness to this part of the city, from the castle looming above to the twisty cobblestone streets to the old-fashioned shopfronts. It was far more relaxed than many other cities Mika had been to, but she still looked anxiously at Rosetta to make sure she wasn't overwhelmed.

Rosetta had moved close to Jamie and followed in his shadow like a baby bird seeking shelter from the cold. She looked shy, and certainly a little unsure, but her eyes were bright with excitement and drank everything in. Instead of making a big deal out of it, Jamie let her follow at her own pace and continued to talk to Ian,

who, as always, was never short of opinions he felt it was impera-
tive he share.

"My mother was a witch," Ian said unexpectedly.

Mika blinked, because it had come out of nowhere, but she
found it wasn't much of a surprise. "That does make a lot of sense,"
she replied. "Considering how little you say Lillian told you, you
do know a lot about us. And you can see magic."

"Can't everyone?"

"Everyone can see *spells*," said Mika. "Or, rather, the result of
a spell. But I'm talking about *magic*, the gold dust that witches
can see and use. You can't use it, but you can see it. That's how
you knew I was a witch just by watching my videos. That's why it
sometimes looks like the girls and I are shining."

"Mother shone," Ian said, smiling softly. "She took *so* much
pride and joy in her power. She considered it such a gift, and it
felt like even more of a gift that she shared it with me."

Mika kissed his cheek, overwhelmed by affection. "You have
a big, wonderful heart, Ian Kubo-Hawthorn."

"Now you're just making an old man blush, Mika Moon."

"I'm glad you told Mika," Rosetta said. "I'm pretty sure Altamira
would have blurted it out any day now."

"I thought it was time to tell her," Ian said smugly. "After all,
she's now one of us."

"I am?"

"I'm making the executive decision to end your two-week trial
period a few days early." Ian raised his eyebrows at Jamie, as if he
expected the latter to object. Jamie rolled his eyes but said nothing, much to Mika's surprise. Ian smiled, and added: "We'll discuss it some more this evening, when Ken and Lucie are with us.

There's plenty to talk about. Until then, you should know that I don't tell just *anyone* about my mother."

"It's Ian's way of inducting someone into his circle of sacred trust," Jamie said drily. "He did it to me, too. Except it came as much more of a shock to me because I didn't even know witches existed at that point."

Mika had a lump in her throat. She had never felt so welcomed and included, so much a *part* of something, and she couldn't rid herself of a lifelong fear that it was too good to be true. That any minute now, like every person who had flashed in and out of her adolescence, they would decide she was *too* something or not *enough* of something else and snatch away their welcome.

But she held back the fear and doubt, and let only her delight show. She put an arm around Rosetta's shoulders and beamed at the two men. "Do I get a cake to celebrate?"

CHAPTER TWELVE

think we're supposed to go that way," Mika said, pointing left
with one hand while holding her phone up with the other. It
was almost impossible to get a proper look at the screen with the
sharp winter sun's glare bouncing off it. "The map says it's—"

"I see it!" Ian said. "Oh, how *darling.*"

The bookshop was indeed rather darling. The shopfront was
bright and colourful, obviously decorated with children in mind,
and there were painted illustrations of unicorns, sea monsters,
and fairies all over the interior whitewashed walls. It was a week-
day afternoon in November, so schools around the city had only
just finished for the day and the shop was still relatively quiet.

Inside, the bookshop was lovely and inviting. It was very clean,
and Mika caught a faint whiff of lemon antibacterial spray (kids,
of course, being veritable hotbeds of germs), but it was also de-
lightfully untidy. Books and cushions were all over the place,
stacked in wobbly piles and scattered higgledy-piggledy, and
someone had left a box of crayons strewn across the rug. Jamie
winced slightly, like he felt he'd just walked into the chaotic hell-
scape of his darkest nightmares, but Mika suspected that the shop

was *supposed* to be messy. This way, a child coming in wouldn't be intimidated by perfectly ordered shelves and untouchably pristine books.

A middle-aged white woman smiled warmly at them from behind the till. "Lovely afternoon, isn't it?" she said, abiding by that ancient and most sacred British law of only ever starting a conversation with a comment on the weather.

After chatting with her for a moment, Ian made a beeline for the one shelf crammed with books for grown-ups, almost all of which were romance novels ("Perfect!" Ian said blissfully), and it took Rosetta less than five seconds to peel herself from Jamie's side and race over to the brightly coloured spines of a mystery series she'd recently fallen in love with.

So passed a peaceful thirty minutes. Mika wandered around the different sections of the little shop, dividing her attention between finding books the younger girls would like and keeping a watchful eye on the mischievous gold dust that had gathered around Rosetta.

Jamie approached her after a while, a crease between his eyebrows. "Will you be okay keeping an eye on Rosetta if I go out for a few minutes? I'll only be round the corner."

Mika could see he was frustrated. He didn't trust her (*yet*, she hoped), but wherever he planned to go, it had to be important or else she was quite sure he wouldn't have dreamed of leaving Rosetta with her. If Ian hadn't been there, too, he probably *wouldn't* have.

"Go," she said sunnily. "We'll be fine."

He hesitated a moment longer, his eyes on the back of Rosetta's tight black curls, and then left with a brusque nod.

Mika turned her attention back to her young companion and

dispelled an especially enthusiastic cloud of gold dust with a wave of her hand. Magic meant well, but it did so want to be used and it had an irksome habit of taking matters into its own hands if witches didn't take the hint.

She and Rosetta were poring over the mysteries when Ian approached them, puzzled. "Where's our handsome escort?"

"He said he had to pop out for a few minutes," she replied.

"Did he?" Ian looked taken aback, and more than a little inquisitive. "Maybe he went to say hello to that friend of his who works in the pub. Stephen? Sam? Something with an *S*. No, I'm quite sure Stephen-or-Sam doesn't work on Thursdays. Hmm . . ."

He continued in this vein for a moment, pondering the mystery of Jamie's whereabouts to an audience who paid absolutely no attention to him. Then he abruptly switched gears and chuckled.

"How interesting." His voice brimmed with humour. "I mentioned a handsome someone and you immediately assumed I was referring to Jamie."

Mika gave him a frosty look, incredibly irked by the fact that her cheeks were reddening. "We all know what he looks like, so there's no need to act like something momentous just happened."

"Someone's tes-*ty*," Ian commented, raising his eyebrows at Rosetta, who giggled.

Mika stomped off, but only to a pile of beanbags by the comic books, where two boys about Rosetta's age, in navy blue jumpers with school crests, were examining the cover of one book in particular.

"Rosetta?" she called back. "Isn't this the sequel to the comic you were reading earlier this week?"

One of the boys looked up. "Did you finish it already?" he

asked Rosetta. "We haven't yet, so don't give us any spoilers, but is the ending as good as everyone says?"

Rosetta's eyes widened in abject terror, and Ian nudged her gently in the boys' direction. "Um, yes," she said, in little more than a mumble. "It's really good. You'll want to have the sequel right there so you can start it as soon as you finish the first one."

"I just want to know if Captain Chaos got the Spear of Fate," the other boy said. "Did she?"

"Zaf! No spoilers!"

Zaf made a face at his friend and waved Rosetta over. "Say it really quietly so Billy can't hear you."

"Zaf!"

Rosetta was smiling now, and her voice was louder and clearer as she said, "You have to read it yourself. It's honestly *so* worth it!"

And that was it. In seconds, Rosetta was on the pile of beanbags with the two boys, arguing passionately about whether someone called Juniper Joy (a name that, improbably, was somehow even *more* twee than Mika Moon) deserved to win the Tournament of Fifteen Crowns.

"Is this what it feels like to be incredibly, absurdly proud of someone?" Mika said to Ian in an undertone.

He patted her fondly on the arm. "It does indeed, my dear. You should go get Jamie. He'll want to see this."

"Can't you text him?"

"He never checks his texts," said Ian blithely, which sounded to Mika like an outright lie.

"Okay, but if someone has to go fetch him, shouldn't it be you? *I* have to keep an eye on, you know, the *magic*."

"I'm an old man, Mika!" Ian tutted. "I can't go traipsing up and down the city!"

Mika scoffed but relented. She glanced once more at Rosetta, just to make doubly sure that the shimmer of power gathered around her was completely in check, and then darted out the bookshop door.

Of course, as soon as she'd made her way down the narrow, twisty cobblestone street and turned the corner, she stopped short because she didn't actually have any idea where Jamie was.

She was just about to turn right around and go back to the bookshop when the door of an old, narrow, two-storey brick office opened and Jamie came out, his brows furrowed. He shut the door with unwonted force.

The angry look on his face didn't budge when he spotted her. "What are you doing out here?"

Mika glanced at the sign above the door behind him. The words SOLICITORS LTD. stood out. "Have you been to see Edward?"

"What?" He gave her an odd look, as if her question had come out of left field. Then he glanced behind him and sighed. "Oh. No. Edward works in London."

So he'd been to see a different solicitor, then. Mika was unaccountably curious, but a voice at the back of her mind piped up, reminding her that it was not considered good manners to ask someone why they'd been to see a solicitor.

She opened her mouth to tell him what Rosetta was up to, but what came out instead was:

"You've committed a crime, haven't you?"

Jamie stopped in his tracks.

"Oh, good God," Mika went on, quite unable to stop the words. "Is it murder? It is, isn't it?"

"You've been spending too much time with Terracotta," Jamie said severely. "Murder is *not* the answer to every question."

Mika found herself collapsing into laughter even as red-hot colour stained her cheeks. "God, I'm fucking ridiculous."

All her life, she had been prone to what Primrose had called *very irregular ideas*. It had not been a compliment. And, really, Mika was starting to think Primrose may have been on to something. Upon encountering a man leaving the office of a solicitor, a regular person would surely have jumped to *it must have something to do with money* and not, instead, to the more outlandish *a murder has clearly been committed and the police will be knocking at the door any minute now.*

Jamie's face was expressionless, but there was something perilously like a smile in his eyes as he said, "You are fucking ridiculous, yes."

"So," she said sheepishly, "At this point, I feel like I *have* to ask why you've been to see a solicitor."

He cut her an exasperated look, but said, "I had a question about my dad's will."

"Oh." Mika felt terrible. "I'm so sorry. I didn't know your dad had died."

"Don't worry about it. I was twelve when he died."

Now Mika was more confused than ever, but it *really* wasn't her place to keep prying. "I never knew either of my parents," she said instead, relieved to find that her mouth was saying the right words this time. "You know that, of course, on account of the witch thing."

"I assume Primrose was the closest thing you had."

Mika choked on a laugh. "I've told you how I grew up. Primrose did exceedingly little parenting."

"But she's important to you, isn't she? She and the other witches in your Society? If push came to shove, they'd still have your loyalty?"

"Of course," said Mika. "If we can't count on each other, who *can* we count on?" She cocked her head to one side, considering him. "Was that your way of asking if I'm going to tell them about the girls?"

"It wasn't subtle," he admitted.

"Not even a little." She smiled. "No, I'm not going to tell them. That would be interfere-y and Primrose-ish of me, and I'd rather not be either of those things. And anyway, even if there was no chance of Primrose trying to convince Lillian to separate the kids if she were to find out about them, I don't see what the point would be in telling any of the other witches." She thought about that for a moment. "I suppose if Lillian refused to come back from South America to recast her wards in the spring, I'd want to tell them. I think it would be too risky to raise three young witches in one place without wards."

"*You* couldn't cast the spell?" He looked away, suddenly interested in something in the middle distance. "If you were still at Nowhere House in the spring, that is."

"No, Lillian's wards are incredibly powerful. I'd need a few other witches to cast the spell with me. But the girls tell me that Lillian always comes back in time, or close to it, so it shouldn't be a problem." Mika felt the edges of her mouth curl up in an irrepressible smile. "You think I might still be at Nowhere House in the spring?"

The faintest hint of colour streaked across the tops of his ears. "I didn't say that." He turned abruptly away, one hand clenching and unclenching into a fist at his side. "We should go."

"If you're lucky, we'll be back in time to see Rosetta with her new friends."

"Yeah, about that," Jamie said, his voice clipped. "Remind me why you left her alone?"

"Bite my head off, why don't you," Mika said, deploying a voice so sunny and sweet, she hoped it gave him a toothache. "She's *not* alone, and I've only been gone five minutes."

"Sorry." He raked a hand over the top of his dark blond hair. "Was she okay when you left her?"

"She was neck-deep in a comic book with two fellow fans. She seemed a bit nervous when they started talking to her, but she'd pretty much forgotten Ian and I were there when I left."

The stormy grey of his eyes softened to something warmer. Then, as they walked back down the twisty street, he absently put himself between her and the icy wind coming from the left.

It was impossible to stay cross with him after that.

Of course, it was also a *little* difficult to maintain the moral high ground when, upon getting back to the bookshop, they found Ian and Rosetta waiting outside with a stack of torn books and rather sheepish expressions on their faces.

"There may or may not have been a small cyclone," Ian informed them. "But not to worry, it's gone now and semi-convincing explanations have been offered. We are, however, in possession of six largely unreadable books because it seemed only polite to buy the books that were ripped apart."

"I maybe lost my temper a bit when Billy said he hoped Captain Chaos never got the Spear of Fate back," Rosetta explained.

Mika didn't dare look at Jamie, whose voice was studiously even as he said, "Did Billy survive the cyclone?"

"He didn't even notice it!" Rosetta said. "It was only a *tiny* cyclone."

Jamie considered her. "Did you have fun?"

"*So* much fun," she said, her sheepish, anxious expression dissolving into an enormous smile.

Jamie shrugged. "In that case, a cyclone seems like a reasonable price to pay."

CHAPTER THIRTEEN

As the days passed, life at Nowhere House settled into a gentle rhythm. This wasn't to say that it was predictable, because it certainly wasn't that; the teaching of young witches was nothing if not unexpected. Mika might find herself brewing potions with the girls on one day, then have to fish Altamira *out* of the cauldron on the next. There was no telling when Terracotta would turn up and, if she did, when she might be in an even more quarrelsome frame of mind than usual. And just as Mika had warned the others on that first day, her presence at Nowhere House had attracted even *more* magic to the area, which demanded more of her attention than she was used to.

But, on the whole, there was a pattern to the everyday lives of the household and, much to Mika's surprise, there was space for her in it. She quickly became the Person Who Made the Tea, as it was universally agreed that she made the best tea ("Of course I do," she said, not very modestly), and she just as quickly became Ken's favourite person to help him in the garden ("Being a witch does have its perks," she said, a little more modestly). When she wasn't teaching the girls or gardening with Ken, she went over to the cottage to help Ian with his dubious beekeeping ambitions, took Circe to the sea, showed Altamira how to properly feed the koi, helped Lucie fix broken odds and ends around the house, and spent an inordinate amount of time napping.

There were game nights and lazy TV afternoons and haphazard football matches in the garden and elaborate adventures involving the tree house and two planks of Ian's beehive wood (apparently, they were supposed to be a pirate ship). There was spellcasting, potion-making, and an entire afternoon's worth of Mika helping the girls make and decorate their very own spellbooks. Sometimes everyone went their separate ways, whether it was Rosetta to the library to use Jamie's computer for some supervised online time in one of her favourite fandom groups, or Terracotta to the kitchen to make pumpkin pie with Ian, or Altamira to the sofa with Lucie and Lucie's laptop for a virtual coding lesson. And sometimes the whole house came together, like the morning everyone abandoned whatever work they were supposed to be doing and they all went down to the beach because Terracotta had somehow coaxed, pleaded, and browbeaten Ken, Lucie, and Jamie into agreeing to a race with one child on each of their shoulders. Mika and Ian, both of whom were spared by virtue of having shoulders Terracotta deemed too flimsy for this purpose, watched from the dunes and cried actual tears of laughter.

A gentle rhythm, indeed. But it was more than that. It was *peace*, the kind Mika was beginning to see she had never known. She hadn't understood how exhausting and heartbreaking it had been to hide such a big part of herself all these years, to reshape and contort herself into something more acceptable. She hadn't realised just how heavy her mask had been until she'd discovered what it was to live without it.

To be at Nowhere House was to put herself in very real peril, so why, then, did she feel safer than she ever had before?

There was a meteor shower on the first night in December. Mika didn't waste the opportunity, and she stayed up late so that she could catch the star shavings falling from the sky. These precious, luminous shards were one of her Can't-Do-Withouts and her tiny vial was almost empty.

Yawning, Circe jumped off Mika's bed and padded closer. She stopped in the open balcony doorway, uninterested in stepping out any farther into the cold.

"I've been thinking about what might happen if I combined star shavings, lavender, pollen, *and* moonlight," Mika said to her. Circe blew out a sleepy breath. Mika nodded. "I know, I know. You think it's a bad idea to put stars and moonlight in the same potion. You think they'll be too powerful together, or that they'll react unpredictably because neither comes from the earth." She clicked her tongue thoughtfully, catching a luminous shard drifting past her. "But what if I combined them and something *spectacular* happened?"

Circe huffed, snuffled her cold wet nose into the side of Mika's neck, and went back to her warm, comfy spot on the bed.

"You're right," Mika agreed. "It's a bad idea. You're such a good influence on me, Circe."

It was always irksome when an idea went nowhere, but Mika knew by now that there would always be new ideas.

She'd just topped up about two thirds of the vial when, from below her attic balcony, she heard a quiet growl of pain. Circe's ears pricked up.

The growl was, of course, unmistakable. Jamie probably hadn't meant for anyone to hear him, but she was on the balcony and he must have had his window cracked open.

She glanced at her clock. Twenty past two. She'd noticed that Jamie slept very little, but this was late even for him. Why was he still up?

"Stay," Mika said to Circe, who was obviously so warm, comfortable, and sleepy that she didn't bother to dignify this with a response.

Laying her tools down carefully, Mika opened her door, slipped down the stairs, and avoided the creaky floorboards (When had she gotten so familiar with the house that she knew which floorboards creaked?) in her path down the hallway. She paused outside Jamie's door, which was open just a sliver, and tapped her knuckles quietly against the frame before sticking her head in.

The room was lit only by a lamp on the nightstand. It was a very Jamie-ish room, which was to say it was perfectly tidy: every book on the shelves was ordered, a laptop and paperback (with a bookmark in, of course, because to leave a book open on its front was practically a capital crime as far as Jamie was concerned) were stacked neatly beside the lamp on the nightstand, and even the soft, round, grey rug was in the exact centre of the room. Incredible.

Jamie was on one knee halfway between the rug and window, picking up what looked like small pieces of broken glass off the floor. There was blood on his left hand.

"Cut yourself?"

He looked up, obviously startled to see her, and then gestured for her to come in. "Watch out for the glass," he said with a cursory glance at her bare feet. Well, she assumed it was *supposed* to be a cursory glance, but then he noticed that the rest of her legs were bare too and he blinked. "Why aren't you dressed?"

"Because it's half past two in the morning?" Mika rolled her eyes. *He*, of course, was perfectly decent in a white T-shirt and grey sweatpants. "Before you call a priest to cleanse my soul, please do behold that my T-shirt is practically down to my knees."

Reluctant amusement tugged up one corner of his mouth. "We'll have to save the exorcism for another day, then."

"A wise decision. I knew you could be sensible when you put your mind to it." Winding a tendril of magic around her finger, Mika summoned all the tiny pieces of glass and collected them together in a neat, glittering ball that hovered in mid-air and sent reflected light dancing across the room. "Disco or bin?"

"I think you know I'm going to say bin," he said, still sounding amused.

"It's true, I would have keeled over dead if you'd agreed to a party. Into the bin it goes, then." There was a rattan wastebasket in the corner of his bedroom, so she floated the pieces of glass into a sheet of loose paper and scrunched the paper securely around the glass. "So what happened?"

"Couldn't sleep. I decided to try that time-honoured tradition of drinking myself into oblivion. Dropped the empty glass before I could even start." He gestured to his desk, where a bottle of whisky and a second glass tumbler still sat.

Over the past couple of weeks, with Edward's visit drawing

nearer, Jamie, Ian, Ken, and Lucie had all, in their own ways, been showing signs of increasing nerves. Ken spent even more time in the garden; when he wasn't flat-out avoiding her, Jamie was moodier than usual; Ian had been getting shrill; Lucie was constantly rushing around the house and keeping herself almost manically busy; and Mika had spotted all four of them in intense, whispered conversation on a few occasions. She had tried to assure them, repeatedly, that the girls were gaining more confidence and control by the day and she had the magic well in hand, but she supposed it was easier for her to say it than it was for them to trust in it.

Mika assumed now that this was at the root of Jamie's insomnia, but she also suspected he wouldn't want to talk about it (not to *her*, anyway), so she kept her mouth shut.

He plucked a shirt out of his hamper of dirty laundry, dabbed away the blood on his hand, and examined it. "It looks like just a few scratches. I don't think there're any glass slivers inside. Thanks, by the way," he added, gesturing to the floor where the glass had been. "Did I wake you?"

"No, I stayed up to collect star shavings," she said, and she smiled at the fact that he didn't even blink. "Come on, I've got a balm upstairs that'll get rid of those scratches in a jiffy."

As she led the way out of his room, she snatched up the bottle of whisky and the remaining tumbler. When he arched an eyebrow, a most enviable trick, she shrugged. "What? I, too, have been known to drink myself into oblivion every now and then."

Back in the attic, she poured out half a tumbler of whisky, drank about half of *that* in one gulp (and deeply regretted it because, no matter how many times she gave it another chance, whisky was *always* horrible), and handed the rest to Jamie. She found the balm in one of her crates of potions and handed him the jar. "Put a little of that on any scratches and let it sit for a few minutes."

He did as he was told. While he waited, he picked up the tumbler. Somewhat appalled to find herself watching the movement of his throat as he swallowed, Mika turned away and went back to the meteor shower. The smaller of her two cauldrons was still bubbling, fortunately, and she gave it a stir, checked the thin curl of smoke coming out of it, and tapped a second silver spoon gently against the side of the cauldron.

"Why are you doing that?"

Mika glanced over her shoulder to see that Jamie was in the balcony doorway, leaning against the jamb with his hands in the pockets of his sweatpants, watching her. There were faint, exhausted shadows beneath his eyes, but he looked curious.

"The tapping? It's like a song," she said, a little too aware of how close he was. "Well, more like a mathematical formula, I suppose. It's all about the pattern. It's how I get the stardust to come to me. The sound and the cauldron smoke draw it out of the sky."

On cue, a tiny, luminous speck drifted down into her free hand, light as a feather and as small as a grain of sugar. She held her palm out to Jamie. He blinked, straightening abruptly.

"Go ahead. It's safe now that it's in my hand. You can touch it."

His hand wasn't quite steady as he reached out.

"Jesus," he said, letting out a short, low laugh threaded with wonder. "We're touching a *star*."

"Just a very tiny sliver of one," she said, unable to stop herself from giving him a radiant smile. It was the wonder that undid her. "Does it make it more or less magical if I tell you that, scientifically speaking, we're all made up of stardust?"

He didn't even hesitate, raising his eyes to meet hers. "More. Definitely more."

Electric energy crackled between them. Mika held his stormy gaze for a long moment, her heart thrumming as fast as a hummingbird's wings.

"I should get some sleep." His sandpaper voice sounded lower and rougher than usual. Very gently, he closed her fingers over the star shard, dimming the light. "Good night."

And just like that, he was gone.

Two nights later, Mika was huddled over her spellbook, the end of her pencil in her mouth, trying to figure out the right rune to cast a tricky Keep Yourself Warm Even When Foolishly Swimming in the Sea in the Winter spell, when someone knocked at the attic door.

From the way Circe perked up, even going so far as to abandon the pig's ear she had been ecstatically chewing a moment ago, the person knocking could only be one person. Mika was so surprised that she almost forgot to respond.

"Oh! Um, come in!"

The door clicked open. "Hey." Jamie said from the doorway, rubbing the back of his neck. There was a bottle in his other hand.

The corners of Mika's mouth curled irrepressibly up. "Hi."

"I, er, could hear that you were still up, so I thought you might want a drink."

"In that case, come forth and make yourself at home," she said merrily, patting the rug beside her. "As you can see, Circe's *very* happy you're here."

So began another pattern in Mika's strange new life. After that second night, there was another, and then another, and so on. Jamie would bring the whisky, and Mika would set him to work helping her with whatever spell or potion she happened to be in the middle of, and they would sometimes say actual words to each other. These words might be about spells, or about the children, or about how the two of them had been mysteriously locked in the pantry together that day and Ian had most unconvincingly sworn up and down that he had had no hand in it whatsoever.

"How does he keep forgetting I'm a witch?" Mika wanted to know. "He *had* to have known I could spell the door open!"

"What did he expect us to do inside a pantry anyway?"

Mika couldn't resist teasing him. "You can't think of a single thing?"

She'd been hoping for a blush or a comically horrified look, but instead he held her gaze for a moment, his eyes dark, and she was the one who looked away first.

Another time, he decided to be irksomely observant and came upstairs with a bottle of pink gin instead of the whisky. Then, while she used her mortar and pestle to grind dried lavender flowers, he scratched Circe's head and said, "How come she doesn't shed anymore? There used to be a lot of golden hairs all over the place when you first arrived."

"Oh, I spell it away."

"Sorry?"

"Her loose fur," Mika explained, examining the lavender with a critical eye. "I use a spell to get rid of it twice a day. That's why nothing rubs off on the furniture or carpets anymore."

He stared at her. "But you didn't used to do that."

"I've always groomed her once a week, so I didn't need to. Anything she shed in between just got hoovered up whenever I cleaned."

"So why are you spelling it away now?"

Mika glanced up, irked. "It's pet hair, not a diamond heist. What's with the inquisition?"

"Curiosity. You seem weirdly reluctant to answer the question."

Great. Now she was going to have to tell him. She pretended the lavender needed more grinding and watched it with the attention one might give a ticking nuclear device. "It bothered you, didn't it?" she said. "The hair? Just like disordered books and chewed pencils and ink stains bother you? Well, I'm a guest in your home. *Not* making your home uncomfortable for you seems like the least I can do."

He didn't seem to know what to say. Mika decided the lavender flowers would be useless if she kept hammering away at them. She emptied the contents of the mortar into her cauldron, then set a witchfire underneath to extract the essence from the flowers.

By the time she was done, Jamie seemed to have rediscovered his powers of speech. "You don't have to do that. I didn't know you'd noticed."

"It's fine. Circe enjoys the spell."

Another pause, and then: "You're not a guest."

Once, after a number of these late nights, they talked about what kind of future witches could expect. "A lot can happen in ten years," Mika said, in response to his wondering what might be different in five, ten, or fifteen years. "I honestly have no idea what's in store for us or what the world will be like by the time the girls are grown. But there's every reason to hope that they'll be able to have almost any life they choose."

"Is yours the life you chose?"

"Altamira told me she wants to make video games when she grows up," Mika said, sidestepping the question. "Which sounds to me like a completely realistic and reasonable dream. Surprisingly so for a seven-year-old. And it'll probably make her a lot of money, which, speaking as someone who had so little of it at one point that I had to sell pictures of my feet to men on the internet, is very useful."

"Rosetta wants to read books and be part of wholesome bookish fandoms."

"Also realistic and reasonable."

"Terracotta wants to be a Pokémon trainer."

"Knowing her, she'll probably find a way to make that happen."

"Mika." His voice was stern. Grey eyes pinned her in place. "Is this the life you would have chosen for yourself?"

"It didn't used to be," she said, and then blinked, flustered by how much truth that revealed. "I mean, I don't know. There's stuff I would want to be different, if I had my way, but there are also a lot of things about my life that I like. It's complicated."

"What would you want to be different?"

She shied away from looking too deeply for an answer. "It would be nice if Terracotta didn't hate me," she said, a cop-out if there ever was one. "Mostly because I can't keep her safe if she won't listen to me. And, to be perfectly honest, I lay most of the blame for her behaviour at your door."

"Of course you do," Jamie said drily. "Why *wouldn't* your inability to win Terracotta over be my fault?"

"You'd let her get away with literal murder," Mika pointed out. "And I say *literal* literally because she quite frequently contemplates *my* murder and I'm pretty sure you would help her hide my corpse."

"I have been known to hide many a corpse in my time."

"Of course you're not taking this seriously. Like I said, you'd let her get away with murder."

"Why do I get the feeling you don't like her very much?" Jamie asked. A muscle twitched in his jaw, and Mika wondered suddenly if they were still talking about Terracotta.

"I like her plenty," Mika said. "She goes out of her way to wind me up, but she's also a stubborn, brave little girl who'd do anything for the people she loves. Why wouldn't I like her? What I *don't* like is the fact that we have very little time, she's determined to waste it, and you're letting her. We talked about this weeks ago. You don't trust me, but you're not supposed to let the kids pick up on that. They have. Terracotta knows how you feel and she takes her cue from you."

His eyes were like metal. "I can't make her trust you. Trust is earned."

"It is," Mika agreed, looking him right in the eye. "But that's only possible if someone's willing to give you a chance."

When disaster struck, as disaster inevitably does, Mika was somewhat distressed to find that, on account of being knocked out cold, she was unable to take any satisfaction in being proven well and truly right.

It was a cold, grey morning, over halfway into her time at Nowhere House, and it started with the resurrection of what had become a frustrating and repetitive argument.

In short, Terracotta, upon hearing the story of Altamira levitating in the attic on Mika's first day and Mika's dire warning about its risks, had promptly decided she had no greater desire in life than to levitate.

Her first approach had been to accuse Mika of inventing tales of peril to cover up the fact that *she* couldn't levitate. Mika, who discovered in that precise moment that she had an immense capacity for pettiness, had responded by finishing the rest of the lesson from a spot approximately six feet off the ground.

Not to be defeated, Terracotta had then demanded that Mika teach *her* how to levitate, too. Mika had explained that it had taken her years to get it right. Terracotta had replied with the opinion that perhaps *she* was a more talented witch and would get it right a whole lot faster. Mika had had to remind herself of every last minute of her thirty-one years in order to resist the childish temptation to suggest a duel so that they could determine who was truly the more powerful witch.

No matter how trying Terracotta might be, and she was very trying indeed, Mika could not help but feel that demanding an eight-year-old meet her with figurative pistols at dawn was not the behaviour of a responsible caretaker.

For weeks, this argument had repeated itself like some sort of ghastly time loop Mika could not break free of. So on that particular cold, dreary morning, when a lesson in the garden devolved into Terracotta dredging up the levitation question again, Mika, who was already somewhat preoccupied with rescuing Altamira from the enthusiastic attentions of a colony of seagulls that the girls had accidentally summoned, lost patience.

"No," she snapped, batting one of the last seagulls away. "I've told you before, you're too young to learn how to safely levitate, *especially* outdoors, so stop asking. Maybe your next tutor, God help her, can have that dubious pleasure in a few years."

There was no response from Terracotta. Mika, now extracting feathers out of Altamira's hair, assumed Terracotta was scowling at her behind her back, which was both familiar and harmless, and so she finished dealing with the aftermath of the gull invasion without worrying too much about it.

But when Rosetta let out an alarmed squeak, and Altamira looked past Mika with enormous eyes, Mika spun around and found that Terracotta wasn't there anymore.

"Up here!" came the joyous, triumphant cry.

Mika's heart dropped like a stone.

CHAPTER FOURTEEN

It was only eleven o'clock, but as far as Jamie was concerned, the day had already started badly. A professor at Durham University had mislaid two rare books; Altamira and Terracotta had had a colossal row over a mysteriously missing jigsaw puzzle, which had ended most ominously with Altamira threatening to hide dead fish around Terracotta's bedroom; Ian had started hatching increasingly batshit schemes to deal with Edward; and, to top it off, Jamie, who was already worn out from far too little sleep, found that he was actually (stupidly, absurdly, senselessly) looking forward to staying awake because he could spend that time in the attic with a certain witch.

(Why? *Why* did he like going up there? She asked questions he didn't want to answer, made fun of his scowl, blamed him for Terracotta's mistrust of her, told him he was made up of stardust, made him laugh, was *outrageously* nice to look at—wait, wasn't he supposed to be thinking of reasons *not* to go?)

Anyway, he had a skull-rattling headache, Ken and Lucie wouldn't be back from the supermarket with the week's shopping and more painkillers for another hour, and somewhere far too close, Ian was hammering screws into a beehive and none too subtly pretending he was hammering them into Edward's head instead. Each ferocious thud of the hammer echoed just as ferociously in Jamie's head, but he knew he probably deserved it.

Then the day got considerably worse.

It was the sound of Terracotta's voice that first got his attention. He was on the upper level of the library, tracking down a book a scientist in Glasgow had requested, when he heard a high, clear voice from the garden outside.

"Look! I'm doing it!" There was joy in Terracotta's voice, but also an edge of savage satisfaction. "You said I couldn't do it, but I am!"

Curious, Jamie looked out of the nearest window. And just about had a heart attack.

Terracotta was a good twelve feet up in the air, sitting astride a fucking *branch* like it was her very own broomstick.

For half a second, he cherished the valiant hope that this was an activity that had been planned and executed perfectly sensibly, but he dismissed that thought at once because he had heard Mika rejecting Terracotta's demands to learn levitation a dozen times. Even if this hadn't occurred to him, the sight of Rosetta and Altamira gazing up at their sister in horror, and Mika's furious, pale face, would have put paid to any foolish hopes.

"Terracotta, get back down here now!" Mika's voice was stonily calm, but Jamie could see the panic she was trying very hard to hide. "It's too windy for you to be up there!"

"Pfft," came the insolent reply. "I seem to be managing just fine! You just don't like that I did this without any help from you at all. In fact," she went on, forcibly struck by the realisation, "I think this pretty much proves that we don't need you, so you can leave and—"

It happened so fast that Jamie didn't even have time to blink. The branch beneath Terracotta jerked, as if tugged by a gust of wind. Mika raised her hands to cast a spell. Terracotta let out an angry shriek of "No!" and tried to wrench herself away from Mika's spell. Mika rose into the air, her hair whipping across her face, pulling Terracotta back.

It seemed to Jamie, remembering it later, that Mika should have had no trouble getting Terracotta safely back to the ground. After all, hadn't she rescued Altamira from an accidental spell or burst of wayward magic countless times already?

The difference, of course, was that she'd never had to fight Altamira to do it. Terracotta, on the other hand, fought tooth and nail. And Mika, who was forced to fight both her *and* the enormous surge of magic around them, was powerless to stop what happened next.

There was a brilliant, blinding flash of light between the two witches in the air. It speared out towards each of them, like Zeus's thunderbolts, and it looked for one awful instant like they were both going to be struck with the magical blowback.

But then, in that single fraction of an instant, Jamie saw one of Mika's hands clench into a fist.

The air trembled. Time held still. Jamie saw every impossible detail: the angle of Terracotta's branch as it fell, Terracotta's wide and frightened eyes illuminated by that brilliant light, the white knuckles of Mika's clenched fist. He saw the light spearing towards Terracotta stop, shudder, and then reverse direction like it was being rewound in slow motion. His heart had time to give a single violent thump.

Then time sped back up and the entire explosion of light slammed into Mika, knocking her to the ground. Altamira screamed.

Jamie ran.

By the time he reached the French doors, Ian was halfway across the garden. Jamie overtook him, arriving first at the scene. One glance told him that Terracotta was safe, back on the ground and trembling like a leaf. Circe was nosing at a terrifyingly still figure on the ground, whining and barking. Rosetta was on her knees next to them. Altamira had tears streaming down her face.

For a moment, Jamie was frozen, ice in his lungs, too afraid to look. Then he was beside her.

"Mika," Rosetta whispered, shaking one limp shoulder. "Mika, wake up!"

"Is she dead?" Altamira sobbed, saying out loud the words Jamie had been trying very hard not to even think.

Ian scooped Altamira up into his arms, making soothing noises. "Nonsense, darling," he said briskly, the croak in his voice betraying his own distress. "She's fine, isn't she, Jamie?"

"J-Jamie? Is she okay?" Terracotta.

Jamie pushed up the sleeve of Mika's oversized white sweater and reached for her wrist. In the horrible heartbeat of silence before the flutter of her pulse beat against his fingers, he had time to see that there wasn't a scratch on her and she almost looked like she was asleep. Eyes closed, face very cold and pale, strands of dark hair sticking to her damp skin. She didn't so much as stir when he touched her, didn't make a sound, but he could feel that stubborn, hummingbird pulse in her wrist and relief made him feel almost light-headed.

"She's alive," he rasped. He pulled his phone out of his pocket and pushed it into Rosetta's hands, then scooped Mika's cold, still form into his arms. "Call 999."

Ian intervened. "We can't do that!"

Back at full height now, Jamie turned to stare Ian down. Mika's head flopped against his shoulder like a doll's, and now that he knew she was alive, his relief was rapidly transforming into panic, fury, and a number of other feelings he wasn't quite sure he could name.

"Why can't we call a fucking ambulance?"

"And say what?" Ian countered. With Altamira on one skinny hip, he reached out with his free hand to press it tenderly against Mika's cold cheek. Jamie resisted the entirely irrational urge to jerk her away. "I don't like it any more than you do, Jamie, but paramedics, doctors, and hospitals will ask more questions than we can answer."

"You know, Ian, I can't help but feel like awkward questions are a small price to pay if they can keep her alive!"

"I don't think Mika will feel the same way," said Ian, but he looked uncertain. "Besides, if magic did this to her, *magic* is the only thing that's likely to fix it and ambulances don't exactly come equipped for—wait a minute!" Ian's tone shifted abruptly, and his eyes sparked blue with recognition. "What's that below her throat?"

They all peered at the base of Mika's throat, where, in the space right between her collarbones, a single, tiny, spring-green leaf had sprouted out of her skin.

"Ohhhh," Ian breathed, sounding both relieved and amazed. "She's *hibernating*."

"She's what?" Rosetta said doubtfully. "Hibernating? Like a bear?"

"I don't know if there's a different term for it, but that's what my mother called it," Ian explained. "It happened to her once when I was a boy. She miscalculated in her potion-making and there was an explosion. When I ran upstairs to find her, she was on the floor, silent and asleep, and a tiny leaf had bloomed at her throat. I didn't know what to do, but my father put her to bed and told me not to worry. Two days later, Mother woke up her usual self and told me she'd been hibernating."

"So it's something witches do when they're badly hurt?" asked Rosetta. "They kind of shut down until they've healed themselves?"

"Exactly." Ian tweaked Altamira's snotty nose. "See? Mika will be fine. She just needs some time to heal."

Jamie listened to all this over the sound of his own thundering heart, and found that it didn't make him feel a whole lot better. But then maybe nothing would until Mika woke up and he was able to see without a shadow of a doubt that she was indeed okay.

His voice was little more than a growl as he turned to Terracotta. "Are you okay? Are you hurt?"

She immediately shook her head. Thankfully, shock seemed to be the worst of what she was experiencing.

"Okay," Jamie said brusquely. "No paramedics, then. We'll take her upstairs."

Rosetta and Altamira ran ahead to open doors. Jamie crossed the house quickly and carried Mika up two flights of stairs to the attic. She still hadn't made a sound, hadn't twitched so much as a toe.

"Ian, pull back the covers so I can get her into bed."

"What can I do?" Terracotta's uncertain voice asked from the doorway behind him.

You've done enough came to mind. Jamie didn't yet trust himself to answer her without saying something he knew he'd later regret, so he clenched his jaw and kept his attention squarely on the reassuring flutter of a pulse at the base of Mika's throat.

Once Ian had pulled back the daisy-patterned duvet, Jamie laid Mika carefully down in her bed. Circe jumped up beside her, putting her wet nose into the crook of Mika's neck. Jamie smoothed the damp strands of hair off her face before he realised what he was doing and took a quick step back, the hand he'd touched her with clenching and unclenching at his side.

This shouldn't have shaken him so badly. *Ian* was the one who panicked, flew into theatrical furies, and lost his head. *Jamie* got irritated, but not much else. And he always, always kept his head screwed on straight.

What the fuck was wrong with him?

He turned to Ian. "So we just let her sleep? That's it?"

"That's what Father and I did," said Ian. "Mother was fine, and Mika will be, too." He put a reassuring hand on Jamie's shoulder, but Jamie shrugged it off, too profoundly on edge to stay still.

"Do you think she can hear us?" Altamira wondered. She bent her lips to Mika's ear and whispered intensely for a minute. Jamie caught the phrases *Very sad* and *Miss you*, which hit him like a kick in the chest.

Terracotta had crept closer. She wrung her hands in front of her. "I didn't mean for her to get hurt," she whispered.

"No one doubts that for a minute, my sweet," Ian said severely, "but let me tell you, you are in a world of trouble!"

"It's my fault, so I *should* be in trouble," said Terracotta without the slightest hesitation. Jamie could tell it was difficult for her to look him in the eye, but she did. "She wouldn't be hurt this badly if she'd let one of those lightning bolts hit me."

"She's older than you are, and more powerful," Jamie said evenly, working very hard to shut down each of the wild, feral feelings rattling around inside his chest. "Frankly, Terracotta, it seems to me that she's kinder than you are, too. There's no telling what the lightning bolt would have done to you. So she absorbed it herself. None of which would have been necessary if you hadn't done something you have been repeatedly and expressly asked not to do."

"I just thought . . ."

"You thought she was getting in your way for her own amusement?" Jamie finished for her. "You thought she was making stuff up because she didn't want to be shown up by an eight-year-old? Yes, you've made that very obvious. And that's on me as much as it is on you because I assumed the worst of her and you took your cue from me." He let out a short, humourless laugh because Mika had said the same thing and he hadn't wanted to listen. "I should have put a stop to it a long time ago, but the choices you made today are all on you, Terracotta. And they were inexcusable. You could have been hurt. You could have hurt one of your sisters. You *did* hurt Mika."

Terracotta nodded again. "I'm sorry," she said quietly. "I owe Mika an apology, too, but this one's for all of you."

"What about my missing jigsaw puzzle?" Altamira wanted to know. "Are you going to say sorry for stealing it?"

"For the last time, I did *not* steal your stupid puzzle!"

"It can't have just walked away!"

"We're witches! Maybe it did!"

"Just you wait," Altamira said bitterly. "Let's see how you feel when your whole room smells like stinky fish!"

"It can't smell any worse than you do!"

"Oh!" Altamira gasped, the light of a Valkyrie in her eyes. "Want to bet on that?"

There was a pause, and then Ian and Rosetta burst into the relieved, hysterical laughter that comes after a big shock. Jamie didn't feel like he was even close to laughing yet, but he put an arm around Terracotta. She wrapped hers around his waist, which of course made Altamira demand an equally sizeable hug, and then Rosetta squeezed her way in, too.

Ian stood, letting out a long breath. "Tea?"

CHAPTER FIFTEEN

In the past, Mika had woken with half a bottle of gin lying on its side beside her, she had woken with menstrual cramps that had come from Dante's worst circle of hell, and she had woken with a dog's tongue halfway up her nose, but she had to admit that she had never, ever woken feeling like she had been hit by a bus.

Not, of course, that she knew what it was to be hit by a bus. But she couldn't believe it could possibly be any worse than this. Every part of her hurt. Her legs hurt. Her arms hurt. Her head hurt. Her *nostrils* hurt, for fuck's sake. Both of them.

She cracked her eyes open and instantly regretted all her life choices.

"What is this evil?" she croaked. "Why have I been engulfed in the fires of a thousand infernos?"

"I believe some call it the sun," a dry voice informed her.

"Take it away. I want nothing to do with it."

"There's irony for you," said the voice, sounding distinctly amused now.

The nerve. Mika was *dying*, and he had the audacity to be amused?

"I'm going to go out on a limb here and say you'll probably survive."

Oh. Had she said that out loud?

"You did, yeah."

"Jamie. The sun. Remove it from the sky at once."

"Anything for you, love," came the wry reply. "Especially when you ask so sweetly. But I'm afraid the removal of the sun is beyond even my powers. Pulling the curtains shut will have to do."

It did *not* do, because there was still far too much light streaming in, but she was a reasonable person and she understood that she had to perhaps make the best of it. Then, before she could resign herself to a lifetime of martyred agony, something warm pressed against her side and a calloused hand settled over her tightly closed eyes, cutting almost all the light out.

"Just until you adjust," Jamie's voice said from close by.

"Oh my god. Don't stop."

"I *will* stop if you keep making sex noises."

"The only reason you think these are sex noises is because you haven't yet had sex with me," Mika felt compelled to inform him.

Yet?

Fucking *yet*?

There was a pause, during which she had the misfortune of not only realising that he, too, had heard the unmistakable *yet* but also of remembering what had happened to make her feel like she'd been hit by a bus in the first place, and then Jamie cleared his throat and said, "You okay?"

"I think I can open my eyes now."

She was rather sorry to lose the warmth of his hand, but she needed to get her head round what was going on. Carefully cracking one eye open and then the other, she blinked slowly. She was in her room in the attic. It had to be the middle of the day, if the sun was any indication. She was still wearing the pink jeans and white jumper she'd had on when she'd last been conscious. Her rocking chair had been pulled up close beside her bed, its cushions wrinkled like someone had been sprawled in the chair for hours. And Jamie was sitting on the edge of the bed beside her.

He stood now. He looked exhausted, the shadows under his eyes darker than usual, and his brown stubble rougher and bristlier than it had been the last time she'd seen him. "I'll go tell the others you're awake."

"Wait."

He paused for an instant, then dropped into the chair. "How are you feeling?"

"Meh," Mika said. "How long have I been out?"

"Twenty-six hours."

"Jesus. I must have been in hibernation." She felt for her throat, for the green leaf that Primrose had once mentioned was a sure sign of a witch's hibernation, and there it was. She plucked it free from her skin and put it down on the bed beside her.

"Ian told us that was what it was called," said Jamie. "I was going to call an ambulance, but he saw this"—he picked up the green leaf—"and he said the same thing happened to his mother once. He was very sure."

"He was right," Mika said. "How come you're here?"

He rubbed his jaw, not quite looking her in the eye. "We've been taking shifts."

"You've been here the whole time, haven't you?"

"I was a little reluctant to leave, yes," he admitted, a faint smile lifting one side of his mouth. "So was Terracotta. She only just left, and only because Lucie made her go downstairs for lunch."

"Neither of you had to do that."

He cleared his throat. "I wanted to thank you. For what you did. For taking all the blowback to protect her."

"Don't be ridiculous. She's a child. I have as many faults as the next person—"

"As *I'm* the next person, I'd say you probably have fewer," Jamie remarked.

Mika laughed, which did her sore ribs no good. "Well, whatever my faults, letting a small child get hurt when I'm perfectly capable of preventing it is not one of them."

"I know. And I appreciate it."

A troubling possibility struck her. "Did anyone's power spiral out of control while I was asleep? Is everyone okay?"

He shook his head at once. "Everyone's fine, I promise. Nothing's happened at all."

Mika cocked her head, searching for the music of the magic around her. As she listened to it, she let out another small laugh. "The magic's feeling very guilty, so it's behaving itself. For now."

"Much like Terracotta, then," Jamie said, cracking a smile. "Can I get you anything?"

"I think I just need to rest," Mika said. Then she reconsidered. "Actually, could you ask Lucie to come help me into the bath?"

"Yeah, of course."

But before he could take so much as a step in the direction of the door, there was a loud bark and Circe ran in joyfully, wasting no time whatsoever before licking Mika's face from top to bottom. Before Mika could protest this assault, the rest of the household had flooded into the attic, too.

"You're awake!" Altamira cried. "I told you she was, Rosetta, I *told* you!"

"Someone's been listening at doors again," Ken said ruefully. His warm, kind eyes smiled down at Mika. "Oh, my dear. You gave us quite a scare. We're so happy to see you awake."

Ian was trying to envelope Mika in the most vigorous of hugs, and Jamie was trying to stop him, when Lucie pushed past both of them and bent at once to press the back of her hand against Mika's forehead like a mother checking a child's temperature. "I don't like it," she said, tutting. "You're too warm. You need a good, hearty lunch and a nice cup of tea."

"Can I have a bath first?" Mika asked meekly.

"Absolutely not," said Lucie. "So you can keel over the moment you try to stand up? Tea and lunch first, then we can talk about a bath."

"What an excellent idea," said Jamie, gripping Ian firmly by the elbow. "Why don't we go get that sorted?"

"I hardly think we need *all* go."

"We do," said Jamie, in a tone that left no room for negotiation. "Because Terracotta would like a minute alone with Mika."

Ian escaped Jamie long enough to plant a smacker of a kiss on Mika's forehead, Altamira followed suit with equal vigour, and then they were all gone and Mika found herself left with a dog wedged up against her side and a small, pink-cheeked girl perched in the chair beside the bed.

Mika had to turn her head away to blink away sudden tears at the unexpected onslaught of their affection, but Terracotta was too preoccupied with twisting the bottom of her T-shirt in her hands to notice. When she finally spoke, it was to say, in a smaller voice than Mika had ever heard from her: "Why did you protect me?"

"Because I like you," Mika said, with a smile.

"Why?" Terracotta sounded baffled. "I've been an absolute *villain* to you."

"You were protecting your family." Mika held out a hand. Tentatively, Terracotta put her smaller one on top of it and threaded her fingers through Mika's. "I wish you'd listen to me when I ask you not to put yourself in danger, and I wish you'd believe that I have no intention of causing your family any harm, but I don't blame you for trying to keep them safe. You never have to be sorry for that."

"But I *am* sorry that you got hurt because of me."

"Really?" Mika teased. "Even after all those times you tried to figure out the best way to murder me?"

Terracotta looked slightly appalled. "I didn't *mean* it!"

"Oh, I see," said Mika, straight-faced. "What a relief."

"Are you really okay?"

"I will be. And I accept your apology."

Terracotta's smile was radiant, and relieved. She gave Mika's hand a tiny squeeze. Then: "Will you tell Altamira that I never stole her puzzle?"

"No," Mika said, sputtering a laugh and wincing at the pain that followed it. "You need to sort that out yourselves."

"What's hurting?"

"What isn't?" Mika replied.

"That sounds a bit rubbish," said Terracotta, "but I reckon I know exactly what you need." And, with a yell that sent an entire troop of drummers line-dancing through Mika's skull: "TRIPLE HUG TIME!"

Rosetta and Altamira, who had obviously not gone far, burst back into the room at once. The next thing Mika knew, she and Circe were pinned to the bed with one child squashed in beside them, another wrapped around Mika's middle, and the third lying on her *other* side with her arms looped around Mika's left.

"Are we hurting you?" Rosetta asked anxiously.

"Not even a little bit," Mika lied, perjuring her soul without hesitation. "In fact, this is actually rather nice for an experience that doesn't allow me to breathe."

"Triple hug," Terracotta said with satisfaction. "Works every time."

"Would you like a lullaby?" Altamira offered generously.

And so, when the others returned half an hour later with a tray of tea, chocolate, and Brie and bacon toasties, it was to find four witches and one golden retriever curled up together in one double bed. Fast asleep.

"Should we wake them?" Lucie looked doubtful. "They could certainly all do with the sleep, but Mika has to eat."

"It can wait," Jamie said gruffly.

It was another two days before Mika could get out of bed without some part of her body feeling like it was about to shut down, during which time the rest of the household were scrupulous in making sure she was fussed over and entertained, both of which were quite unprecedented experiences in the whole of her life.

When she tried to get up to make her own tea, she was kindly and firmly deposited back in bed. When she mentioned the children's lessons and Edward Foxhaven's ever-nearing visit, she was immediately overruled and told in no uncertain terms that she was to do *nothing* except get better. When boredom so much as dared to encroach, someone was always miraculously there with a chew toy (Circe), books and video games (the children), a story about the stage (Ian), a complaint about Ian (Lucie), a potted plant in need of nurturing (Ken), or a disastrously honest critique of her wan appearance (guess who).

Which was how, on the day reality rudely interrupted this idyll, Mika found herself whiling away most of the evening after dinner upstairs, back in bed, listening to Rosetta read out loud from *Persuasion*.

One of the consequences of growing up in a house with no real company, not to mention Primrose's rather narrow and archaic ideas about what constituted a well-stocked library, was the fact that Mika had read just about every classic there was. Twice. If it was written by somebody called Austen or Shelley or Brontë, Keats or Dickens or Eliot, Christie or Rossetti or Blake, she had read it. (Indeed, lest anyone accuse Primrose of not being worldly, she had also made sure names like Homer, Rumi, Dumas, Tolstoy, and Seth appeared on her shelves.)

A handful of Mika's tutors had attempted to introduce her to new books, handing over comic books, highly masculine epic fantasies, and even, on one memorable occasion, a romance so steamy that Mika had read it three times in one night. But, for the most part, the literary worlds she'd visited growing up featured ballrooms, governesses, pickpockets, men who went by their last names only, the London fog, and not a whole lot else.

So Mika could quite safely say that she already knew *Persuasion* very well, but Rosetta was more than a little obsessed with Captain Wentworth at the moment and Mika didn't have the heart to part her from him.

"Just listen to this," Rosetta was saying dreamily. "*You pierce my soul. I am half agony, half hope. Tell—*"

Terracotta and Altamira, who were disgusted by notions of romance, made distraught sounds at this and begged Rosetta to pick a book about pirates instead.

"No," Rosetta said firmly. "The two of you are supposed to be practicing your spellwork anyway, not listening to me read."

Over the past weeks, all three girls had mastered the simple animation spell Mika had set them to work on in their first lesson. Now that they could make a single pebble do whatever they wanted it to, she'd moved them on to a more advanced version of the spell, one that would require more concentration and control. She'd given them each a small wooden doll, the articulated kind that artists often used to create poses for their reference, and she had asked them to cast a spell that would make the dolls stand, sit down, and walk independently.

"You can animate a single, rounded object," she'd explained when she'd handed them the dolls. "Now it's time to animate something more complicated. When you animate a doll, the only way to create smooth, natural movements is by enchanting its hands, arms, legs, waist, and neck separately *and* simultaneously. If you can master that, you'll be well on your way to controlling your power."

Now, the younger girls grumbled as they concentrated on their dolls. Rosetta, who had already spent an hour practicing with hers, went happily back to *Persuasion*.

She didn't get much further before they were interrupted by Jamie, who marched in, sent the girls away on an errand that Mika was quite certain he'd made up on the spot, and shut the door firmly behind them once they were gone.

"Listening ears," he explained. He picked up the copy of *Persuasion* Rosetta had left behind, briefly distracted. "It was *Pride and Prejudice* last week. I hope she gets to *Emma* soon. That was always my favourite."

"Mine too," Mika said, surprised. "My enthusiasm for the classics is usually tepid, but I'm a sucker for Austen."

She noticed that Jamie had her phone in his hand. She must have left it downstairs the day of the Disaster, as the children were now referring to it, and she hadn't given it so much as a moment's thought since. (Which was unusual, and a sign of just how successfully she had been entertained.) How the battery hadn't died yet was anyone's guess. Maybe Lucie, that model of efficiency, had plugged it in.

"You got a text," Jamie said warily.

Yes, such was the barren wasteland of her social life that *this* was the first text her phone had received in three days. (And the one before that had been from her service provider, reminding her to pay her bill.)

But Jamie's mood and the fact that he'd shut the door told her it wasn't just any old text. As she took the phone from him and the screen lit up, a tiny knot of dread formed in her chest.

Let's have tea on Thursday. 3pm. You may choose where.

Primrose, of course.

"It's Wednesday," Mika said. Which was nothing if not stating the obvious.

"I assume from the expression on your face that Primrose doesn't often demand you meet her for tea?"

"I wouldn't use the word *often*, but she does ask me a couple of times a year. And she always texts like she's the Queen bestowing a great favour on an unworthy subject." Mika rolled her eyes, but said firmly, as much to convince herself as it was to convince him, "It doesn't mean anything."

Jamie didn't look convinced. "You don't think it's a bit of coincidence that she's inviting you to tea now? Right after what just happened?"

"It's possible that the wards couldn't completely contain such a big surge of power, and it's possible other witches within a hundred miles or so noticed it," Mika admitted. "You know how storms hit Wales, but we just get a bit more rain than usual? It's kind of like that. The power ripples out, fading away the farther it gets. Agatha Jones lives this side of London, which is still pretty far away, but she's also very old and we get more powerful as we get older, so she *could* have picked up on the disruption in power and mentioned it to Primrose. Who *could* have assumed I was the one to blame. But that's a lot of very woolly maybes, and it's more likely that this is just an innocent invitation. Either way," she added, wanting for some reason to take away that worried crease between his eyebrows, "there's absolutely no way Primrose can possibly know about the kids, so you don't have to worry about that."

"But I do have to worry about you," he said, and he sounded so irritated by this that she had to hide a smile. "You've barely been out of bed in three days. Are you really going to tea with her tomorrow?"

"It'll look a lot more suspicious if I don't," Mika pointed out. "And it'll be fine. I'll pick somewhere far away from this house—"

"Once more, the problem is *you*, not this house."

"—and the Broomstick will get me there in no time at all," she finished merrily. "Primrose won't ever know where I've been these past few weeks."

"Are you being deliberately obtuse?" Jamie demanded.

"Are you actually worried I'm going to keel over and die if I go to tea?" Mika demanded right back. "It's *tea*. The nation's favourite activity! I promise I can survive its lethal trials. Look," she went on, softening her tone, "I know you're worried about me because you feel guilty about what Terracotta did and you're afraid my untimely death will be on your conscience, but I really—"

He stared at her. "Do you actually think that? That I'm concerned because I feel guilty?"

"Well, you don't particularly like me," Mika reminded him reasonably. "As such, guilt seems like the likeliest explanation for your concern. Why? Am I wrong? Oh!" Face-palming as realisation struck, she laughed. "Of course! You're afraid that if something happens to me, I won't be here for Edward's visit. No, honestly, I'll be fine. I'll be here."

He seemed to be at a loss for words. The incredulous expression on his face had turned into something she couldn't decipher.

"Are you okay?"

"Hasn't *anyone* ever been worried about you just because?" Jamie asked, his voice low and rough. "Because, to be perfectly honest, this conversation suggests no one's ever cared about you."

Mika's smile vanished. "I've told you about the way I grew up," she said tightly. "Do I really have to explain it again?"

"No," came the gravely quiet reply. "I think I get it."

"Okay. So I'll see Primrose tomorrow, then, and I'll let you know how it goes when I get back."

"Okay," he said, and that was that.

CHAPTER SIXTEEN

Mika picked a café in a formidably posh hotel in Cambridge, the kind of place that met Primrose's exacting and snobbish standards, and, when it was time to leave the following afternoon, used the Broomstick's speed spell to get her there in fifteen minutes.

She regretted the folly of this as soon as she stumbled out of the Broomstick on wobbly legs, feeling nauseated, exhausted, and entirely too weak to put on a convincing show. The Disaster had fucked her up in a big way, casting and maintaining a powerful spell for several minutes had done her no favours, and, much as she hated to admit it, Jamie had probably been right to tell her it was too soon for her to be gallivanting about the country.

But she was here now, and she had to get her mask firmly in place. She glanced at her watch. Two-fifty-five. She took a few deep breaths of damp, cold, clean air (well, clean-*ish*, considering she was in a hotel's carpark), then ducked back into her car to reapply her eyeliner, dust her face with setting powder, twist her hair up into an approximation of elegance, and text Ian to let him know she'd got here safe and sound. (She didn't bother texting anyone else because she had no doubt Ian would tell them himself. He was probably already shouting at Lucie across the house and texting Jamie and Ken, who had gone out earlier in the day.)

Primrose, who subscribed to the belief that if you weren't five minutes early, you were late, was already at a frilly, dainty corner table when Mika entered the café. Pinning her sunniest smile to her face, Mika joined her. With the exception of an impeccably polite greeting, Primrose said nothing more until they'd ordered a pot of Earl Grey—and Mika had ordered an entire plate of scones with jam and clotted cream—before throwing down the gauntlet.

"So it *was* you," Primrose said, looking rather satisfied. "I suspected as much."

"What was me?" Mika asked innocently.

"The surge," said Primrose, raising her eyebrows. "On Sunday morning. I didn't feel it myself, but Agatha says there was a distinct disruption from somewhere north of Essex. You came to mind at once."

"Of course I did."

"Don't give me that look, Mika. Your recklessness this past year has not gone unnoticed. That said," Primrose went on, cocking her head to one side, "I noticed your social media accounts have been deactivated, dear. Dare I assume I have finally had some influence over you?"

Mika crammed her mouth full of an excessively jammy, creamy scone to make herself feel better about the indignity of having to allow Primrose to believe *she* was the reason Mika had stopped posting witchy videos online. And a happy bonus: the ludicrous quantity of sugar made her feel just a teeny bit less like a tired, delicate flower about to crumple beneath a stiff breeze.

"I was puzzled by the surge," Primrose went on, sipping her tea in the daintiest of fashions, "because you've been living in Brighton these past few months, haven't you? Or do you live somewhere else now? Frankly," she tutted, "it seems to me absurd that you keep moving around like an overenthusiastic mayfly when there's a perfectly good house going to waste."

This was not a new complaint, and from Primrose's point of view, Mika knew it was a reasonable one. After all, there *was* an empty house on a quiet street in the city of York, and it did indeed seem like madness not to use it. But it was the house of Mika's childhood, and she did not know how to tell Primrose that *nothing* could convince her to go back to the ghosts and memories that haunted it.

"In any case," Primrose went on, impervious to the thoughts clattering around Mika's mind, "I did wonder if perhaps you weren't the cause of the surge after all, but now that I see you, it's obvious you were. If you don't mind my saying so, dear, you look positively sickly."

"I can always count on you to bolster my self-esteem, Primrose," said Mika in her most cheerful voice.

"Well? Are you going to explain what happened?"

"Are you going to give me a choice?"

Primrose looked taken aback. And was that even a bit of *hurt* in the flattening of her lips? "I only ask because I can help, if you need help," she said crisply.

"I don't need help," Mika said. Fortunately, she had a cast-iron excuse for her presence in Norfolk, one that would distract totally from a beautiful, lonely house on the coast. "I went to UEA over the weekend. A class reunion."

Primrose blinked. "Do they invite you to reunions if you don't graduate?"

"Apparently," said Mika, her smile just this side of robotic. Primrose knew exactly why she'd dropped out of university a year early. "Anyway, while I was there, I saw him."

"*Him*," Primrose repeated, in the voice she might have used if she'd said *bird shit* or *full-fat milk*.

For once, Mika was in complete agreement with Primrose. "Yep. Him. We had a bit of a row. I'm not proud of it, but I lost my temper. Not in front of him, or anyone else, but outside."

"I see," said Primrose, and she actually sounded sympathetic. Mika almost felt guilty for the lie. "That is regrettable, but understandable. You're quite certain no one noticed anything? Because I can—"

"Wipe their memories?" Mika said a little bitterly. "No, that won't be necessary. No one saw me."

There was a pause, during which Mika demolished another scone, drank a full cup of tea and poured a second, and Primrose took all of two dainty sips. After a moment, Primrose said, "We all have types of magic we excel in. For me, it's the manipulation of memory. I am aware that you don't like it, but it has gotten you, me, and a number of other witches out of tight spots over the years. You, on the other hand, excel at potion-making. And my late sister, may she rest in—"

Mika blinked. "Sorry, what?"

"My late sister?" Primrose repeated doubtfully. "Yes, she—"

"No, what you said before that."

"Oh. Potions, dear. That's what *you* excel at."

"You think I'm good at potion-making?"

"Of course. You've always had such a knack for the creation and conjuring of potions. Your teas, in particular, are extraordinary. Indeed, at least a third of the most powerful potions in my spellbook are yours."

Mika felt like she'd fallen into a parallel universe between one bite of scone and the next. "Is that a compliment?"

Primrose sniffed. "You needn't act like I've never given you one before."

Mika was quite certain she never *had*, but resisted the temptation to say so. Instead, she said, "So you're not cross, then, that I lost control of my power?"

"It happens," said Primrose. "I wish *that man* didn't still have so much power over you, but it is what it is."

Mika would have liked to tell Primrose that *that man* had no power over her at all anymore, but that would put rather a big hole in her carefully constructed lie. She swallowed another mouthful of scone. "I expected you to be more judgy."

"You know my views," said Primrose primly. "As a child, I instructed your nannies and tutors very specifically not to tell you what to drink, what to eat, and what to wear. That is because I believe what you put in your body is your business, and that," she added, raising her teacup to her lips, "includes penises."

Mika almost dropped her own teacup, betrayed into a fit of schoolgirlish giggles.

Primrose eyed her askance. "You're thirty-one, Mika. Do try to act like it. And if you *would* care for my opinion, perhaps you might choose a worthier penis next time."

Mika did not at all like the fact that a certain scowly someone came immediately to mind.

"Damn it, Primrose," she muttered under her breath.

"What was that?"

"Nothing," Mika said too quickly, then backtracked, seizing on the first thing she could think of that had nothing whatsoever to do with Jamie Kelly. "I just asked if you ever knew a witch with the last name Hawthorn?"

"Minerva Hawthorn?" Primrose said, pausing to signal imperiously for another pot of tea. "Of course I knew her. Lovely woman. She contracted a particular aggressive form of cancer about thirty years ago. She had a child," Primrose added, stirring the dregs of her tea with a faraway look on her face. "A little boy. I met him once. I wonder what became of him."

Mika kept her face studiously blank.

"How do *you* know about Minerva Hawthorn?" Primrose asked, those sharp eyes skewering Mika in place.

Mika took a chance on the fact that the second-oldest witch in the Society might also have known Ian's mother. "Oh, Agatha mentioned her, but you know what Agatha's like. Most of the stuff she says is only half-remembered." And then, suffering only the smallest qualm of guilt for throwing Agatha under the bus, she added: "She also told me why we're all orphaned."

It was a shameless attempt to find out more about their history. Primrose had only ever referred in the loosest terms to a spell that once went wrong, and according to the girls, Lillian had done much the same.

Primrose looked unimpressed. "You know why we're orphaned. The spell."

"Yes," Mika said, irked. "So you've always said. Agatha, on the other hand, told me a little more. At our last meeting, while the rest of you were talking about Zuzanna's peonies." She thought fast, sent a silent apology Agatha's way, and fibbed: "She said the Witchfinder General cursed us."

This was a throwaway gambit, a piece of infamous British history she'd plucked out of thin air in the hope that Primrose would be so annoyed that she would pooh-pooh this theory and tell Mika the *real* story.

Instead, the response Mika got was: "I wouldn't put it quite like that, but yes, the blame lies with him. And others like him."

Primrose said this so matter-of-factly, so nonchalantly, that for a moment Mika was stunned into speechlessness, her cup frozen halfway between her mouth and the saucer. "It's true?" she spluttered at last, astonishment giving way to indignation.

"More or less."

"And you never thought about mentioning this before?"

"You never asked, poppet," said Primrose serenely.

Mika had to very sternly remind herself that it was not polite to throw teacups at people. Teeth gritted, she pointed out the obvious. "You always told me not to ask questions."

"Naturally, dear. That was for your own good."

Mika tightened her grip on her cup, genuinely concerned that if she relaxed her hold a fraction too much, the teacup would fly out of her hands and knock Primrose out cold. She took a handful of deep breaths before saying, in what was frankly a voice of heroic calm, "So you're saying witch-hunters cursed us? That's why we're orphaned soon after we're born?"

"Don't be absurd," said Primrose, sniffing. "The Witchfinder General and his ilk wielded a great deal of power, but it was the power of politics, not enchantment. How could they possibly have *cursed* us?"

"But you just said—"

"I said the blame lies with them, not that they cast a curse on us."

Somewhere in the mess of Primrose's half-explanations and woolly maybes, Mika thought she could see a glimmer of the truth. "They hunted us, so we tried to defend ourselves," she guessed, tracking the inevitable sequence of events to its tragic end. "Only we cursed ourselves instead."

"Which is just as I've always said," said Primrose. "A spell went wrong, for which we can thank the prejudices of an uncaring, patriarchal society that went out of its way to punish anybody it deemed too wilful, too powerful, or too different." Her lips twisted. "Not unlike the society we live in today."

"But what kind of spell was cast? How could it go so badly wrong?"

"You are irksomely inquisitive today, Mika," Primrose replied, looking very put-upon. "There isn't much more to tell you. The seventeenth century was a time of growing prejudice and peril all over the world, and young witches were particularly vulnerable. The spell was supposed to give newborn witches greater protection. It went wrong, and essentially did the opposite. It killed the parents of new witches, a curse that has persisted in every generation since."

Mika was baffled. "But *all* new witches are orphaned, not just the ones in a certain place or country. I'm struggling to believe any one witch could have had the power to cast such a timeless, far-reaching spell."

"Well, of course not," said Primrose, tutting like Mika should have somehow known the impossible. "It wasn't just one witch who cast the spell, was it? It was fifty-three."

"*Fifty-three*—" Mika broke off, incredulous. A fourth scone seemed like the only logical next step. "Fifty-three *witches*? Cast a spell? *Together?*"

Primrose didn't reply immediately because the stiff, butler-like waiter had returned with the second pot of tea. Once he had left, she poured a fresh cup and said: "Haven't you ever wondered why witches never spend too much time together?"

"Yes," Mika said tartly, "and I have also asked the question many times, only to be told *We would attract too much attention, poppet* and *Dangerous things happen when too much magic gathers in one place, poppet.*"

"Both true," said Primrose. "But both of those things were true back then, too, and yet witches took those risks because they believed the benefits were greater. Then the spell went wrong, proving that some risks are just not worth taking, and we scattered." She took a sip of her tea. "For centuries, witches formed friendships with other witches. Every few months, representatives from every part of the world met to share spells, offer each other advice and assistance, and *chat*. Just as we do now, but on a much bigger scale."

"But it must have taken forever for everyone to travel to one place!"

"Hardly," Primrose sniffed. "They were witches. They flew."

"On actual broomsticks, you mean?"

"Well, the specific tool depended on the culture, but yes, broomsticks were the most common. It was a simpler time. There were no aircrafts, no satellites, nothing in the sky to catch them out. Our ancestors were free to travel as fast as their magic could take them."

Mika pictured this rather wistfully, this world where witches from all over the world were *friends*. She couldn't help thinking it a terrible, beastly pity that here they were, centuries later, in a world where, no, it wasn't possible to ride broomsticks across the skies without attracting an awful lot of attention, but a group chat on a phone that fit in their pockets could serve exactly the same purpose. How long were generations of witches supposed to let an old spell dictate the way they lived their lives?

"So when the witch-hunters started gaining a lot of political power, a generation of witches decided to cast a spell together, one that was supposed to protect all new witches across the world," Mika said, thinking out loud as much as anything else. "Primrose, please tell me *you* weren't one of the witches who cast that spell!"

Primrose's expression was glacial. "You really do have the most irregular ideas," she said severely. "You may find this hard to believe, Mika, but I was *not* alive four hundred years ago. I know the story because I heard it from an older witch, who heard it from an older witch, and so on. It's how we preserve our histories, you know."

"I don't know, actually," said Mika, goaded. "How do you expect all this to survive *your* death when you don't tell anyone anything?"

"I'm telling you now, aren't I?"

Mika prayed for patience. "What did the witches do after the spell went wrong?"

"It took a generation or two for the reality of what they'd actually done to sink in," said Primrose. "Once it did, it was decided that witches would stay apart. It was inevitable, between the deaths of so many parents, the orphaning of new witches, and the ill will that followed the spell. I can't speak for elsewhere, but here in Britain, the witches chose to continue the tradition of meeting every few months. Careful consideration was given to the risks, and rules were imposed to reduce them, and, so far, our existence has remained safe and secret."

"And we have no contact with witches anywhere else."

"I wouldn't say *no* contact," said Primrose. "I have been known to correspond with other witches on occasion. Your grandmother, for example."

Mika hastily swallowed a mouthful of scone, startled. "You actually *knew* my grandmother? I mean, I knew you had to have known *of* her if you knew she and my mother had been witches, but I didn't realise you knew her."

"She was the head of *her*—"

"Society?" Mika couldn't resist asking.

"I would prefer to use the term *group of witches sharing a similar geography*," said Primrose coldly.

Mika rolled her eyes. "Yes, that sounds much better."

"Your grandmother, Sita, occupied the same position I do. So we corresponded."

"She was the leader of all the witches in India?"

"Just the south of India," said Primrose. "It's a big country. It has at least six groups of witches. Your grandmother was the leader of one. She died shortly after your mother was born, of course, and I took it upon myself to look in on your mother every now and then." She paused, and then added almost kindly: "Neither your mother nor your grandmother ever planned to have children. I think they would have liked to if it hadn't been for the spell, but they did not have the luxury of choosing in the end."

Mika felt absolutely no resentment at the likelihood that she wouldn't have existed if her mother had had a choice in the matter. She was very glad she was alive, of course, but she also wished her mother *had* had a choice. *Everyone* deserved a choice.

"How did I end up with you?" she asked curiously. "Why didn't one of the witches in India take me instead?"

"It was the early nineties," Primrose explained. "By the time you were born, all the adult witches your mother and grandmother had known were married, with their power kept secret from husbands and in-laws, and none of them could afford the risk of taking in an orphaned child who would inevitably display uncontrollable bursts of magic. It was not so different here, either," she went on, "but I was unusually privileged. I had money, and I was beholden to no one, so it seemed only right that I take you into my care. And for what it's worth, Mika, I have never regretted it."

This was quite possibly the most astonishing revelation of the entire hour. Mika demolished the last scone to cover up her surprise.

"Am *I* supposed to pass all this history down to other witches once you're dust in the ground?" she eventually asked.

Primrose let out a peal of ladylike laughter, so long and full of mirth that Mika would have been downright offended if she hadn't had such a ready sense of humour. "No, poppet, I don't expect that of you," Primrose said, dabbing at the corners of her eyes with her napkin. "Our tradition is to pass our history down from eldest witch to eldest witch. I use the term *eldest* loosely, as each leader chooses her successor and it does not necessarily have to be the next witch in age."

"Is this your subtle way of telling me you won't be appointing me leader of the Very Secret Society of Witches anytime soon?"

"The fact that you persist in calling it that should give you your answer," said Primrose acidly.

Mika hid a smile. "Out of curiosity, who *are* you going to pick?"

"I don't expect to shuffle off this mortal coil for a while yet, dear, so I haven't settled on anybody. At the moment, however, I am inclined to choose Belinda."

"She'd be good at it."

"I'm aware. Believe it or not, I *do* know what I'm doing."

Mika toyed with her teaspoon, studying her warped reflection in the back. One last question nagged at the back of her mind and she knew that if she didn't spit it out now, quickly, she'd lose her nerve. "Have you ever considered breaking with tradition and letting witches spend more time together?"

"Why would I do that?" Primrose asked, her eyes instantly shrewd and suspicious. "Even if the old spell hadn't shown us exactly what happens when too many witches get together and lose their heads to arrogance, you know accidents are inevitable when too much power gathers in one place. Look around you," she went on, lips pursed as she indicated the phones clutched in almost every hand. "In this world, someone's always watching. How long do you think we could keep our secret?"

"But—"

"No, Mika," said Primrose, and she was utterly unyielding. "You know how this works. Alone is the only way we survive."

CHAPTER SEVENTEEN

It was a little after five o'clock when Mika said goodbye to Primrose and wobbled back to the Broomstick on legs of jelly. It was cold, dark, and wet, an utterly wretched December evening, and not even the insistently merry sound of festive music from inside the hotel could cheer her up. Like the fairies of old, who were repelled by cold iron, she felt like she'd spent too much time in the crowded, brightly lit, fast-paced world normal people inhabited and she longed for a crackling fireplace, the click of knitting needles, and the lullaby of ocean waves.

She longed for Nowhere House.

Mika fumbled with her keys, feeling leaden, shivery, and dizzy with exhaustion (and perhaps also from an excess of sugar. That fifth scone might have been overkill.). Once she'd gotten the car unlocked, an almost impossibly difficult task, she almost fell into the driver's seat. The heating came on immediately, but it didn't do much for her shivering. She leaned her heavy head back against the seat and groaned silently. There was absolutely no way she could pull off a speed spell right now, but just the thought of over two hours of driving made her want to crawl into the back seat and just go to sleep there.

Actually, that wasn't a bad idea.

She was just trying to figure out if she even had the energy to get to the back seat or if she was just going to have to stay right here for the rest of her days, when the door on the driver's side was yanked unceremoniously open and a tall someone glowered down at her.

"Hey!" Mika protested. "It's cold!"

"Then move over." Impossibly, that was Jamie's voice, stern and unsympathetic. "I'll shut the door once I get in."

She moved like she was fighting quicksand, her muscles protesting as she clambered over the handbrake and fell into the other seat. As promised, he slid into the driver's seat and shut the door. She blinked dizzily at him. Half his face was in shadow, the other lit only by the ambient light spilling out of the hotel, and she was quite certain there were two of him.

Mika wondered if she was hallucinating. "How are you even here? Didn't you and Ken go off on an errand earlier today?"

He rolled his eyes. "Yes, this. This was the errand."

He pointed. Blinking at the misty windshield, Mika just about made out the shape of Jamie's black sedan in the space opposite hers. Ken was behind the wheel. He gave her a smile and a wave.

Her brain was mush, so it took her a minute to crack this riddle. "You're saying you and Ken left Nowhere House two hours before I did just so you'd get here in time to find me?"

"We had a hunch you wouldn't be in a fit state to get yourself home. Looks like we were right." Jamie arched an eyebrow. "If only someone had warned you before you embarked on this unnecessary escapade."

"Be honest. You came here just for the pleasure of being able to say you told me so."

His mouth twitched, but the furrow between his eyebrows didn't budge. "Would you rather Ken drove you home?"

"No," she said before she could think better of such disastrous honesty.

"Well, good, because he just drove off."

Mika laughed, but her teeth were chattering so hard that the sound came out all wrong. She felt damp and clammy, from cold sweat rather than the drizzle outside, and she was about to make the herculean effort of reaching out a hand to turn the heating up even higher when she saw Jamie shrug off his coat. He manhandled her into it, to which she didn't object in the slightest. His coat was butter-soft and radiated the heat from his own body. She drew her knees up to her chest, turned sideways in the seat to lean back against the door, and snuggled deeper into the coat. The shivering quieted down at last.

"Pine needles and the ocean," she said sleepily. "It smells like you."

"So I've been told."

"By me?"

"No, it must have been one of the *other* witches who make a habit out of sniffing my neck."

"Once does not a habit make," Mika objected, but couldn't quite suppress a tiny smile. That worried line between his straight, dark brows was still there. Quite beyond pedestrian concerns like propriety, she raised one hand and smoothed her thumb over the furrow, trying to make it go away. "You'll get wrinkles if you frown like that."

His eyes were almost silver. He reached for her hand and drew it away from his forehead, but didn't let it go. Instead, he turned it over to trace a scar on her palm. Her skin tingled. "What's this from?"

"Thorns." She moved her hand out of his and back to his face. He stopped her, his hand tightening around her wrist as she drew her fingers over the line of his jaw. "It's as hard as it looks," she marvelled.

Jamie cast his eyes heavenward and muttered something under his breath that sounded a lot like *It's not the only thing.*

Melting bonelessly into the warmth of his coat, her heart thumping unevenly, she smiled fuzzily, beyond all hope. "Come here."

"Absolutely not."

"But I want you to kiss me."

"I got that, which is why I'm not moving so much as one inch closer."

Mika felt this was distinctly unfair, but then it occurred to her that maybe she'd misinterpreted his expression and she was actually being politely rejected. "Do you maybe not want to kiss me? Because that's okay."

He moved his jaw gently out of her reach. "It's not about what I want."

"I think you're avoiding the question."

"And I think you're delirious, and not even *close* to thinking straight," Jamie said, his voice low and not quite steady. "So no, I'm not going to kiss you."

"Well, fuck."

"Yeah, I'm not going to do that to you, either. Not like this."

Not like this.

He seemed to realise what he'd said the same moment she did. Her heart thudded and her mouth opened, lips forming a soundless *oh*. He stared at her mouth, made a soft sound in his throat, and looked away. His hands clenched the steering wheel.

"Time to go," he rasped, starting the car. "You should probably eat something before we drive back."

"Oh, I have already. I had a whole plate of scones."

There was a bit of amusement in his voice now. "Something other than a whole plate of scones."

"There was a pot of jam and clotted cream, too."

"You're not making this sound any better."

"Heathen," she said, yawning.

Her eyes drifted closed to the sound of a seatbelt clicking into place, and when they opened, it looked like some time had passed because they were pulling out of a drive-through and Jamie had deposited a cheeseburger, fries, and, hilariously, one of those child-sized bottles of juice on her lap.

"Is the fruit juice supposed to balance out all the salt and sugar?" she asked, popping a fry in her mouth and closing her eyes blissfully at the taste. "Because I feel like I should tell you that it's a Band-Aid over a bullet hole. It's going to take two lettuces, three carrots, and a whole pumpkin to offset the heart attack that plate of scones and this dinner is on its way to causing."

"And yet," he said, stealing one of her fries, "you appear to be eating that dinner with little to no concern for said heart attack."

"You only live once." Glancing out of the window at the spires of a cathedral, she tried to picture Jamie in his twenties. "Do you miss living here?"

He looked surprised. "Cambridge? No, not really. I spent most of my years as a student pretty much blackout drunk, which, considering I'm Irish, is saying quite a lot. And teaching didn't suit me." His eyes cut to her, a smile flickering across them. "Turns out I was too grumpy, if you can believe that."

"You? Grumpy? Impossible!" Mika leaned her heavy head on her elbow, finished the last of her cheeseburger, and studied his profile. "Was it hard? Coming back to Nowhere House and becoming a de facto parent to an infant witch at the age of, what? Twenty-six?"

"The witch part did come as something of a surprise because Lillian didn't bother to warn us before turning up with a baby in tow, but Rosetta, you'll be unsurprised to hear, was a placid, easy baby. Altamira, on the other hand"—here he shuddered, which made her laugh—"well, let's just say that when she hit the terrible twos, I was ready to put her in a boat and set her adrift on the sea. Ian had the boat practically ready to go."

"I assume, as Altamira is still safely ensconced in Nowhere House, that the more level heads of Lucie and Ken prevailed."

"It takes a village." Jamie turned right, cutting across traffic. Mika, who was very possessive of the Broomstick, found she rather liked watching him behind the wheel of her car. "How did it go with Primrose?"

"It was the most peculiar thing. I lied about where I've been and I don't think she suspects anything, so that's all fine, but she also told me a whole lot of other stuff." Mika gave him a brief description of Primrose's various revelations. "It was *so* weird. I must have asked her the same kinds of questions dozens of times as a child, only to be told each time that my curiosity was obnoxious and unbecoming."

"Have you asked her those questions since then?"

"No," Mika said, thinking back. "I gave up years ago and usually stick to small talk when we meet, but this time, I don't know. I asked. Maybe it was because I've spent so much time with the kids, so it feels like there's more at stake now that it's not just me. I want to be able to give them more of our history. More than I had growing up, anyway. But I really didn't expect her to tell me as much as she did."

"Maybe she did it because you're an adult now," Jamie said. "There's a lot we'll say to other adults that we won't tell a child."

"You think she finally sees me as an equal? Well, almost equal," she amended, her mouth twisting ruefully. "She was as imperious and inflexible as ever when I went so far as to suggest tweaking the Rules. Like Icarus, I flew too close to the sun and have been brutally cast back down."

The sound of Jamie's laugh vibrated across the car. "You've been spending too much time with Ian." He cut her a shrewd glance. "You look like you're having a hard time keeping your eyes open. Don't stay awake on my account."

"I could attempt a speed spell to get us back faster," Mika offered.

Jamie's only answer was a glare.

Burrowing happily back into his coat, Mika breathed in, leaned her head on the window, and closed her eyes.

"I like you when you're stern," she said drowsily, and drifted into a deep, dreamless sleep.

~

I like you when you're stern.

Jamie cut an incredulous look at Mika's sleeping face. What the fuck was he supposed to do with that?

Do you maybe not want to kiss me? He'd almost laughed when she'd said it, a dark and mirthless laugh. If she only fucking knew.

When Mika next woke, it was because Jamie had stopped the car. She ached all over, but the shivery, dizzy ickiness was gone. Rubbing her eyes, she saw that the Broomstick was outside a mostly dark Nowhere House. Only the upstairs hallway and kitchen lights were still on.

"Home," Jamie said quietly.

Home. It sounded right, which was frankly terrifying because it *wasn't* her home. Sooner or later, she'd have to leave. It was wildly foolish to get attached, to *care*, because she had never belonged anywhere and had never been enough for anybody, and it was only a matter of time before the people of Nowhere House figured that out.

A glance at the clock told her it was past ten. "Wow," she said, her voice a little croaky from the impact the word *home* had had on her. "We must have been on the road for, what? Five hours?"

"There was an accident just outside Cambridge, and it took ages to clear it. Are you okay? Can you walk?"

"I think so. I don't feel as wobbly." She watched him, brows knitted. "Are *you* okay? You must be exhausted."

"I'm fine."

"As if you'd say so even if you weren't," Mika scoffed. He smiled. She opened her door, letting the cold, sharp sea air in, and clambered out. She teetered for an instant but she didn't keel over, so that was an improvement. "Do you think Ian's up? Is that why the kitchen light's still on?"

"He said he'd wait up for us," Jamie said, handing her the car keys and starting up the path to the front door.

"Jamie."

He hesitated, but turned back.

"You came to get me," Mika said. "No one's ever done that. Thank you."

He looked at her for a long moment, then nodded without replying and unlocked the front door. They got rid of their shoes and went straight to the kitchen, Mika still huddled in a coat she had no intention of getting out of anytime soon, where Ian was busy removing trays of oatmeal-raisin cookies from the oven.

"Stress-baking," he explained, beaming at them. "Cookie?"

"I could definitely do with more sugar today," Mika said gravely. Jamie's mouth quirked. They each accepted a cookie from Ian. "Is the kettle on?"

"Popped it on the moment I heard the car outside," said Ian proudly. "A nice, hot cup of tea before bed is just what you need, my dear. Jamie? Tea?"

He nodded, dropping into a chair at the table.

"You could probably do with some warming up, too," Ian remarked, his eyes bright with unholy mischief. "What with you losing your coat and all that."

"*Were* you cold the whole way?" Mika asked Jamie, feeling guilty and horrified.

Jamie cut Ian a glare before answering her. "Don't be ridiculous. You had the heating up all the way. I was fine."

Ian hummed merrily to himself as he busied himself with the tea. He had way more energy than any man in his eighties had any right to have this late in the day. In minutes, he had three cups brewed and brought them over to the table, along with a plate of the cookies. "So?" he prompted. "Should we expect the Bogeywoman at our door any day now?"

Mika choked on her cookie, immensely tickled by the idea of Primrose as a bogeywoman. "Nope. She did figure out I was to blame for the surge in power, but I gave her a pretty good excuse for my presence in these parts."

"Really? What did you tell her?"

"A class reunion at UEA."

"Of course! You were a student there, weren't you? What a clever excuse!"

Jamie gave her a wry look. "Are class reunions often the cause of massive surges in magic?"

Mika could have dodged that or simply lied, but she didn't. "No, but reunions with horrible ex-boyfriends can be."

His eyes narrowed, his expression darkening. Ian, on the other hand, perked up. "Well, now you have to tell us all about this fiend!"

"No, you don't," said Jamie.

"Hush, you."

Mika laughed. "It's really not that exciting. It's just that Primrose knows about him, so he was a convenient scapegoat." She clutched her teacup between her hands, unburying a memory she had tried very hard not to think of for the best part of a decade.

"We met while I was at UEA, and we were together for about four months."

"Was he your first dalliance?" Ian asked.

"He was not," Mika said, grinning at the ridiculously archaic turn of phrase. "I'd gotten around a bit by the time I met him. But he was my first and last actual boyfriend."

Ian's face gentled. "Were you in love?"

"I don't think so," Mika mused. "Looking back now, I don't think it was anything so powerful as *love*, but I did care a lot more about him than I had about anyone else I'd been with before. And I was twenty, with stars in my eyes and a song in my heart, so I decided to tell him the truth. About me."

Ian gasped.

"Not all of it," Mika added. "I told him I practiced magic, but I didn't tell him other witches existed. He, um, he asked if it was some weird cultural thing. His words, not mine." She didn't dare look up at them, but she heard someone's breath hiss through his teeth. "I laughed it off because I thought that was what I was supposed to do. Then I showed him a few spells."

"And then?" Jamie asked quietly.

The pain was unexpected, like an old, almost forgotten bruise that surprises you when it's pressed. It wasn't as bad as it used to be, but it was still there because she understood that it wasn't about one ex-boyfriend. It was about so much more.

"I still don't quite understand *how* it happened," Mika said, her eyes fixed firmly on the teacup in front of her. An old sense of shame threatened to rear its head, but she knew it was a lying sort of feeling and she knew how to deal with it now. She said the words out loud: "I know now that it wasn't my fault, but at the time, it felt like it must have been. It was like one day, I was *me*, and the next, I was casting spells *he* wanted me to. He was at an ATM getting cash out one time and he got me to enchant the machine so that it malfunctioned and gave him a few hundred quid that wasn't his. Another time, I cast a basic warding spell over his phone so that he could take it into exams and look the answers up without anyone noticing. I did things like that for weeks. Because he wanted me to. Because I thought if I did enough, he'd love me."

"Oh, Mika," Ian said, upset, putting a hand over hers.

"Anyway, there was a moment, one day, when it just hit me that I didn't like myself very much anymore, and that mattered more than whether or not *he* liked me, so we broke up. I reported everything he'd done, admitting I'd helped him but obviously leaving out any mention of spellcasting, and then I left. I could probably have stayed on at UEA and finished my final year, but I wanted him to forget all about me and about what I'd been able to do."

There was silence in the kitchen when she finished speaking. Mika bit into another cookie, inordinately interested in the pattern of the wood grain on the table.

Ian tightened his grip on her hand. "I can't imagine how much it must have hurt to be used like that, but surely, *surely*, you don't plan to let one slimy cretin affect the way you live your life?"

"One slimy cretin, and a host of nannies and tutors before him," Mika reminded him, her smile a little wobbly. "I'd seen ugly reactions before. That ATM spell? I'd used it before. One of my nannies asked me to." She stopped, startled. "I've never said that out loud before. I try not to even think about it."

"It's okay," Jamie said quietly.

Mika looked up at him. There was no judgement or censure in

his eyes, just an anger that she could tell wasn't directed at her, and it gave her the nudge she needed to tell them the rest. "When my caretakers found out I was a witch," she explained, "some of them were afraid, some thought they were hallucinating, and, on one memorable occasion, one tutor was convinced I must have been experimented on by a secret government agency and insisted I go public. But most often, the reaction I got was a whole lot like *his*. I became something that could be used."

A muscle jumped in Jamie's jaw. Ian looked unhappily at him, then turned back to Mika with a firm: "Not everyone is like that, my darling. There is someone out there who will accept you as you are, who will allow you to just be Mika."

"Is there?" Mika asked. "Because the way I see it, to be a witch is to be exploited when it's convenient and turned against when it isn't. I'd *love* to just be Mika, but the rest of the world has yet to give me that privilege."

"Yes, I see that," Ian admitted. "I understand, I do. There was a time when Ken and I weren't allowed to just be ourselves, either."

"I know," Mika said, squeezing his hand. This time, her smile was brighter and a lot less wobbly. "Believe me, if there's one thing that *might* be able to convince me that there's a better future ahead, it's you and Ken."

Jamie pretended to scowl. "Oh, Christ, don't get him started on his stories about the pair of them!"

"Scamp," Ian said fondly.

"Fossil."

Mika interrupted this loving volley of insults. "How long *have* you and Ken been married?"

"As long as we've been allowed to," said Ian. "Which is to say, not very long. But we've been together over fifty years." That seemed like an unfathomable amount of time to Mika. With a dreamy sigh, he went on: "You know, love at first sight sounds like a lot of nonsense, but I swear to you, I knew I loved Ken the moment I laid eyes on him. He took a bit more convincing, I'm afraid. I can be a trial."

"We know," Jamie said drily.

"My father had died a few years before, but my mother and Ken's parents knew about us. They were the only ones we told at the time. To everyone else, we were confirmed bachelors. That was what they'd call us back then. Well, to be more precise, that was the *nicest* thing they'd call us."

"But you loved each other anyway," Mika said, suddenly aware that she was not just in awe of them, but also envious. Her heart ached with a terrible, passionate yearning. "And you still do, even after all this time."

"I could have another hundred years with Ken and still want more," Ian said simply.

CHAPTER EIGHTEEN

Mika spent most of Friday fast asleep, drifting in and out of peculiar dreams about snowy nights, stormy grey eyes, and pine needles. She'd locked the attic door to prevent anyone from coming in to check on her and finding her asleep wearing a coat that most certainly was not hers, so when she woke at last, it was to the sound of loud, resolute knocking at the door.

"Just so you know," Terracotta's voice hollered from the other side of the door, "you *have* to teach me the spell to lock and unlock doors."

"And me!" Altamira chimed in, not to be outdone. "Are you awake yet? We miss you!"

Hastily putting Jamie's coat on her chair, where it might have been all night and all day for all anyone knew, Mika let the girls in. Circe, who had been inadvertently locked out of the attic as well, followed them in with a rather petulant bark. Mika immediately set about soothing her offended temper with hugs and scratches.

"Lucie says you have to come down to dinner," Rosetta informed Mika. "She says she doesn't care how tired you are, you're *not* missing another meal."

Mika grinned at this spot-on imitation of Lucie's tone. "As it happens, I feel a lot better and I'm *starving*, so Lucie's summons couldn't have come at a better time. Lead the way, small ones."

But Terracotta, that irksomely hawk-eyed child, paused. "Why is Jamie's coat on your chair?"

"Because he let me wear it last night when I got very cold," Mika said in what she hoped was an entirely unconcerned tone of voice. "Now move it, buttercup, or I might get so hungry I'll have to make do with nibbling on you."

"Don't you want to get dressed?"

"Are you sure you're eight years old?" Mika demanded. "Not, perhaps, eighty? Or eight hundred? No one is going to faint at the sight of a pair of bare legs, I promise you."

"I thought you might get *cold*," Terracotta replied, giving her an odd look. "Why would bare legs make anyone faint?"

"Never mind."

They traipsed downstairs together, Mika knuckling sleep crust out of her eyes while the girls showed her the progress they'd made on their spellwork. Rosetta could now make her jointed wooden doll tap-dance on her palm, while Terracotta and Altamira had joined forces to animate a handful of origami paper swans. Mika was terribly impressed and terribly proud of all of them.

Surrounded by a flock of merry paper swans fluttering around their heads, they joined the others in the kitchen. Ian was crouched in front of the oven, his back to them, but Jamie looked up as they came in. His dark eyes snapped quickly to Mika's, then snapped just as quickly away.

Ken stood at the table, filling up glasses with apple juice he and the girls had made themselves, and Lucie came directly over to get a good look at Mika.

"Well, you're not feverish," said Lucie, her cheeks rounding in a relieved smile. "You're still a bit pale, but that's probably because you haven't eaten anything since Ian's cookies last night. How do you feel?"

"Almost human," Mika said cheerfully. She didn't care one bit that she was a fully grown adult. She'd happily sink into Lucie's embrace and be fussed over any day.

"It sounds like you were in a bad way yesterday. Do you remember much?"

Lucie's eyes were completely guileless, the question utterly innocent, but Mika's cheeks went hot and she forced herself not to shoot a look over at Jamie as she said, "I remember all of it."

I remember being so delirious I forgot that restraint exists. I remember asking Jamie to kiss me and being very soundly rejected. What I don't remember is him suffering from any such delirium, which makes me tragically certain that he remembers all of it, too.

She did not, of course, say any of this.

Instead, she went over to Ken and gave him an impulsive hug. "Thank you for yesterday."

"It was no trouble at all," Ken said softly, his arms tightening around her. His warm brown eyes crinkled in a smile.

Altamira peered up at them with something like concern. "Why are you hugging? Is someone sad?"

"The opposite, actually," Mika explained. "Ken was very kind to me yesterday."

"It was at Jamie's insistence, but I must admit he didn't have to do much to persuade me."

"Oh! Was that when they came and picked you up after you saw Primrose?" Altamira asked, and immediately followed this up with a fervent, "Damn it, Primrose," as if the mere mention of Primrose's name was such an ill omen that it necessitated the latter to dispel the curse.

Dinnertime conversation was familiar, mundane, and comforting: Lucie wanted to spend the weekend reading a stack of deliciously steamy historical romances she'd found at the charity shop, but Ian wanted her to help him build a beehive instead; Ken settled this argument by reminding Ian that he was almost out of his beloved flamingo pink wool, so Ian immediately made plans to drive to his favorite wool shop, The Lost Sheep, to stock up on supplies; Altamira and Terracotta tried to negotiate an extra hour of screen time out of Jamie, who was unmoved and reminded them that the only reason Rosetta was getting an extra hour was because *she* had actually cleaned her bedroom without being asked; and Mika said she'd be spending her Saturday in the woods, foraging for ingredients she'd noticed she was running low on.

"The Winter Solstice is just a few days away," she explained, neglecting to point out the obvious fact that this meant Edward's visit was only a few days after *that*. "It's one of the most powerful days of the year for witches, so I try to get as much potion-making done as possible."

"Not too much *this* year, I hope," said Lucie. "You can't possibly shut yourself away in the attic all day! We don't do much for Christmas at Nowhere House, but we always make the Solstice as festive as possible. In fact," she added, with a pointed glance in Altamira's direction, "Santa's even been kind enough to adjust his schedule and bring the girls their presents on the Solstice!"

"Really?" Excitement and delight coursed through Mika. "I mean, I suppose I should have expected it, considering this is a house full of witches, but I've never celebrated the Solstice with someone else before."

"So you *have* to join in," Rosetta said earnestly.

"How could I possibly refuse?"

"You should take the kids out foraging with you tomorrow," Jamie suggested. "They always enjoy that."

"A very good idea," Ian approved, and added innocently, "You could go, too. To, er, keep an eye on things."

Mika raised her eyebrows at this, amused by such a shameless lack of subtlety, but Jamie only said, "I can't. I'm away tomorrow."

"Away?" Ian blinked. "Away where?"

"I'll probably be back before the girls are in bed," Jamie went on, ignoring the question.

Ken and Lucie exchanged wary looks, which suggested to Mika that such caginess was unfamiliar to them. Ian eyed Jamie askance. "But where are you going?"

"Yes, where?" Terracotta put in, her tone even more suspicious than Ian's.

Jamie scowled at them. "Liverpool."

"*Liverpool*—" Ian's eyes almost bugged out of his head. "You're planning to go four hours each way? In a day? Why? Is there a

208

stupendously rare book there that you can only pick up in person?"

"Sure, let's go with that."

"Jamie!"

"Oh, for fuck's sake, Ian," Jamie snapped. "It's my mother's sixtieth birthday tomorrow. She loves art galleries. She's spending the day at the Tate. She asked me if I'd go. Can we drop it now?"

There was a moment of absolute silence. Mika looked around the table, confused, and saw that even the girls looked shocked.

"Will your brothers be there?" Ian demanded.

"Ian," Ken warned. At the same time, there was a thump under the table, as if Lucie had given Ian a swift kick.

"She's their mother, too, so I expect they will be there, yes," Jamie replied in a clipped tone.

"You've lost your fucking mind," said Ian succinctly.

"Ian."

Mika attempted a question. "Why shouldn't he go see his mother on her birthday?"

No one answered her. Mika knew it wasn't fair to grudge anyone else their secrets, but she felt like she was on the outside again, looking in at something she wasn't a part of, and she was amazed at how much it hurt.

Ian glowered at Jamie, who simply looked back, unmoved and implacable. Mika was only slightly surprised when Ian looked away first.

"Fine." Ian crossed his skinny arms over his chest. "If you insist on this foolishness, you should at least take Mika with you."

"What?" Jamie demanded. "Why?"

"What he said," Mika agreed. She was quite certain that when she'd wished she weren't on the outside looking in, she hadn't meant she wanted to be involved like *this*.

Ian looked at them like the answer was the obvious. "Mika is excellent company, *and* she knows a speed spell. Why drive eight hours in one day when you can do it in two?"

"An annoyingly fair point," Mika admitted. "And I'm much better now, so I should be able to cast spells without needing a sugar rush and an eighteen-hour nap right after."

"Excellent," said Ian, looking decidedly perkier. "Jamie?"

Jamie scowled at Ian, his jaw clenching and unclenching like he was irritated with the logic laid before him. Then, almost reluctantly, his eyes moved across the table to Mika. "Would you mind going?"

"Not at all," she said. In fact, whatever the opposite of minding was, *that* was pretty much how she felt. The idea of spending a day with him was much too appealing. A thought struck her. "I don't have to go *inside* the Tate, do I? Because crowds and enclosed spaces are a combination I don't partake in if I can help it. I'd prefer to wait in the car. With a book. And snacks. *Many* snacks."

A faint, crooked smile replaced the scowl on Jamie's face. "Sounds like a plan to me."

Jamie was in a mess of a mood as he clattered his way into Ian and Ken's cottage the following morning, shutting the front door behind him and rocking back and forth on the balls of his feet for a moment to shake off the cold. Mika still had his coat, and it was only a minute's jog across from the house to the cottage, but Christ, it was freezing out there.

"I see your feathers are ruffled," came Ken's deep, amused voice from the tiny, firelit front room.

They *were* ruffled. Not that he would ever admit it to Ian, but he was genuinely questioning his judgement in agreeing to go see his mother and brothers. On top of that, he was aggravated and exasperated and a number of other synonyms besides.

"Ian's feathers, on the other hand," Ken went on, as Jamie threw himself into an armchair, "are about as thrilled as any feathers can be."

"Colour me surprised," said Jamie irritably. "Where is he, anyway? I came to have words."

"I think he suspected you might," said Ken, sipping his morning coffee in an unsubtle attempt to hide his smile. "He nipped out to the wool shop just a few minutes ago, so I'm afraid, sweet boy, that you'll have to make do with me."

Ken was the only person in the entire world who used the term *sweet boy* to refer to Jamie, completely without irony, and it made Jamie love him all the more. While also questioning *his* judgement because Jamie was many things, but he was quite sure *sweet* was not one of them.

"Jamie." Ken prodded gently. "Are you sure you want to do this? You don't have to go."

"I think I need to."

Ken's face was full of understanding and compassion. "As long as you remember that they have absolutely no power over you anymore."

"I know." Jamie didn't want to think about it any more than was necessary. "Anyway, I didn't come to talk about them. I came to talk about Ian's godforsaken pigheadedness." He glowered at the empty spot on the sofa where Ian usually sat. "This thing with Mika. *You* know this is a terrible idea, don't you?"

It was a long shot to hope that *someone* on this property was still sane, and this pessimistic expectation proved correct when Ken said, "I did think so at first, but I'm not so sure anymore." He put his coffee cup down and reached across the space between their chairs to pat Jamie's arm. "You understand why Ian's doing this, don't you? He's beginning to feel his own mortality and, between you and me, the idea of leaving you alone terrifies him."

Jamie found his chest was too tight to allow a reply. The idea of a world without Ian and Ken was not one he allowed himself to think about. As far as he was concerned, Death had taken enough from him and every person here was going to live fucking forever.

"Jamie," Ken said tenderly. "You must understand why he's so determined to find you the same kind of happiness he and I have had. You've been *our* boy since the day you arrived, *ours* to love and protect and give the world to. And I know you're an adult now. In his more reasonable moods, Ian knows that, too. But you must remember that while twenty years have come and gone, we haven't forgotten the brave, wounded boy who stormed into our lives that day, utterly alone, and we will do *anything* in our power to make sure you never have to be that boy again."

"I know that," said Jamie. "It's just that Ian may have miscalculated this time. If anyone has the power to tear me apart, I think it's her."

Ken's smile crinkled the corners of his eyes. "That might be true but, you know, I don't think she will."

"She'll leave."

"I expect so, yes," said Ken, considering. "Mika has been so deeply hurt that she has taught herself to run before she can lay down roots, but the thing you have to remember, Jamie, is that when someone leaves, all *you* can do is leave a window open for them so that one day, if they choose, they can come back."

CHAPTER NINETEEN

The trip up north started uneventfully. By the time Jamie and Mika left Nowhere House in his car, the sky was the kind of blinding white that promised snow (but this was Norfolk, so it probably wouldn't deliver on that promise).

Jamie had been more curious about Mika's speed spell than he'd let on, especially considering they were taking *his* car and *he* was the person behind the wheel who had to somehow cover just under three hundred miles in a little over an hour. When he said this to her, though, she explained that the term was a bit of a misnomer.

"It's tidy and alliterative, calling it a speed spell," she said, toying with a chocolate bar (she'd already made a start on the snacks Lucie had stuffed the car with). "But it would probably be more correct to call it a spell that bends the rules of space and time. Which is much more of a mouthful."

"So it won't make the car go faster?"

"Not quite," she said. "It's more like, at intervals, the car will sort of *bend* the space between one point and the next. Like this." She dropped the chocolate bar back into the box of snacks and

214

plucked a piece of luminous gold thread out of the air. He glanced over, keeping one eye on the winding road ahead. "Let's say this thread is the distance between Norfolk and the Midlands. If I stretch it taut and you run your finger along it, it'll take you a few seconds to get from one end to the other. But if I fold the thread and put the ends together, like *this*, your finger will get from one end to the other almost instantaneously."

"So you'll have to cast the spell more than once?"

"Probably a few times each way," Mika replied. "It's easier to bend fifty miles a few times than it is to bend two hundred miles all at once, if that makes sense." She vanished the gold thread and retrieved her chocolate, smiling. "Tiny bites, not one ginormous gobble."

"Tell Terracotta that," said Jamie wryly. "You can laugh now, but have you ever seen her eat a cheeseburger? It's downright terrifying, like watching a python unhinge its jaw."

He saw the speed spell in action about ten minutes later, and almost didn't notice. Mika told him that was because he was *in-side* the spelled car, so to him, it felt like he'd just driven down one quiet country lane and turned into another. Only the satnav built into his car, scrambling to recalculate the route, gave away just how much distance they'd covered.

They paused in a thick, brambly wood for twenty minutes so that Mika could gather a few of the potion ingredients she hadn't been able to forage at Nowhere House like she'd planned. Jamie offered to help, so Mika pointed out what she needed: chestnuts, sloe berries, rosehips, honeysuckle, winter heather, and any winter-blooming flower.

"Are you sure you don't want to go back to the car?" she asked, sitting cross-legged on the mossy forest floor to snip stalks of heather. "You're not cold? Or bored?"

"No."

"See, I actually believe you," she said merrily. "Because you're kind, not nice. You'd never say you weren't bored to be polite."

"You're the only person I know who says the word *nice* like it's a bad thing."

"It's not a bad thing at all, except when it's *all* there is. A lot of nice people stop being nice when they don't get exactly what they want." She got back up and walked a couple of steps ahead of him, so he couldn't see her expression as she added: "When I'm around people like that, I feel like curling up into a little ball, like a hedgehog. I've been taught all my life not to draw attention to myself, not to make people angry, not to let anyone notice how peculiar I am. Sometimes, even now, I have to remind myself that I'm stronger than they think. That I have power." She turned her head and smiled over her shoulder at him. "You can't see it, but there's gold dust curling like smoke all around us. It's a constant reminder that even when I'm alone and afraid, I always have magic."

It was such an unexpected confession that Jamie heard himself give her one in return: "I had my father's journals. After he died, when *I* was alone and afraid, those pages covered in his handwriting got me to the other side of it."

Her smile right then was brighter than the fucking sun, and he had to look away, pretending there was nothing on his mind apart from a very pressing need to find honeysuckle.

Back in the car, Mika cast another speed spell, demolished another chocolate bar, and started typing furiously in the Notes app of her phone. She looked up, rubbed her cheek absently, muttered something under her breath, and then went back to typing.

Jamie was fascinated by this opaque process, and had to remind himself to pay attention to the road. Mika looked up at him after a while and gave him a sheepish smile. "Sorry. I got distracted."

"You don't have to be sorry for that. What were you doing?"

"I noticed a pink camellia as we left the woods," she explained, her eyes lighting up with an infectious excitement he'd noticed before, on those late nights when she'd been collecting pieces of stars or brewing a potion. "You know how some people think flowers have meanings? Well, I've heard that a pink camellia means you miss someone. And it got me thinking about whether I could use that. Like maybe if I combined the essence of a pink camellia with white lily petals, moonlight, and something else I haven't yet figured out, I could create a potion or tea that would soften that feeling of missing someone."

One side of his mouth lifted in a smile. "You know, I've never heard the kids talk about magic the way you do."

"Give them time," Mika said fondly. "They're only just learning not to be afraid of their power. Of course, they might never feel the same way I do. Witches don't always fall in love with magic. Like anybody else, we each have our own relationships with our identities and our power."

"What about the rest of the Very Secret Society of Witches?"

"I don't know any of the others very well, but based on what they've said over the years, it sounds like we've all chosen to live our lives in very different ways. One of us just got divorced, and another is about to get married, and another has been happily married for thirty years or so. I know a witch who works as a barrister, and one who has her own patisserie, and another who teaches at a primary school." Mika winced, as if struck by an unhappy notion: "Honestly, Primrose is the one I'm probably most like."

Jamie gave her an incredulous look, trying to match warm, merry Mika with the gorgon he assumed Primrose was. "Why?"

"In all the time I've known her, she's been alone," Mika said. "Like me. And she likes to say it's because of the Rules and the Sacrifices We Must Make for the Good of All, but I know it's more than that. Zuzanna, the witch who has been married for thirty years, says that she almost never does any spellwork at home because her husband doesn't know the truth about her. She doesn't seem to mind at all. Or take Sophie, the teacher. She lives alone, but she hardly ever uses her power and she says it's because she's just not that interested in it. But Primrose and me, we're not like that. We need magic the way we need to breathe."

"I get it," Jamie said. "That's kind of how I feel about books. When Lillian said she needed someone to run the library, I jumped at it."

"I bet. I'm glad you get to work with the thing you love."

There was a wistful note in her voice. It tugged at his heart-strings, but all he did was nod.

"I think that's why I've never settled down to any one kind of work," Mika mused. "Why I've cleaned houses and waited tables and served drinks behind bars. It's not just because they're temporary jobs I can find and leave easily. It's because magic is the only work I've ever been passionate about."

"And what would you do if you could?" Jamie asked. "If being a witch were a job, what would it look like?"

Mika gave him a doubtful look. "Do you actually want to know?"

"I wouldn't ask if I didn't, Mika. I'm not nice, remember?"

That made her smile. As she considered her answer, her forehead creased in a way that was, frankly, adorable. "I'm not sure. I think about it all the time, but I suppose I've never really let myself get too attached to any one idea." Her face softened. "Except for this one: I used to dream about having my very own enchanted tea and potion shop. A small, storybook kind of place, with potions and jars of tea leaves on the shelves, and a mortar and pestle on the counter, and a cauldron bubbling away."

The instant she said it, he heard how right it was, how *her*. And he heard something else, too. How, underneath the love of magic and the joy of living without having to hide who she was, what she wanted more than anything was *people*. Visitors she could befriend, friends she could help, a family she could share the thing she loved with.

"That was the place you created in your videos." Her alter ego. "I only watched one of them, but I remember the cauldron, and the potions in the background, and you, the wise and mischievous witch."

She laughed. "I suppose it was the closest I was ever going to get to the real thing."

"You could make it happen, you know."

"I don't think so," she said. "Not here. Not yet."

Quiet descended over the car. Jamie could tell she had something on her mind, so he waited patiently.

"Sometimes," Mika said after a moment, "I wonder what it's like to be a witch in other places in the world. Like in India, where

I was born, or in America or Norway or Egypt. Wherever. I some-times think about the ugly things, like I wonder if witches are still hunted in places with more deeply rooted superstitions, but mostly, I think about families and communities. Is there a place out there where witches live their lives in the open? Are there entire communities where the townspeople know about the friendly local witch, who maybe works with the friendly local doc-tor so that, together, they can fix pretty much anything?" She smiled a little sheepishly, like she expected him to laugh at her, but it was the furthest thing from his mind. "I suppose *that* place, if it exists, is where I might be able to have my tea and potion shop."

"You could go looking for it."

At that, she shook her head decisively. "I don't think so. I like learning about other places, and I'd love to find out more about witches in other parts of the world, but . . ."

When she hesitated, Jamie filled in the gaps. "But you've spent so much of your life moving around, you just want somewhere you can stay put?"

She nodded, her eyes wide with surprise, like she couldn't quite believe he'd understood this about her. "More than anything, I just want *one* place I can be myself. I just want a home."

"Home is worth finding," he said quietly. "Even if it takes a while."

"Did you?"

He'd known that was coming, but still, all the muscles in his body locked up. "Yes. I did."

She didn't say anything else for a while, and when she did, her voice was soft. "Why did you leave Belfast?"

There had been a time when the idea of opening up to her had been absurd, but now he found that he wanted to. There were truths he hadn't told her, and they lived in a hollow space inside his chest that echoed with guilt and regret, but maybe this was one truth he *could* share.

He let out a slow breath, and looked for the least thorny path through his past. It helped that she wasn't looking at him, that she'd turned her eyes to the window. "My dad was a rough, burly man," he said. "Rough like he was scruffy and salt of the earth-ish, not rough like he was mean. He was the gentlest, sweetest man you'll ever meet. And you've met Ken." She smiled. He rolled his shoulders, trying to unknot the tension in them. "I have two older brothers, but I was his favourite of the three of us. I'm not sure why, because Ryan and Matt were burly, boisterous copies of him, but they didn't have his heart. They were a fair bit older than me. They never liked me. It was partly because I came along late, and partly because I was small, skinny, and preferred to stay indoors with a book rather than go outside and play football or rugby with the other boys. More than anything, though, it was because Dad liked me best. *He* preferred playing football and rugby, but he'd stay in with me, let me ramble on about my favourite books."

"It sounds like he loved you very much."

"When Dad was alive, Ryan and Matt pretty much just pretended I didn't exist. Then, when I was twelve, Dad died. It was an accident at work. He was a builder."

"I'm sorry. I'm sure losing him just about killed you."

"Well, it didn't," said Jamie, with dark humour. "So my brothers did their best to finish the job."

Dark, long-lashed eyes grew wide.

His voice was wooden. "It was the usual kind of stuff. They'd rip up my books. They'd fuck up my room because they knew how much the mess bothered me. They'd hide Dad's journals from me." He took a deep breath. "They'd use Dad's old belts and take it in turns to hit me with them. They'd laugh the whole time because they were *his* belts and they'd say it was the same as if he'd done it."

"That's not what anyone would call the *usual* kind of stuff," Mika said passionately. The sheen of unshed tears in her eyes had turned into a fearsome rage. "And you lived like this for four whole years before you left?"

He shrugged.

"Where was your mother while all this was going on?"

"Dad was the light of her life," Jamie said. His teeth were clenched so hard, they ached. "My brothers had always been *her* favourites because they looked just like him. After he died, she fell apart. She was a ghost. She barely got out of bed, barely ate, barely spoke. She couldn't do anything for me." He smiled mirthlessly. "The day I came here, Lucie insisted on calling Mum to tell her I was safe. When she got off the phone, she told me Mum sounded relieved that I was gone. I think she knew I was better off."

"You know that's *massively* messed up, right?" Mika said.

He switched lanes, jerking the wheel a little too aggressively. "It wasn't her fault. She was in pain."

"So were you. She should have protected you."

Jamie's teeth snapped together. He wished he hadn't said anything. He was too raw for her unrelenting honesty. "She was—"

"Grieving," Mika finished for him, and the gentleness of her voice was almost worse than her anger. "Heartbroken. Depressed. I do understand that. But—"

"Mika, just stop, okay?"

"You were her family. She had a responsibility to all of you."

"Remind me," Jamie heard himself say as if from very far away, his voice low and icy and alien. "What exactly do *you* know about families?"

It was a knife that went right between her ribs, a thrust that drew blood. And hadn't he meant it to? Hadn't he wanted her to bleed the way he was bleeding?

So why, then, did he wish he could take it back?

Mika's face was very pale, but she looked him straight in the eye. "It's true that I have never had a family," she said, and the tremor in her otherwise tight, even voice almost undid him. "I don't think I have ever been loved by anybody. But I would argue that, despite what you think, that makes me uniquely qualified to know what it is to be treated poorly, and it means I know what I'm talking about when I say you deserved better. You *deserve* better."

His voice cracked. "I shouldn't have said that. I'm sorry."

"I know," she said quietly. Her arms were tightly folded across her chest, but some of the colour came back into her face as she gave him a faint smile. "I'm sorry, too. You asked me to stop, and I didn't. I should have."

"It doesn't excuse what I said."

"Can I just ask one thing?"

"You want to know why we're going today," Jamie guessed.

She nodded.

"I haven't seen any of them since I left Belfast. I've talked to my mother a few times over the years, but she's never asked me to meet her before. She said she wanted to, but she always chickened out. Until now, with the whole sixtieth birthday thing giving her a push. I think she thought I'd refuse to go, but I didn't. She's my mother, and I left her at a time when she was in pieces. I owe her this."

The expression on Mika's face told him she had some choice words for him in response to that, but she didn't say them. Instead, with heroic effort, she only said, "And your brothers? They'll be there, too, won't they?"

"I don't think about them much these days, but when I do, they always seem so *large.*" He shrugged. "You know how when we're little, we're afraid of monsters under our beds? We think they're huge and terrifying, but then we turn on the light and look and all we see are a few cobwebs."

"And you're hoping that's what today will be like?"

"Pretty much," Jamie said. "It feels like the least I can do for the boy who was afraid of what was under his bed. I'm hoping that when I see the monsters today, they'll just be cobwebs."

CHAPTER TWENTY

The Tate in Liverpool was in a converted dock right on the River Mersey. It was a long brick structure with wide arches and red columns, with a stream of visitors trickling in and out of the doors, and Mika felt not the smallest desire to join them.

They had found a tiny carpark a few minutes' walk away, and instead of staying in the car, Mika had accompanied Jamie to the entrance of the gallery. His shoulders were tense, his posture rigid, and she wished they'd never come.

"Will you be okay?" Mika asked at exactly the same time Jamie said, "Are you sure you'll be all right?"

"Yes," they both answered, also at the same time.

Mika laughed. Jamie even cracked a smile.

"I won't be far," she said.

She watched him enter the gallery, and once he was out of sight, she gathered up the friendly gold dust around her and let it guide her to a spot where it was quieter. There she found a low waterfront wall to perch on in the bright, cold sunshine, and fished her phone out of the pocket of her knitted yellow coat so that she could reply to the stream of texts Ian had sent her in the last hour or so.

The first seven texts were anxious queries about whether Jamie seemed himself, while the eighth seemed to be an ode to his grief that there had been no flamingo pink wool in stock at The Lost Sheep.

If you see a reputable wool shop while you're up there, dearest, the text ended by saying, **please get me all the flamingo pink. All of it.**

Mika was just about to reply to this request when she noticed a familiar prickly sensation start in her thumbs and spread slowly up her arms until they were covered in gooseflesh.

There was a witch close by.

She hopped off the wall, took a step away—

—and walked right into a perky, blue-haired Korean cannonball, who was holding the hand of a shorter, perkier, black-haired Korean cannonball.

"M-Mika?" Out of breath, the cannonballs came to an abrupt halt, stopping their relentless forward momentum with such speed that they nearly fell over. The blue-haired one gave Mika a single panicked look before hugging her. "What a surprise to see you here!"

"Hilda?"

"Of course, silly!" Hilda had grown up in Liverpool, so her chirpy Scouse voice would have been unmistakable even if the hair hadn't given her away. "Who else?"

Mika was stunned. The sight of another witch in the wild, outside of the familiar, specific setting of a Very Secret Society gathering, was so alien that she just blinked a few times. Were they even allowed to speak to each other? Hilda, too, seemed at a loss.

"Hiya," said the other cannonball, coming to their rescue. "I'm Kira, Hilda's fiancée. Are you the same Mika from the book club?"

"I—" Mika looked helplessly at Hilda, so startled to hear that Hilda actually *talked* about her at home that she didn't know what to say.

"Yes," said Hilda quickly, and pointedly. "This is Mika. From my book club. My *virtual* book club. She lives in, er—"

"Norfolk," Mika filled in, at exactly the same moment Hilda said, "Brighton."

Hilda paused. "You moved again?"

"Just last month. What are you doing here?"

"We live here," Hilda said, eyebrows vanishing into blue hair. "What are *you* doing here?"

"A friend of mine is visiting the Tate. I'm just waiting for him."

"We were just about to go in there to meet someone about our wedding plans," said Kira. "Hilda, why don't you stay out here and catch up for a few minutes while I go in?"

In a blur of dizzying speed, Kira was gone.

Mika blinked. She and Hilda looked at each other.

"Um," Hilda started.

"So," Mika started.

And, at exactly the same time: "Primrose can never know!"

There was a beat, and then they both burst into the slightly giddy giggles of two schoolgirls who know they're up to no good.

"Fuck me sideways," Hilda said, wiping tears of mirth from her eyes. "We're grown women quaking in our boots at the idea of an ancient crone."

"An ancient, *powerful* crone."

"There's that."

"It's nice to see you, Hilda," Mika said, looping her arm around Hilda's. She jerked her chin in the direction of the gallery. "A book club? She still doesn't know?"

Hilda's face fell. "I'm afraid to tell her the truth."

"Because of how she might take it?"

"That, and I'm afraid of what Primrose will say if she finds out I told her, and of Kira not loving me anymore." Hilda toyed absently with a blue curl. "I love her. I hate hiding this from her. And I really, truly believe I can trust her. But every time I think about saying the words, I hear Primrose's voice. *They've turned on us for centuries, poppet*"—Hilda's imitation of Primrose was eerily accurate—"*They'll do it again if we give them a chance.*"

"Alone is how we survive," Mika said under her breath.

"I hear that one, too."

Mika hated to see the uncertainty and distress on Hilda's face. "From what I just saw," she said, "Kira looks at you like you climbed up into the sky and put the moon there yourself, so I think there's a very good chance she's going to love and accept you for exactly who you are. That's the fucking Holy Grail. Tell her the truth. What you two have is worth Primrose's wrath."

Her brown eyes dewy with emotion, Hilda smiled a wobbly smile. "That was a really good pep talk."

"I thought so, too, if I do say so myself." Mika gave her a little nudge. "You should go. Talk to her. Plan your wedding. And tell me all about it at the next meeting."

Blowing her a kiss, Hilda darted off. Mika wondered if she *would* tell Kira the truth. It was easy to talk about taking such a big, terrifying step, but actually doing it was something else entirely.

She hadn't been alone more than ten minutes or so when she looked up to see Jamie coming her way. How long had he been gone? Less than an hour? She straightened up, immediately searching his face for signs of distress. Instead, he smiled at her, a slow, crooked smile that did obnoxious things to her heart.

Then she noticed that he had a stack of books under one arm, and that they were old, worn volumes covered in battered leather. She gasped. "No way! Are those—"

"Dad's journals."

"You got them back!"

He nodded, his eyes twinkling with an electric, giddy sort of high. He'd walked into an arena unsure if he'd be devoured by lions, only to come out unscathed. Even better: he'd come back with something precious, something that had been taken from him a long, long time ago.

"You didn't want to stay a bit longer?" Mika asked as they started walking back to the car.

"I think all my mother and I needed was just to see each other one more time," Jamie said, his energy damping as he thought about it. "Too much has happened for anything to go back to the way it was before Dad died, for either of us, but I think we were the loose threads in each other's lives. The moment I saw her, it hit me that all I'd really wanted was to make sure she was okay. I'd left her in pieces, and I wanted to know that she was now whole. Or close to it. And she is. I think she wanted the same."

Mika gave him an affectionate nudge. "I'm glad you got what you needed."

"Were you okay? What did you do while I was inside?"

"*I* met a witch," Mika announced.

Jamie gave her a surprised look. "A new one?"

"No, a witch from the Society. Hilda. I might have mentioned her before." Mika gave him the highlights of her conversation with Hilda, and finished with, "I hope she tells Kira. She seems so unhappy, keeping something so big and important a secret from her."

A shadow crossed Jamie's face, damping some of that light in his eyes again, but he only said, "Holy Grail?"

Mika shrugged, sheepish. "Well, it *is*. To be loved and accepted exactly as we are? Isn't that the thing we're all searching for?"

"Maybe," Jamie said, almost to himself, "but we don't always know it when we've found it."

They'd reached the carpark where they'd left Jamie's car. It was almost deserted, the winter dusk creeping in early.

"You haven't mentioned your brothers," Mika observed. "Weren't they there?"

"They were." Jamie's eyes drifted thoughtfully out to the water. "I thought they'd take up all this *space*, that I'd go in there and all I'd be able to see was them. But it wasn't like that. I almost didn't notice them at all."

Mika smiled. "Cobwebs?"

He smiled back. "Definitely cobwebs."

"A trip worth taking, then."

Jamie nodded. "I think it helped that I started putting myself back together a long time ago. Ian, Ken, and Lucie get a lot of the credit for that. But I'm glad I came. Maybe some kinds of trauma can't be revisited—and some *need* to be."

He unlocked the car as he spoke and Mika was about to get in her side when he caught her by the elbow, stopping her.

"If you hadn't come with me, I'd have spent the whole drive up here wading neck-deep into the most glass-half-empty thoughts known to humankind," Jamie said wryly, and she laughed at how dramatic yet extremely accurate that description was. "So thank you."

"I'm glad I could help."

He held her gaze for a moment, then went around to the other side of the car and got in.

Mika blew out a breath and followed suit.

She cast her first speed spell once they got out of the city, watching as the ever-present gold dust around her frolicked in pleasure. Magic did so love to be used.

"You do that a lot," Jamie commented, watching her idly twirl gold dust around her fingers. To him, it probably looked like she was moving her fingers around for no reason.

"I've done it since before I can remember," she said. "Magic is a witch's familiar. It likes attention. I've told you before about how it can be mischievous if it doesn't get the attention it wants, but most of the time, it's a loyal friend that tries to help. Like when Ian first reached out to me, I don't think I would have paid him any attention if it hadn't been for the way my power gave me a little nudge. His request *was* very peculiar."

"It was certainly that," Jamie said drily.

"I could have ignored the nudge, of course. Because it *was* just a nudge. It's not like we don't make our own choices. But I didn't ignore it, and here I am."

There was a tiny crease between his eyebrows. "Don't you wonder why your power gave you that nudge? It seems like a weird thing to do, doesn't it? According to the Rules, you're supposed to stay away from other witches, and yet it wanted you to come to us.

What if it's trying to tell you the Rules aren't working? What if it's saying the same thing to other witches? Maybe it wasn't just a co-incidence that you bumped into Hilda back there. I know there are real risks to witches gathering together, but if you ask me, it seems like magic, the force that binds you all together, doesn't *want* you to be alone."

This hit Mika right in the heart. Over the years, when there had been nobody and nothing else, she and magic had always had each other. But what if they both wanted—*needed*—more?

What if that wasn't possible?

"I can't transform the world, Jamie. The world's too big and too messy and too stubborn."

"Who said anything about transforming the world?" He shrugged. "What about just making it a little better? And then a little better? And then a little more, until, one day, maybe long after we're gone, it *has* transformed? You deserve more than what you're allowing yourself to have."

She wrapped her arms around herself, a flimsy bit of protection from the weight of her feelings. "I'm afraid."

"Of what?"

"Of the heartbreak when I fail," she said simply. "Of rejection. Of wanting too much. Of discovering again and again that I'm unlovable. All those nannies came and went, and not one of them loved me. And, thanks to Primrose, not one of them remembers me, either. People are usually like the sea, a constant, unerasable part of something bigger, but I'm more like a single wave that washes over the shore, ebbs away, and doesn't leave a trace behind."

He swallowed, his knuckles almost white on the wheel.

Mika looked away. "I'm afraid I'll never leave a mark on anybody."

It was quiet for so long that Mika wished she could take the too-reckless, too-honest words back, but then she heard him, rough and uneven and so quiet she almost missed it:

"It's a little late for that, I'm afraid."

CHAPTER TWENTY-ONE

Six chocolate bars, three speed spells, and thirty minutes later, they stopped in the woods again. Jamie didn't pretend to understand why the Winter Solstice was more powerful than the days before or after it, but he did know that it mattered to Mika. So when he saw the sign for the woods, he followed it.

"Jamie, we really don't have to—"

"You can either sit here or you can come look for rosehips and chestnuts and whatever else," Jamie said, opening his door. "I'd suggest coming, though, because I wouldn't know a rosehip if it bit me, so I probably shouldn't go alone. Unless you *want* all your potions to become poisons, which is a perfectly reasonable choice no one would blame you for making."

Mika almost fell right out of the car laughing, and gamely followed him off the winding country lane and into the tree line.

They talked as they worked, or at least Mika did most of the talking (about plant lore, why *Northanger Abbey* was a valid contender for Austen's second-best work, and how to brew the perfect cup of tea) while Jamie did most of the listening, which suited him just fine because in spite of the dwindling light and the fact that even his *eyelashes* had gone numb from the cold, he could have stood out here and listened to her all day.

There was a recklessness in him, one that was partly down to the adrenaline of putting his past to rest at last and partly down to the novelty of being out here alone with her in the middle of fuck-off nowhere. And he *knew* it was utterly, catastrophically, fucking foolish, but right then, in that moment, he couldn't bring himself to *care*.

"Do you ever think about going back to Belfast?" Mika asked him, and he was so used to her habit of saying whatever popped into her mind no matter what they'd been talking about before, he didn't even blink.

"Sometimes. I'd like to visit. My father loved it, and I sometimes miss the sound of Irish voices." The space between them had all but vanished, and he was very, very conscious of the fact that they were standing so close, he could see every freckle scattered across her nose. "But I'm not sorry I left. It got me to Nowhere House."

She smiled. "Where you found a family."

"I did."

And now I've found you, his mind added silently. And entirely without his permission.

It was a stupid, reckless thought. He *knew* that this couldn't end well.

Their eyes held a long, *long* moment. There was doubt and hope and *wanting* in her eyes, and it matched his so perfectly, his breath caught.

"Hi," he said quietly.

Her smile broke the little willpower he had left. "Hi."

He could feel himself coming undone, a shattering between the pieces holding him together. He searched the glossy, inky dark of her eyes, watched the golden afternoon light dance on her brown skin.

He took a shaky step forward. One hand tangled in her hair. She closed the rest of the distance between them and he ran his thumb over her lower lip. Her breath hitched. His heart stuttered.

For one moment they were suspended, like they were both bracing themselves for a cataclysmic shift in the ground beneath their feet, and then, in the space of a heartbeat, his mouth was on hers and her palms were flat on his chest and his thumb was on the wild flutter at the base of her throat. They were wild, ravenous, untethered.

She tasted like sea salt and sugar, and lightning, too, if lightning had a taste. The cold wind, the past and the future, the terrible secrets he had been guarding—none of it mattered. Christ, he was drowning, and he didn't ever want to come back to the surface. She was pressed so hard against him that he could feel her heart racing right beside his.

When they broke the kiss, he dropped his head and leaned his forehead in the crook of her neck, breathing hard. One of her hands played with the hair at the back of his neck, sending electricity shuddering across his body with each stroke of his fingers.

"I refuse to have sex in the woods," she said, startling a laugh out of him. "Even *I'm* not magical enough to keep dirt out of places dirt should never be."

He felt something like awe. "How do you do that?"

"Do what?"

"Make me laugh."

"I work *very* hard at it."

"Well, as it happens, I wasn't assuming we *would* have sex."

"You *should* assume that," she said firmly. "You should absolutely, definitely assume that."

"Come here," he said, and kissed her again. By the time he was done, she was trembling, her soft, impossibly warm body pressed right against the hard, aching ridge in his jeans. He was so dizzy with desire and longing that he could barely think straight.

And that, of course, was the moment it began to rain.

Mika looked up at the sky, her shoulders shaking with laughter. "Fucking typical."

The sandpapery rasp of Jamie's own laughter vibrated right through her body, which was frankly incandescent with desire and frustration. She glanced up at the gold dust dancing mischievously in the air around them, like a hundred unhelpful fireflies, and felt, unjustly, that the least it could have done was keep the storm at bay for a *few* more minutes.

"Let's go." His eyes silver with humour, Jamie took her hand. They were both soaked through already.

They had to watch their step on the wet, slippery path, so it was slow going getting back to the car, but Mika didn't usually mind the rain and, in any case, the cold was helping to dampen her very earnest desire to jump Jamie's bones. She did, however, cast her recently perfected keep-warm spell and let it seep from her fingers to his.

"I thought you didn't want me," she said, the end of the statement curling up like a question.

He rolled his eyes. "I don't think there's been a single moment since the day you told me we're all made up of stardust that I haven't wanted you."

Her heart gave an astonished, delighted thump, but she shook her head. "You turned me down in the car just two days ago."

He raised an eyebrow. "When you were delirious with a fever? That time?"

"That is an annoyingly good point."

The sound of their shoes sloshed in the wet undergrowth. Jamie closed his eyes. "God, Ian can never find out about this."

"Can you imagine?" Mika didn't know whether to laugh or cry. "The smugness might kill us on the spot."

The rain had quieted down by the time they got back to the car. Inside, Mika scrabbled in the box of snacks until she found a thermos of hot water and two teabags. She let the bags steep in the water while Jamie got the car back on the road, and then cast her last speed spell of the day.

"Here." She handed him the thermos. "Drink that."

He obeyed and looked down at himself in astonishment as, with each sip, his clothes grew drier and drier until it was as if he'd never been caught in the rain at all.

She grinned and took the thermos so that she could polish off the rest of the tea. "I looked up the weather forecast last night. I thought this particular brew might come in handy."

"You know you're *really* good at what you do, don't you?"

The words, and the wonder in his voice as he said them, found their way deep into Mika's heart and warmed a part of that that even the tea hadn't been able to reach.

"There's this tiny town about fifteen minutes away," Jamie

commented, pointing out the window. They were quite close to Nowhere House now. "The gardens all have flower borders. Every lamppost is decorated with two basket planters overflowing with flowers. There's a red telephone box, which is out of order these days and stuffed with flowers. There's a statue of a horse pulling a cart loaded up with flowers, and the cart's been artistically tipped over so that it looks like the flowers are spilling out. Basically, you can't take a step without tripping over a fucking flower."

Mika laughed. "That sounds like my kind of place."

"Exactly." His voice was more serious now, and she glanced sideways at him, confused and curious about where this was going. "Someone in that town loves flowers the way you love magic. They went all in, and you should, too. You should open that enchanted tea and potion shop."

"It just isn't possible," Mika objected. "I don't know of a single place in the world where I could do that."

Perfectly on cue, the car turned in at a pair of iron gates. The storm had blown over and the air had that wonderful, earthy scent of wet grass and new possibilities. The low, golden sun gleamed over the gables and chimneys of Nowhere House. A sense of complete rightness filled Mika.

"It's not always enough to go looking for the place we belong," Jamie said, his eyes on the house ahead. "Sometimes we need to *make* that place."

CHAPTER TWENTY-TWO

In the days before the Winter Solstice, while Ian and Lucie made shopping lists and bought enough food to feed the entire county, and Jamie and Ken set about the decidedly perilous task of stringing fairy lights all over the tall peaks of the house, Mika squeezed in a few extra lessons with the girls.

While there was no way to tell what effect the stress and nerves of Edward's visit would have on the children's control over their power, Mika knew from experience that the only way to maintain *any* control at all was to practice so much that it became second nature. So she set the girls the task of animating an enormous metal horse Mika and Ian had made out of wire. The sheer size of it made it a good progression from the little wooden dolls and paper swans that the girls had been working on previously; it was the size of a real horse, jointed in about twenty different places, and she asked the girls to work together to make it gallop up and down the pebbled driveway.

So far, the poor horse had been pulled in three different directions, distorting its frame terribly, and Mika had had to magically restore it.

Altamira, who had been in an unusually morose mood before they'd even begun, now abandoned the horse, flopped down on the grass beside Mika, and looked up at the house, which was half-decorated with fairy lights. "Nothing feels wintry and festive this year," she admitted. "Ian forgot to post my letter to Santa. There's no snow. And there are still sunflowers in the back garden!"

"He *has* posted it now, so Santa should still have time to make you a present," Mika assured her. "The lack of snow is a pity, I grant you. As for the sunflowers, they *do* seem very stubborn for a flower that should not be blooming past August." She tugged affectionately on the end of Altamira's light brown braid, and added gently, "I think it's just difficult for us to think about anything but Edward's visit right now, what with it being so close and all. But I promise we'll forget all about it for one day and have a perfect Solstice together. If you're lucky, I may even brew you a cup of *very* special fairy wine."

"Fairy wine?" Altamira squeaked, her hands flying to her mouth. "What's that?"

"You'll have to wait and see, won't you?"

"Oh, I'm *so* excited!"

Rosetta and Terracotta joined them. "Excited about what?" asked Rosetta.

"Mika says she's going to brew us fairy wine on the Solstice!"

"Is it *really* something fairies drink?" Rosetta asked eagerly.

"Is it *really* going to be wine?" was what Terracotta wanted to know, even more eagerly.

Mika bit back a laugh. "Like I told your sister, you'll have to wait to find out. Why aren't you two practicing on the horse?"

"That horse is stubborn," Terracotta said roundly.

"*You're* stubborn," Rosetta corrected her. "We're supposed to be working *together*."

"We always got told *not* to cast spells together, remember?" Terracotta replied. "Before Mika, we never would've even tried."

"Before the three of you, I'd never tried it, either," Mika admitted. "In the Very Secret Society of Witches, we share spells with one another, but we never *cast* them together. The four of us are unusual that way. In fact," she added, as a thought struck her, "one might even say we're *irregular*."

"Irregular?" Altamira repeated.

"Primrose always says I have the most irregular ideas," said Mika. "It occurred to me that maybe it's time to embrace that. We can all be irregular together."

"Maybe we could have our own Very Secret Society of Witches," Rosetta offered.

"Yes!" Altamira cried. "Just for the four of us!"

"The Very Secret Society of *Irregular* Witches," Terracotta said, grinning. "What do you think, Mika?"

"I think it's perfect," said Mika, her heart too full to say anything more.

It was a beautiful moment, but it was also proof of just how badly she'd failed at the one promise she'd made to herself for almost all her adult life: *don't get attached*.

She wanted that promise not to matter anymore because, after all, this place and these people were not like any of the others she'd known before. They knew who she was. They knew her secrets. Here, she was accepted, understood, and even *liked*. So would it really be so bad to get attached? Would it really be so bad to admit to herself that she really fucking loved it here, and she loved these people, and she wanted nothing more than to stay?

But she couldn't stay, could she? This was Lillian's house, and when she came back, she might not want Mika here. And even if she did, even if she decided that Mika's lessons with the children were worth the risk of having another witch living in her house, who was to say that the others would feel the same way? In a month or three months or six, who was to say they wouldn't decide, like everyone else she'd tried to love before, that she was simply not worthy of being loved in return?

These were thoughts that crept in when it was dark, and the sea was too quiet, and she got trapped on the hamster wheel of her own mind. She tried not to think of them in the light of day, but there were some things she couldn't ignore even then.

Some irksome, devastatingly attractive, Jamie-shaped things.

She'd hardly seen him in the days since the woods, and they hadn't been alone once. This could admittedly be a coincidence, but Mika was quite certain he'd deliberately pulled away and had gone back to avoiding her. When they'd got back to the house that day, there had been something like panic in his eyes. Panic, and guilt.

They were adults. If he regretted what had happened in the woods, he could just say as much. So why hadn't he?

Once the mayhem and festivities of the Solstice were done, she decided, she'd ask him.

And it did indeed promise to be full of mayhem and festivities. On the eve of the Solstice there was still so much to do that Mika's mind boggled. There was a winter-themed paper tablecloth for the girls to paint and decorate so that it could adorn the table on the day; they hung up a bird feeder and filled it with a winter feast of nuts and berries; and a large, fluffy spruce was lugged in from the garden and promptly decorated in the ugliest, most ostentatious manner possible. The house and garden were festooned with fairy lights, porcelain ornaments in the shapes of penguins and polar bears, and metal statues of reindeer that lit up when plugged in (or when spelled by a witch, thereby removing the necessity of needing them to be in range of a socket). Ken, having never had the privilege of an enchanted greenhouse before, was over the moon about harvesting all kinds of unseasonal herbs, veggies, and fruit; Jamie cloistered himself in the library to plan a snowflake hunt; and Ian and Lucie's activities in the kitchen led to the entire house smelling wonderfully of apple cider, boozy pudding, a slow-roasting ham, and cinnamon. For her part, Mika helped whoever needed it at any given time, finding it the most natural thing in the world to fit into spaces that seemed to be made for her.

Circe, on the other hand, was most displeased. She was a sweet, placid, lazy creature who loved her routines, her companions, and, above all, her naps. She disapproved strongly of all the noise and activity, and expressed her displeasure by retreating to the relative peace of the library to sulk and demand Jamie's attention.

At the stroke of midnight, the very beginning of the Solstice day, Mika set two different potions bubbling in her cauldrons to make the most of how much stronger each infusion would be on this extra magical day. (One of the potions was the fabled fairy wine, a treat that had by this point reached the proportions of a hallowed myth akin to Excalibur. She did not, of course, tell the girls that the fairy wine was just a sweet, syrupy lavender and stardust tea with added Solstice pizzazz.)

She went to bed, then woke up early to bottle her completed potions and set two new ones going. By the time she got downstairs, she found that despite the early hour, everyone was already awake, the promise of presents being too great to keep the girls in bed a moment past dawn.

But the atmosphere was perilously fraught. Mika walked into what looked like Terracotta and Jamie in a towering row, and it was only when Rosetta edged closer to her and whispered in her ear that she found out what she'd missed: Altamira had, happily, found the jigsaw puzzle she'd been missing for weeks. Terracotta hadn't taken it after all. Unhappily, this discovery had come a smidge too late because Altamira had already placed a basket of rotting fish in Terracotta's bedroom.

To Mika, this sounded like a lot of silliness and tomfoolery, the kind that could be expected from children of the girls' age, but it seemed that Terracotta had then taken it a step too far. Infuriated by the injustice of being accused of something she hadn't done, and by the persistent smell of rotting fish in her bedroom even after the fish had been disposed of, she had dumped a colour-shifting potion on Altamira's head, turning the latter's brown hair a lurid, ghastly shade of green.

Which was how Jamie and Terracotta had come to be arguing in the middle of the festively decorated front room.

"You get a *lot* of leeway, Terracotta, but I draw the line at you hurting someone else on purpose!"

"Pfuee," said Terracotta scornfully. "It's just her *hair*."

"That is not a word, and that is not the point!" Jamie snapped. "Don't ever do anything like that again! Are we understood?"

"No, we're not," said Terracotta, crossing her arms over her chest. "I'm not promising anything."

Jamie, obviously, seemed to feel that such impertinence deserved some kind of clever and quelling retort, but before he could come up with one, he was distracted by the fact that Altamira had wrapped her arms around his waist and was bawling into his jumper.

This proved to be more effective than any cross words; Terracotta's face transformed instantly. "Oh, *no*, don't cry, Altamira! I was just so cross with you because my room smells horrible, but I'm sorry! We can fix it! At least, *Mika* can fix it, can't you, Mika?"

"I can," Mika said at once, crouching down to Altamira's eye level. "Why don't you go wash off the worst of it, and then I'll spell the colour away, okay?"

Once Altamira was gone, Terracotta looked at Jamie out of the corner of her eye and blew out a breath. "I know I shouldn't have done it. I *am* sorry."

"Are you?" Jamie asked shrewdly. "Or are you just saying you are because you think it's what we want to hear?"

"I'm not terribly sorry right this minute," Terracotta admitted, a little sheepishly. "I told her I didn't steal that puzzle, but she wouldn't believe me. But I went too far, and I know I'll be sorry in a little while, so I didn't see any harm in getting a head start on the apology part."

Rosetta tried and failed to stifle a giggle. Even Jamie's mouth twitched. Mika, biting her quivering lip, managed somehow to maintain a straight face. "That's very efficient of you," she choked out. "If nothing else, you've saved so much time."

"Exactly," said Terracotta, pleased.

"Come on," Rosetta said to her, still giggling. "Let's go make sure Altamira's okay."

As the two of them trotted out of the room, it struck Mika that she was alone with Jamie for the first time in days. He looked down at the tearstains on his jumper and gave her a wry look. "It was too much to hope we might have a day without some kind of dramatic upheaval, wasn't it?"

"I'm sorry," Mika said sheepishly. "I've been so determined to teach them that magic can be fun that I've obviously neglected the part where I teach them to be responsible with it."

"They're happier than they've been in a long time," Jamie said, his voice low. "Don't be sorry for that."

"Jamie, if you—"

But it was impossible to say anything more because it was at that precise moment that the front door opened and Ian torpedoed in, shouting "Haaaaapppy Solstice!" so loudly, it was doubtful anyone in the county could have failed to hear him.

So Mika left the conversation with Jamie until later, and went upstairs to fix Altamira's hair *and* spell away the stench in Terracotta's bedroom.

And indeed, once these torments were removed from their lives, the girls forgot they were cross with each other and launched themselves wholly into the festivities. Apple cider and fairy wine flowed freely, and Ian presented everyone with striped rainbow sweaters he'd knitted himself (and lest they worry that any of them might outshine him, he assured them, he had elevated his own outfit somewhat by adding a Santa hat to his head).

Gifts were passed around: books, video games, toys for Circe, new wool for Ian specially from The Lost Sheep, and much more. Mika, deeply touched by the lovely potted plants and gorgeous vintage journal she'd been given ("Your spellbook looked like it was running out of pages, so Jamie and I thought you'd like this," Rosetta said shyly), barely had the presence of mind to hand over the jars of tea leaves she'd concocted for each of them, labelled with their names and a silly, whimsically inaccurate list of the ingredients that had gone into them.

Mika watched Jamie, more than a little nervous, and saw the way his mouth kicked up on one side as he read the words beneath his name on his label.

12 of the most attractive scowls
½ tablespoon of sandpapery laughter
the best heart
and a whole lot of stardust

He looked up at her then, and the expression in his eyes took her breath away. Her heart stuttered.

Around them, as everyone else read their own labels, there was a chorus of sniffs, laughter, and even the sound of Lucie noisily blowing her nose. Both moved and embarrassed at having provoked such a response, Mika ducked her head, cheeks glowing warm, and ran her fingers over the old, crisp pages of her new spellbook.

After that, it was time for the snowflake hunt: Jamie had constructed a hundred beautiful, delicate, *unique* snowflakes out of thin craft wood, painted them with iridescent paint in shades of silver, white, and pale blue, and come up with clues to point the intrepid seekers to where they'd been hidden all over the front and back gardens.

As he'd hidden the snowflakes himself, with Lucie's help, Jamie and Lucie felt it was only fair that they sit out the actual hunt. Mika pointed out that their absence made the teams very uneven, so she joined Ian and Ken with the children's blessing, and a happy hour was spent scrambling around the frosty gardens trying in vain to find more snowflakes than the kids did. (No, they didn't try very hard, but Mika couldn't help feeling that finding *eleven* snowflakes compared to the girls' eighty-nine was a tad mortifying.)

Pink-cheeked from the cold and a sense of well-earned triumph, the children rushed inside to lay out the tablecloth they'd painted, and then it was time for Ian's labour of love: a deliciously salted roast ham; mashed potatoes; fries; a crisp salad straight from the greenhouse; roasted parsnips with a honey glaze; a handful of perfect, fluffy Yorkshire puddings; homemade candy canes; and two gooey, dome-shaped cakes with chocolate, sea salt, and, in the one that was only for the adults, a *lot* of brandy.

After all this, a food coma was inevitable, so the rest of the afternoon was spent watching snowy, wintry movies about lost sticks, penguins who befriended lonely boys, and other sweet, soppy stories. Then there were leftovers for dinner, board games late into the evening, and at last, when the girls were pretty much falling asleep on the sofa, bedtime.

Mika and the other adults stayed up a little longer, drinking far too much apple cider and eating an awful lot of boozy pudding, and when it got to the point that it looked like Jamie might go to bed before the others did, Mika decided it was time to take matters into her own hands.

"Can we talk?" she said to him, and made a swift exit from the room before he had an opportunity to refuse.

The instant Mika left the room, Ian was drunkenly, unapologetically ecstatic. He was about to say so when he encountered a steely, grey-eyed glare, at which point he decided it might be best to wait until Jamie had followed Mika out of the room before crowing.

Their trip up north should have led to *something*, but Ian still hadn't recovered from the disappointment of Mika and Jamie coming home and proceeding to say nary a word to each other. It was downright obnoxious of them.

So when Jamie followed Mika out a moment later, Ian had every intention of trailing after them and eavesdropping from a decorous distance, but Ken and Lucie, those long-suffering bastions of good sense, would not let him. Ken even went so far as to threaten to make Ian sleep on the sofa if he persisted (when he *knew* that Ian's back needed the perfectly springy memory foam of their bed!).

It was with a distinctly sulky air, therefore, that Ian sat back down to finish his glass of cider, resigning himself to the agonies of ignorance until the morning.

CHAPTER TWENTY-THREE

Jamie was only a step behind Mika as she walked out into the garden, to the back gate, past the sunflowers, and out on the dunes. He followed, about to protest that it was almost pitch-black out here and one of them would break an ankle, but then she waved a hand in the air and a thousand soft, glowing, firefly-like lights lit the way.

He knew what was coming. When he'd pulled away after the woods, hating himself for it but certain he'd hate himself more if he didn't, he'd seen her confusion and hurt. She'd hidden it well, but he knew her, knew the widening and narrowing of her inky eyes and the way she held her body depending on how she was feeling.

When she stopped at last, they were on the pebbly beach. The artificial fireflies hovered around their heads, making her face flicker golden, the way it did when she was sitting in front of the firelight in the front room of the house.

He broke the silence, his voice only a fraction louder than the crash of the waves. "Well?"

"Something's bothering you," she said.

He hadn't expected her to start *there*. He recalibrated, clenching his fists at his sides because the temptation to touch her was almost irresistible. "Edward will be here in just a few days."

She looked unimpressed. "It's more than that. It's something else. You weren't pretending to want me in the woods, but you've gone out of your way to avoid me since then. If you don't want to repeat what happened, just tell me and I'll drop it."

If she only knew.

Jamie was fighting against a pull that felt like a force of nature. It *hurt* to fight it. He tried to memorize every detail of her standing there, haloed in fireflies and winter starlight, the cold sea wind whipping her hair across her face, where strands of it caught on a mouth he wanted to kiss. He swallowed. God, she was so fucking beautiful.

He took a shaky breath. "It wouldn't work, you and me."

Her eyebrows drew together. "Why not?"

"You don't do serious." He looked out at the sea, impossibly dark and endless. "And I don't think I can do anything *but* serious. Not with you."

Her smile was gone. He saw her throat work. "You know who I am," she said. "You know the truth about me. All my usual reasons don't hold up with you."

"Except I think you'll find new reasons," Jamie said quietly. "You've never been enough for anyone before, so I don't think you're going to believe that you're enough for me. As soon as I do something to hurt you, and I *will* hurt you because you don't know the half of how fucked up our lives are, you'll leave."

"Is that it, then?" Her dark, inky eyes were glossy with tears.

"Trust doesn't come easily to either of us, so we're not even going to try?"

"There are things you don't know—"

"Then tell me."

"I *can't*."

"Because it's not just about you," she guessed, her eyes searching his. "Because you're protecting someone, or something."

"I'm protecting *everything*."

For a moment, she said nothing. Then, very quietly: "Okay. I won't ask again."

She stepped around him and started to walk back to the dunes, her shoulders too straight, her hands tucked under each arm, her light all but extinguished.

He understood what it must have cost her to accept his poor explanation, to be pretty much told outright that she was once again on the outside, to see once and for all that she was *not* one of them and would never be, and it occurred to him, watching her walk away, that none of this was worth it if it meant doing that to her.

She had never been loved. No one had ever chosen her.

But Jamie could choose her now.

He could give her this, even if it meant he never saw her again.

"Wait."

Mika stopped, but she didn't turn around.

"We lied to you," he said.

And then he told her everything.

CHAPTER TWENTY-FOUR

Mika strode up the dunes. Somewhere inside her, there was a dark and hollow dread, and an impossibly deep sea of anguish, but they were buried so deep that she hoped they'd never find their way out.

She marched past the heather and sea holly, the glow of a thousand firefly-like lights lighting her way. By the time she entered the garden gates, the stars were ablaze in the wintry sky and the peculiar, persistent sunflowers were glowing so brightly, they looked like they were on fire.

There was a swan on the koi pond. This wasn't terribly unusual because wild ducks and swans had been drawn to the pond before (and had always, in the polite way of wild things with a good understanding of magic, left the koi alone), but the still, silent, ghost-white shape did nothing to keep Mika's dread away. Behind her, the sea whooshed, a lullaby that steadied her as she approached the patch of sunflowers.

She held her hands up, palms out, like she was holding an invisible ball in front of her. What she was *actually* holding was the magic around the sunflowers, and she threaded it around the stems and petals and roots of the flowers until she had control of them. Slowly, the entire patch of sunflowers lifted out of the ground, along with two feet of rich, dark soil, and Mika gently brought the patch to rest on the grass nearby. The sunflowers dimmed as the gold dust left them and curled around her wrists and waist instead.

Mika cast a new levitation spell, this time on the object at the bottom of the long, dark hole she'd unearthed. Something pale rose into the air.

So it was true.

Mika lowered the pale thing to the grass at her feet and immediately drew her hands back to tuck them in the warmth under her arms. The glow of gold dust and fireflies hovered around her, making it impossible for her *not* to see the pale thing for what it was.

It was a skeleton, white and pristine, wrapped in the remains of a soft, striped wool blanket that Mika was almost certain Ian had knitted. A skull, a spine, a femur, toes. Bones. There was no stink of decay and no suggestion of rot, just the damp, earthy scent of soil and rain.

It was almost funny. She, with all her irregular ideas, had never once suspected *this*. Honestly, all this needed now was an old locket, and it would be the perfect Gothic tale of—

Ah. There it was.

Around the neck of the skeleton was a tarnished silver locket with an engraved letter *L*.

She'd had to see it for herself. It wasn't that she hadn't believed Jamie when he'd told her, exactly, but some things you just have to see with your own eyes. And he'd been telling her the truth, for once: here in front of her, retrieved from where she'd been buried and hidden beneath the impossibly perfect sunflowers, was all that was left of Lillian Nowhere.

Mika had been here for weeks, and there'd been a *corpse* beneath the sunflowers the whole time.

"Where's the rest of her?" Jamie sounded hoarse and haunted, his voice right behind her. He'd followed her up from the shore, quiet, waiting. "She shouldn't be just bones so quickly."

"She's a witch," Mika said numbly. "The earth took her, and gave you the sunflowers in return."

And, just like that, the dread and anguish found her.

She spun on her heel to face him. "When did she die?"

"June," Jamie rasped. "It was the night before she was supposed to leave for South America. She was walking across the kitchen to get a cup of tea and she just *dropped*. She was gone before she hit the floor. It must have been a heart attack, or maybe an aneurysm."

"So Lillian's been dead the whole time I've known you," Mika said, keeping her rage and anguish contained in as low and tight a voice as she could muster. "Do the girls know?"

"No. Just the four of us, and now you."

"Why?"

Jamie looked out across the night, his hands clenched tightly in the pockets of his coat. "For most of the time I've known her, Lillian was very open with us about her will. It was one of the few things she *was* open with us about. She let us see it. It said that when she died, Ken and Lucie would get some money, I'd inherit her house and the rest of her possessions, and the legal guardianship of the girls would go to her sister Peony."

"Peony? This is the sister you mentioned once, the one you've never met?" Mika asked incredulously, something like horror and pity finding space in the middle of all the pain. "She wanted *her* to take them?"

Jamie nodded. "We tried to talk to her about it, but she was adamant that she wanted the girls to have an adult witch in their lives, someone who could protect them if she wasn't around anymore."

"Someone to cast wards," said Mika. "Like the wards she cast, the ones that will break in the spring."

"Except the best possible life isn't always the one where you're safest," Jamie said quietly. "You, of all people, know that."

"I do."

"Taking the girls away from the only family they've ever known will do more harm than anything that might happen when the wards break. We tried to tell Lillian that, but she refused to listen." A muscle flickered in his jaw. "The girls are ours and we're theirs. *We're* their family. We can't lose them. But there's absolutely nothing we can do to fight the will. I asked."

"*That's* the real reason you were at the solicitor's office that day in the city? It wasn't about your father's will?"

"I wasn't expecting you to ask me why I was there, so I just said the first thing that came to mind. I'm sorry. But yes, I was there to ask them if there was any way around Lillian's will. There isn't. The only way I'd get guardianship of the girls would be if Lillian's sister refused to take them, and that's too big a gamble."

"So instead of reporting Lillian's death, you buried her."

He nodded. "Honestly, I don't know what we hoped for long-term. That we could somehow hide Lillian's death for a *decade*, until the girls were too old to need a legal guardian? It sounds ridiculous and half-baked, and it *was*. We panicked, and we did the only thing we could think of. We buried her. We needed to buy ourselves time to come up with a better plan."

"And Edward?"

"Edward has the will, so he knows exactly what's in it and has the power to act on it." Jamie's breath fogged white between them. "About a month before Ian sent you that message, Edward rang saying he hadn't been able to get hold of Lillian for months and he was concerned. We tried telling him she was somewhere with no phone service, we said she was busy, we pulled just about every excuse out of a hat, but it didn't fly with him. He sent us a formal letter informing us that he'd be here on the twenty-sixth of December and he expected Lillian to be here, too. If not, he'd report her as missing and us as covering up that fact."

"Okay," Mika said, still bottling every wild, painful feeling up as tightly as possible. "Maybe I'm wholly lacking in moral fibre, but I actually *get* all that. You couldn't let anyone find out Lillian was dead before you figured out a way to keep the girls, and you can't let Edward find out she's dead *now* because you'll lose the girls *and* he'll be able to report you for committing a crime. And you can't let him report her as merely missing, either, because that'll lead to the police pretty much camping out here, which will in turn lead to them most likely finding Lillian's remains and will probably end up exposing the girls' magic to boot."

"That's pretty much it."

"The part I don't get," she said, and her voice cracked as all that bottled anguish threatened to explode, "is me."

"We were out of ideas," Jamie confessed. "Then Ian saw your videos. We'd already been talking about how restricted the girls' lives were and how little they knew about their own power, so the part about needing a tutor was true. But the timing of Ian's message to you was because of Edward. We hoped you'd able to help us. Ian thought that if we could just get you here, then maybe, once we'd gotten to know you and knew we could trust you, we'd tell you the truth. And maybe you'd be able to disguise yourself as Lillian to get Edward to back off."

"Which explains why Ian was so keen to find out if I could glamour myself," Mika remarked rather bitterly, the sense of betrayal almost too much to bear. Had there been an ulterior motive in *every* conversation she'd ever had with these people she'd grown to love?

"Mika—"

"You *did* get to know me." She cut him off. "You got to know me so well that I told you I've been used and manipulated and lied to before, and I told you what that did to me, and at no point, not *once*, did you stop me and admit that you were doing exactly the same thing. Jesus, Jamie. We kissed in the woods, for fuck's sake. Why didn't you tell me any of this before? Why did you keep lying to me?"

Jamie's eyes were stormy with guilt and regret, and it took him a moment to say it.

"Because we couldn't trust you not to tell the other witches."

Ah, there it was. She had put herself at risk by coming here, she had put her whole soul into teaching three wonderful children how to use their power, and she had let every person in this house into her heart—and still, they hadn't trusted her. Nothing she'd done had been enough. *She* hadn't been enough.

It was the obvious explanation for the lies she'd been told, of course, but she'd needed to hear him say it, just as she'd needed to see the bones beneath the sunflowers.

Quietly, feeling almost as if she was in a dream, she returned the bones to the grave in the ground and moved the sunflower patch back into place. Gold threads of magic dug deep into the soil, twining the roots of the flowers back into the earth.

"I'm done," she said, very softly. "You were right. You hurt me, and I'm leaving. You know us both very well."

"Mika, *please*—"

"I can't be here," she said, and added, as an afterthought: "I'll come back on the twenty-sixth, just for Edward's visit."

"Forget about Edward for a minute. Just listen to me—"

But she couldn't listen. She couldn't bear to. So she just kept talking. "I don't know how to glamour myself, but there might be another way to trick Edward into thinking Lillian's still alive and buy you some more time. I'll see what I can come up with. It's the least I can do for the girls. Then I'll get the rest of my stuff and leave for good."

He said nothing more.

"Thank you," she added. "For telling me the truth, even if it's come just a little too late."

When she walked away, he didn't stop her.

She crossed the dark, silent house she'd come to love, past the girls sleeping soundly in their bedrooms, and went up to the attic that had, for so short a time, been the most wonderful home she'd ever had. There, she packed up a random assortment of clothes, the smaller of her two cauldrons, and her potion-making supplies. It was only when something dripped into the cauldron that she noticed she was crying.

She packed one more thing: a silver key, taped to the inside of a copy of *Sense and Sensibility*, Primrose's favourite book.

Then she dried her tears, woke Circe, and they left the house together.

Outside, the night sky was a pale, wintry white, still promising a snowfall that probably wouldn't come. There was a silent figure out by the barn where the cars were parked, and Circe ran to him, whining piteously. It was a sound Mika wanted to echo, a forlorn, distressed cry of confusion and betrayal and anger, but she just quietly put her things into the boot of the Broomstick.

"Tell the girls I'll be back to say a proper goodbye to them on the twenty-sixth." Mika's voice wobbled, but she forced herself to speak. "Circe, it's time to go."

With another heartbreaking whine, Circe left Jamie's side and clambered into the back seat of the car. As soon as Mika shut the door, she pressed her wet nose to the window glass.

Jamie put a hand on the glass, but his eyes were on Mika. He swallowed, his voice cracking. "I'm so sorry. I lied for a lot of reasons, but I never, *ever* wanted to hurt you."

In the pale half-light of the Solstice night, Mika had the fleeting impression that his eyes were shining like diamonds, unshed tears refracting the light.

She got in the Broomstick, and left.

CHAPTER TWENTY-FIVE

Mika drove for over three hours. She could have used her speed spell, of course, but she didn't *want* to go any faster. In fact, if it were possible to simply drive the Broomstick forever, she would have done that.

There was only one place she could go. She couldn't go back to Nowhere House. She couldn't go to Primrose, who would ask questions Mika could not and would not answer. She had no one else.

But there was a tall townhouse on a quiet street in the city of York, and she had a key.

It had struck Mika, packing her clothes in the attic, that no matter what she did, she always found herself right back in her childhood, so she might as well use the house it came with. She was thirty-one, but here she was again, just as she'd been as a child, trapped on the hamster wheel of her mind, conducting a postmortem on every memory to find out what, if anything, had been *real*. She had always understood, at the end of the previous postmortems, that the answer was nothing. Nothing had been real. Her caretakers had been paid to look after her, and some had been kind and some merely nice and she had not mattered to any of them. Some had left without hurting her and some had left after Mika had been shunned, used, or lied to. And always, in the end, she had been forgotten.

Over the years, Mika had embraced all the things that made her different and had discovered that she liked herself very much. But what was that worth without human connection? How was it possible to live, truly *live*, without the companionship of other people, without a family formed in any of the thousands of ways families could be formed?

It was a bit like that old philosophical question about a tree falling in the woods, wasn't it? If no one remembered her, and she didn't matter to anyone, did she really exist?

She had been a ghost until Nowhere House, leaving no trace of herself on anybody, but she had thought for a few precious weeks that maybe she had at last come alive. Maybe, like Pinocchio or the Velveteen Rabbit, she had at last been made real.

And now she didn't know. She didn't know *what* had been real. Had those late nights in the attic with Jamie been part of the bigger scheme to save his family? Had every kindness from Ian, Ken, and Lucie been underpinned by probing questions to determine how useful she could be?

So went the hamster wheel, round and round, until she brought the Broomstick to a stop in a tiny driveway in front of the familiar white door of a townhouse.

Circe poked her head between the two front seats and gave the house a long, unimpressed look.

"I know," Mika agreed. "But it's all we've got."

Inside, the house was exactly as it had been the day she'd left for university and never returned. The furniture was old, simple, and spare. The walls were blank, the floors dusty, the corners strung with cobwebs, but Mika could see past all that to the crayon scribbles artfully concealed under a cushion; to the long-faded smudges of a child's face pressed against the window to catch a glimpse of the world outside; to the tiny, walled patch of grass at the back where a little girl had collected daffodils and daisies. She saw echoes of the coats that had once hung from the hook by the front door, tweed coats and puffy coats and waterproofs, and she saw the scratched edge of the kitchen table where that same little girl had once knocked out a wobbly tooth.

It was a house riddled with ghosts.

"Maybe we could live in the Broomstick," Mika said to Circe. "It has the space." Circe snuffled sleepily. "You're right. We need indoor plumbing. I guess we'd better stay, then."

The heating, water, and electricity were all working because Primrose would never dream of letting a house she owned go to *total* ruin, so Mika took down the dusty curtains, stripped off the faded cushion covers, retrieved a set of bedding from the airing cupboard on the landing, and set all of it to wash in the washer-dryer in the kitchen.

She spent the rest of the night hoovering the carpets, scrubbing the surfaces, and spelling away the spiders and dead moths that had taken up residence in the house. She moved the furniture around, put the freshly washed curtains, covers and bedding back in place, and scattered the few books she'd brought with her. By the time she was done, the house didn't look like the one she remembered anymore.

She was so tired by then that she couldn't think straight,

which was exactly the point because the hamster wheel had finally stopped. She stumbled into the shower, had a good, long cry, and fell asleep in the bedroom that had once been hers.

The best way to keep the hamster wheel from turning was to distract herself with a useful, practical task, so Mika allowed the next few days to blend into each other as she focused obsessively on the problem of Edward. She got the food shopping delivered, left the back door open so that Circe could have a run in the walled garden whenever she wanted to, laid out her cauldron and potion-making supplies, checked her spellbook, and brainstormed.

She didn't know the runes for a spell that could glamour her to look like somebody else, assuming such a spell existed in anything but theory, but was it possible to brew a *potion* that could do the same thing? What would she need? What plants and ingredients did she know of that might produce the effect of a very specific illusion?

But with just four days available to her, she didn't think she had the time to concoct a potion as unfamiliar and complicated as that. It was more likely to backfire than not. On the other hand, a simpler potion, one that was less effective than a glamour but far less risky, might work. She could adapt a potion she already had in her arsenal, which would allow her to make the most of the little time she had.

She scribbled on scraps of paper, switching between a dozen open tabs of research on her phone. Maybe she could brew a tea to confuddle the senses and make the drinker more likely to believe a lie?

At no point did it even cross Mika's mind to abandon the

inhabitants of Nowhere House to the consequences of their own choices. She was still too raw to interrogate her complicated feelings for the adults of the house, Jamie in particular, but the way she felt about the girls was not complicated at all. Rosetta, Terracotta, and Altamira deserved the best, most joyful lives possible, and that would only *be* possible if they stayed together, in their home, with the people who loved them so much that they'd literally hidden a corpse in their back garden.

So Mika checked and rechecked her spellbook, studied plant lore, and experimented over her cauldron.

At first, the riddle of the potion kept her wholly in the moment, lost in a dreamworld of tinkling spoons, luminous stardust, and gentle bubbling. She was hyper-focused on the riddle that needed to be solved, so there was no space for anything else.

It didn't last, of course. In the quiet moments, with Circe looking mournfully out of the window, Mika couldn't get away from how much she missed the home she'd had for so brief a time. She missed the gables, the crash of the sea, the salt on the air, the *people*.

How could she possibly miss them this much if none of it was real?

Before she knew it, it was Christmas, a fact she noticed only because the townhouses on either side of her were suddenly reverberating with laughter, clinking cutlery, and carols. Mika, who did her best to be sunshiney every other day of the year, found herself feeling downright *grinchy*. She couldn't help it; Christmas had a way of dialling everything up in intensity. Yes, there was the joy, goodwill, and kindness, but there was also loneliness.

She ignored the festivities on the other sides of the walls and stayed curled up on the sofa, a cup of tea in one hand, Circe at her feet, and the cauldron simmering gently on the kitchen table.

The sound of a knock at the door took her by surprise. Quite certain that it was a well-meaning neighbour coming to drop off a gingerbread cookie their toddler had decorated, which was the only reason anyone had ever knocked on Mika's door on Christmas Day in the past, Mika uncurled herself from the sofa, mustered up a smile, and opened the door.

Oh.

Pine needles and sea salt.

Jamie rocked back on his heels, one side of his mouth lifting in a faint, crooked smile. "Hi."

The sight of him on her doorstep, *this* doorstep, did something funny to her. Her breath caught, and for the space of a heartbeat, she forgot that she was angry, she forgot that she'd been lied to, she forgot that she was in pain. She wanted to throw her arms around his neck and sob. She wanted to lose herself entirely in his lean, solid warmth and rough, sandpapery voice and his stupid, irresistible pine-needle-ness. She wanted to look into his anguished, stormy grey eyes and see something *true*.

So for the space of that beat, as her heart shuddered violently against her ribs, she just imprinted every detail of him on her memory: the tiny white scar at his hairline, the way the dimming afternoon sunlight brought out the blond in his brown hair, the muscle twitching in his angular jaw, the hope and longing in his grey eyes, the way his whole body was braced as if he expected a blow to fall.

Then the heartbeat was over, and she took a deep, shaky breath and remembered.

"I told you I'd be back in time for tomorrow," she said evenly. "You didn't need to come here to convince me."

"That's not why I'm here."

"Then why are you here? No, *how* are you here?" Her brow furrowed. "How could you possibly have known where to find me?"

"You put this address down on the contract you signed for Ian." Jamie's eyes searched her face. "I'm sorry for just turning up out of the blue. I would have called first, but I didn't think you'd answer."

Her heart felt like it was going to burst, and her feelings were all over the fucking place. Circe, with perfect timing, pushed her way past Mika and bounded into Jamie with a joyful bark, giving Mika the opportunity she needed to wrestle her messy, chaotic heart under control.

She turned away, leaving the door open. "I guess you'd better come in."

CHAPTER TWENTY-SIX

M ika put the kettle on, and waited for it to whistle. Around the corner, she could hear Jamie and Circe in the front room, a mixture of low, deep murmurs and joyous barks. She closed her eyes, resting her forehead on the cool surface of the fridge door, fighting the urge to walk back into the other room, burrow into his arms, and hold tight.

By the time the tea was done, she felt like her calmest, coldest mask was in place. She took the cups out to the front room.

"The girls miss you," Jamie said quietly. "We all miss you."

"Did you tell the girls why I left?"

"We told them everything. They're furious with us." He smiled faintly. "Not for lying about Lillian. For taking *you* away from them."

Mika swallowed. She returned to her spot on the sofa, holding her hot, comforting teacup close. "Why are you here, Jamie?"

"I'm leaving a window open."

"Am I supposed to understand what that means?"

He sat down on the opposite end of the sofa, giving her space. He didn't look at her, staring instead at the cup of tea in his hands.

"It means we know we fucked up. We know why you might leave for good. But we wanted you to know that we want you to stay. Not just for now. Always. So we're leaving a window open so that, if you ever want to come home, you'll know you'll always be wanted."

God, he'd only been here ten minutes and she was already about to fall apart. She swallowed, the lump in her throat almost too painful to bear. "The thing is, it would be so easy to forget the lies and the tricks," she said. "Because I know why you did it. You did it for those three children and for the weird, wonderful family you've made together, and that's something I understand. You didn't want a spell to break an ATM. You wanted me to help you save your family. I can forgive that. I *have* forgiven that."

She stopped, her breath shuddering out of her. He waited, knowing she wasn't finished.

"The part I'm struggling with," Mika said, "is the fact that I can never know how much of it was real."

He put his cup down with a thump and turned to face her dead on, his brows knitted. "It was *all* real. Mika. Look at me. The only thing we lied to you about was why we needed your help. Everything else, *everything*, was real. *Is* real. The way we feel about you is real."

A wayward tear escaped, and she dashed it off her cheek. "No, I don't believe that. If you really knew me, if you really trusted me, you would have told me the truth a whole lot sooner. But you didn't. You thought I'd tell the other witches!" Her voice throbbed with anger. "*Why* would you think that? I didn't tell them the girls existed! Why would I tell them this?"

"Because of the wards," Jamie said hoarsely, and understanding struck her like a blow to the chest.

"The day we took Rosetta into the city . . ."

He nodded. "We were going to tell you everything that night. Then you and I talked about the other witches."

"And I said something like, if Lillian wasn't around, it wouldn't be safe for the girls to grow up together without the protection of the wards," Mika finished for him. She sank back against the fluffy throw pillows behind her, suddenly exhausted. "I said you'd need help."

"We were afraid that if you knew Lillian was gone, you'd feel differently about keeping the girls' existence a secret from the Society," Jamie said quietly.

Mika was quiet for a few minutes, the hamster wheel running wild, her tea growing cold in her hands. She put it down.

She wished she hadn't left Nowhere House the way she did. She had a right to be angry that she had been lied to and manipulated, and the sense of betrayal had been viscerally real, but sitting in this house now, this house with all its ghosts and all its monsters under the beds, she knew her abrupt flight had been a kneejerk reaction to the pain. She'd reacted as if it had been just like every other time she had been used and betrayed, but it hadn't, had it? Because nobody at Nowhere House had lied to her or betrayed her for their own gain. They'd done it to save their family. Mightn't she have done the same if she'd had a family to save?

"I only had part of the picture, Jamie," she said at last. "If you'd told me everything, I might have said that I *do* think you need help recasting those wards, but I agree that keeping the girls with you, in their home, is more important. I wouldn't have told them."

"I know that." He shook his head. "I knew weeks ago, but I didn't want to admit it. Because if I admitted it, it would mean you mattered a whole lot more than I ever wanted you to."

"I wish you'd told me the truth sooner," Mika said softly. "You *did* tell me in the end, and that means something, but you were right about me. About the way I run when I'm hurt. I have to. Because everything here, deep inside me, says I should trust and believe that Nowhere House *was* real, but I don't know if I know how. I'm *afraid*."

"I know that, too," Jamie said. He got off the sofa and knelt on the rug in front of her, his hands on her knees. "You're afraid of feeling like this again. You're afraid that if you come back, if you climb through the window we've left open and let yourself *belong*, you won't survive if it's taken away from you."

Mika nodded, tears spilling down her cheeks. "I care far, *far* too much about all of you already, and it makes me *dangerously* happy to be somewhere where I can be myself, but it's also *way* too easy for me to be hurt by you, even if you don't mean to hurt me." The words spilled out of her in a rush. "I should have stayed to talk this through, but I don't know if I can come back for good. I don't know if I can gamble my stupid, fragile heart again."

His voice was very, very low. "Your heart's the strongest fucking thing I've ever known. It makes me want to be braver, and *happier*." His eyes held hers. "Stay. Stay with me."

"Would you still want me if I wasn't a witch?"

Jamie's eyes lit with laughter. "No."

"Christ, you could say nice things *sometimes*, you know."

"No, I couldn't. I want you, Mika. There are a million things that make you *you*, like your laugh, and the fact that you care about Primrose in spite of everything, and the colour of your skin, and the fact that when you decided you needed a mask to fit into the world, you chose one that was sunny instead of scowly like mine. Those are a few things. You know what another one is?" He raised an eyebrow. "The fact that you love magic. You need it like you need to breathe. You wouldn't be *you* if you weren't a witch. And it's *you* I want. All of you."

The room fell quiet. Circe had gone to nap beside the oven in the kitchen because it was the warmest spot in the house, so even her usual sleep snuffling was absent. The clock on the mantelpiece ticked. Mika scrubbed at her wet eyes, her heart full and raw and still desperately afraid.

But also desperately *wanting*.

"We're going to need new cups of tea," Jamie said, giving her space again. He straightened up, took their cold tea out to the kitchen, and flicked the kettle back on.

Mika got off the sofa and went to the fireplace to light it. It was one of those electric ones, with fake brickwork. Mika watched the artificial flames flicker and frolic for a moment, then ran her finger over one brick that was a lot redder and chalkier than the others. She'd gotten red crayon on it when she'd been six or seven years old. She had expected to get in trouble for it because Primrose, who had been here at the time, liked things just *so*. Instead, Primrose had only shrugged and said, "Art is art, poppet.

Show it off with pride. In fact, why don't I help you colour in the rest of that brick?"

She'd forgotten that small kindness, and others like it. Even in this house of ghosts, there was a little bit of light.

"The tea's steeping." Jamie came to stand beside her. "You okay?"

"I think so."

"You know, when I first got to Nowhere House, I was fractured." Firelight flickered in his eyes. "I flinched at the slightest noise. Refused to let anyone touch me. Locked myself in my room. Lillian gave me a home, but it was Ian, Ken, and Lucie who put me back together, piece by piece. It took me a long time to let them in. I was afraid, too; afraid of what it would do to me if I lost them. It's a leap of faith to love people and let yourself be loved. It's closing your eyes, stepping off a ledge into nothing, and trusting that you'll fly rather than fall. I can't step off the ledge for you, Mika. It's something only you can do. And I know you will. It might not be right now, but I know you. Sooner or later, you'll fly."

Mika had no difficulty with the loving part. She loved him, loved all of them, with a ferocity that hurt. She had known that for some time.

But to allow herself to *be* loved? That was so much harder. That required bravery and trust and the vanquishing of the monsters that lived under the bed. Jamie had said, rightly, that he couldn't step off the ledge for her. Only she could do that.

Could she? *Could* she go to the very edge of that ledge and, even knowing there was always a chance that she would fall, still jump?

"What if I can't?" Mika asked out loud, her voice little more than a whisper.

"Then I'll take anything you *can* give me," Jamie replied. He took a step closer. "But just so you know, you can have all of me. If you want it."

"I do want it. I want it more than anything."

He smiled crookedly, but he didn't touch her. Instead, they had their tea, and Mika showed him the potion still simmering in her cauldron and explained her hope that it would confuddle Edward into believing whatever lie they told him, and for a little while, they both let themselves hope that this would work, that after tomorrow they'd never again have to worry about a spiteful solicitor or a pile of bones hidden in the garden.

And for the first time in days, Mika laughed—really, properly laughed—when Jamie told her what the girls had said when they'd told them the truth about Lillian. "I think we expected them to be suitably solemn and respectful about it, but in hindsight, that was an absurd expectation." He paused. "Altamira said we should have buried Lillian in the woods."

"No, I don't think so," Mika said wisely. "Foxes dig things up in the woods, you know. It's a terrible place to hide a corpse."

Jamie gave her a wry look. "Yes, that's exactly what Terracotta said, too."

They opened a bottle of mulled wine, demolished a lemon cheesecake for dinner, and played a drinking game that involved taking a swig out of the wine bottle every time someone next door shouted "Jesus fucking *Christ*, Granddad!"

By the time the night quieted down at last, they were tipsy and Mika was feeling just a *bit* braver, and Circe had wisely taken herself off to the kitchen for the night.

"I'm going to bed," Mika said, pausing at the bottom of the stairs. "You want to come?"

"Fuck, yes."

He kissed the back of her neck halfway up the stairs and caught her as she stumbled. She turned, pressing her mouth to his, and for a few minutes, it looked like they wouldn't even get all the way upstairs.

But they did. Jamie pressed one hand into the door by her head, the other tracing her kiss-swollen mouth with his thumb. She bit his thumb, then licked it. He groaned. She reached up, playing with the edge of his rolled-up sleeves, tracing a finger down the muscles in his forearm.

"Forearms are my ruin," she said dreamily.

He kissed her brow. "You're *my* ruin."

"If you keep saying things like that, we won't make it to the bed."

"I promise to nobly bear that sacrifice."

She laughed and darted under his arm. He pivoted, catching her around her waist, and pressed the length of her back against him. He used his other hand to sweep her hair over her shoulder, the soft, silky strands slipping through his fingers, and then he lowered his head to the back of her bare neck.

They made it as far as the rug on the floor. She pushed him down on his back and sat astride him, her hair curling over one shoulder as she kissed him. Her fingers fumbled with the buttons of his shirt and she rocked against him, needing the friction. His hands clenched on her hips to hold her in place. He broke the kiss and dropped his head back, his breathing ragged.

Mika straightened to pull her dress over her head. She didn't have a bra on. His body jerked and he flipped them, getting her beneath him while he shrugged off his unbuttoned shirt. A groan slipped between his teeth as he hovered over her for a moment, unmoving, just gazing in wonder at every inch of golden, sweat-salty skin she'd uncovered.

She let him look until she grew impatient and bit softly at his mouth. He made a low sound, partly a moan and partly a laugh. "Sorry."

"I don't think you are," she whispered against his mouth.

He kissed his way down her neck, pausing at the wild pulse fluttering at the hollow of her throat, and then his mouth was on her breasts. He nipped and licked and kissed until she was writhing and whimpering and nothing more than *fuck* and *please* and *so fucking good*.

"God, I could watch you coming apart all day." He whispered the words between kisses, his voice low and raspy. "I want to see it again and again and again. I want bruises on my shoulders from your fingers. I want my tongue between your legs. I want to be inside you."

"James Kelly," she whispered. "You're really good at this."

He tore himself away long enough to grin at her, a shy, boyish grin that splintered her heart. She couldn't believe she'd ever thought him scowly, cold, and unreachable. He was the purest alchemy, lead to gold. Each time he looked at her, it was like he was looking at her for the first time, and each time he looked at her like that, she was lost.

She skimmed her hands down the lean, muscled planes of his torso, delighting in the way he shuddered at her touch. It seemed only fair, considering every part of her that he'd touched and kissed had turned electric. "We should probably get on the bed," she said. "You're not in the first blush of youth, you know. You could do your back in if we stay down here."

Eyes twinkling, he licked her nose. Mika curled her fingers around the back of his neck and pulled him back down to her, kissing him until her body softened with heat and his eyes went hazy. He broke the kiss and kissed his way down her neck, then kept going, making her laugh helplessly as he nuzzled her along her ribs. She'd never known sex like this, this absurd, bewildering mixture of lust, mind-boggling pleasure, laughter, and *silliness*, but it was perfect.

He hooked her legs around his waist and scooped her into his arms, and then they were on the bed. He kissed her, one hand between her legs. He swore under his breath. Her hands were on the button of his jeans. "Now," she whimpered, writhing beneath him. "Please."

He kicked off his jeans. His eyes held hers. "Are you sure you want this?"

"I don't know, Jamie," she said solemnly. "You're the one with your hand between my legs. What do *you* think?"

He made a low noise, his fingers still stroking her, and then he pulled his hand away and braced his arms on either side of her head. In one thrust, he was inside her. She bucked at the wild surge of pleasure. He shuddered, pulling out and thrusting in again, his eyes falling closed like he was helpless.

It was too much and not enough and everything.

After, Mika buried her face in his damp neck, breathing in sweat, pine needles, and the ocean. Jamie pressed a kiss to her hair. She yawned, stretching like a cat. He pulled his jeans back on, watching her with such awe and tenderness that she had to look away or else be knocked down by a wave of emotion too powerful to hold at bay.

"Stay."

He climbed back into the bed with her, smiling crookedly, one hand fitted to the curve of her waist. "I'm not going anywhere."

CHAPTER TWENTY-SEVEN

Edward Foxhaven was an ordinary man. From his ordinary height to his ordinary grey hair to the ordinary crows' feet clustered around his ordinary blue eyes, there was nothing at all about Edward that would catch the eye of a passer-by. His suit, tie, and shoes, all expensive and neat and in sensible dark colours, were always worn with a precision that he extended to every other part of his life. He paid as much attention to the position of his cuffs as he did to the small print on a contract.

His one extraordinary quality (the adjective was his, nobody else's) was his meticulous attention to detail. Where some solicitors (and he was not naming names, but one did not need to look further than two of the more undeserving partners of the firm) might simply glance over a brief or pass on some of the more tedious legwork to a subordinate, Edward took pride in the fact that nothing escaped his eye. Some people might complain that his patience and diligence was an excuse to charge his clients more money, but they were mistaken. His clients *wanted* him to be thorough. They *wanted* to pay him a great deal of money. (Apart from, of course, those few impoverished clients he was obliged to work with to fill a firm quota. Irksome, but Edward would dispense with that quota when he was made partner. Which he would, as soon as someone bothered to take notice of the excellence of his work.)

Take Lillian Nowhere, for example. Lillian was a charming, wealthy client who trusted him to look after her affairs and paid him handsomely to do so. Edward had no intention of failing to live up to that trust, especially considering poor Lillian had decided to open her home to a number of highly questionable persons.

When pressed, he had found he couldn't articulate exactly what it was about these people that he questioned. He *knew*, of course, but there were just so many things one wasn't allowed to *say* these days. It was extremely inconvenient.

But while he might not be able to *say* certain things, he could certainly *act* on a very real concern. A wealthy, elderly English woman had fallen mysteriously out of touch and he had no doubt who was to blame. He was, therefore, determined to root out whatever sketchy goings-on were going on at Nowhere House.

It was in this frame of mind that Edward knocked on the front door of the house on the morning of the twenty-sixth and started to question its inhabitants, only to encounter a stumbling, unsteady skeleton wearing a navy pantsuit and a flowery hat.

Everything from *there* proceeded to go well and truly to shit.

By the time Mika and Jamie pulled into the barn, just thirty minutes later, they were too late.

Mika got out of the Broomstick seconds before Jamie got out

of his own car, her sense of glorious, perfect homecoming short-lived. The unfamiliar, expensive car in the driveway was the first sign that something was wrong.

"Edward's here already?" she said to Jamie in an undertone, alarmed. "Wasn't he only supposed to be here this afternoon?"

Jamie's face was grim. "He probably came early to start us off on the back foot. Trust him."

As they approached the house, Mika spotted the girls perched side by side on the fence, entirely preoccupied with staring at the small garden shed where Ken stored his tools. At the sound of their footsteps, they turned. Altamira leapt off the fence at once, shrieking "Mika!" and rushing over to her. Rosetta hung back a bit, looking distressed.

And Terracotta said, "Good, you're here. There's been a *bit* of a situation, but we've fixed it by locking Edward in the garden shed."

Mika and Jamie stood frozen for a moment, then looked at each other, then looked back at the girls.

"You did what?" Jamie said at last, very, very calmly. "And where the hell are Ian, Ken, and Lucie?"

"Inside," said Terracotta. "Panicking. Because of the aforementioned situation. They don't seem impressed with the notion of locking Edward in the shed as a long-term solution."

It was at this precise moment that Mika noticed something out of place. Just outside the front door of the house, lying in a jumbled heap, was what looked like a navy pantsuit, a hat with satin roses on it, and *bones*.

"Jesus fucking Christ," Mika said. "You unburied Lillian, didn't you?"

"Well, yes," said Terracotta. "Now before you get cross, we

know it wasn't our most brilliant idea ever, but neither of you were here and we didn't know what else to do."

"Anything, Terracotta!" Jamie exploded. "You could have done literally *anything* other than unburying the corpse we've been trying to hide!"

Mika squinted at the pile. "Why is she wearing clothes?"

"We didn't unbury her just for *fun*," said Terracotta, offended. Neither Rosetta nor Altamira had said a word so far, both looking a lot more sheepish and a lot less matter-of-fact than their sister. "Edward was horrible. He looked pleased when he got here and there was no sign of Lillian. *Pleased*. He started asking Ian, Ken, and Lucie all kinds of questions and said he knew they'd done something to her. So Rosetta, Altamira, and I went to Lillian's room and got some of her clothes. Then we went into the garden and got all her bones out of the ground. Then we assembled the skeleton, dressed it, and animated it."

"You *animated*—"

"We worked together, Mika!" Altamira told her proudly. "We cast the spell together! Just like you taught us!"

There was absolutely nothing Mika could say to that except: "You did very well, sweetheart."

She meant it, too. She was incredibly proud of them.

She was also slightly horrified.

"I think we got the skeleton wrong," Rosetta admitted. "We put some of the bones in the wrong places. It didn't look right."

"It was a dead woman's skeletal remains wearing her clothes, Rosetta! It was never going to look right!" Jamie pinched the bridge of his nose, his jaw clenched so tightly, Mika was afraid he'd crack his teeth. "What exactly did you think you were going to achieve by parading an animated corpse in front of Edward?"

Terracotta gave him a look like the answer should be obvious. "We thought we might be able to convince him that it was really Lillian."

Mika could see from the expression on Rosetta's face that at no point had *she* thought any such thing was possible, but she was too loyal to say so.

"Terracotta," Mika said firmly, her heart giving a thump of dread. "Does Edward know those bones are real? Does he know Lillian is dead?"

For the first time, Terracotta's bravado cracked. She nodded. "Yes. He knows."

"That's why we locked him in the shed!" Altamira chimed in. "He went bonkers when he saw the skeleton, so Lucie tried to calm him down by explaining the truth. He wouldn't listen. He called us freaks, so we made the skeleton chase him into the shed, took his phone, and locked him in."

"He called you what?" Jamie demanded, furious. "You know, I was going to object to you locking him in a garden shed in the middle of winter, but I'm not sure he doesn't deserve it."

"Deserve it or not, we're not so unkind," Altamira said reproachfully. "We left the big blanket from the tree house with him, the one Mika enchanted with a heating spell."

But Mika was unable to spare a thought for cold sheds and enchanted blankets. She kept repeating Terracotta's words over and over inside her head.

Yes. He knows.

Mika looked at Jamie, whose clenched jaw and ashen face were the only outward signs of the horror and despair he had to be feeling. He'd been so afraid of this, of the moment when the truth would come out and Lillian's will would have to be honoured.

Everything they'd *all* been afraid of had happened.

They were going to lose the children.

"The three of you need to stay right here," Jamie said. "Don't go in the shed. Don't leave this exact patch of grass. Don't do *anything*. We'll be back in a minute."

Mika followed him into the house. As soon as the front door shut behind them, the sound of distressed whispers drifted out from the kitchen. Jamie leaned back against the door, like he couldn't stand on his own two feet anymore, and Mika saw that his hands were unsteady.

"I don't suppose"—his voice cracked—"I don't suppose your confuddling potion can fix this?"

"No," Mika said softly, regretfully. "It was supposed to help us convince him that Lillian's safe and well in South America. It can't undo everything that's just happened." The look on his face was almost too much for her to bear. She reached tentatively for him, and his hands settled on her waist, a whole shudder going through his body. "I'm so sorry."

There was a clatter of footsteps as the others, obviously hearing them, rushed in from the kitchen.

"Mika!" Ian's smile was wobbly and voice was choked. "You came back. Oh, my dear, dear girl."

Lucie burst into tears. "We should never have lied to you! We're so, so sorry!"

"Lucie, no! It's forgotten, honestly. We have bigger things to worry about now!"

Ken and Ian both put their arms around her. "It's so good to see you," Ken whispered. Ian's shoulders shook.

"We should go back outside," Jamie said, his voice hollow. "The kids are waiting."

So they joined the girls and Circe in the garden, the shed casting a long shadow over them. The sun was pale and white, the light cold, and Mika rubbed her arms to keep the cold and heartbreak at bay.

"We need to decide the best way to deal with this," Ken said quietly. "We can't leave Edward in the shed forever."

"I recommend we murder him," said Ian.

"I second that," said Terracotta.

As everyone was quite certain they were at least semiserious, Lucie and Ken had to state in the plainest terms that Edward's murder was not on the table.

Ian huffed. "Then I'll go in there and speak to him."

"Absolutely *not*," said Ken and Jamie at the same time.

"I'll go," said Mika.

"No," said Jamie at once. "Edward's never met you. He has no idea you exist, or that you're involved in any of this. If he sees you, he'll find a way to pin something on you, too. What you *should* do is get in the Broomstick and get the hell away until all this blows over."

"Until which part blows over?" Mika asked sarcastically. "The part where the girls get shipped off to someone named Peony? Or the part where you're all standing up in court accused of murder, witchcraft, and who knows what else? Seriously, why would I go?"

"You should," said Ian, and the others nodded.

Mika glared at them. "You've decided *now* is the time to protect me? Really? Why?"

"Because you've been protecting us since you got here," said Terracotta.

"Because we want you to be safe," said Altamira.

"Because we love you," said Rosetta.

Jamie shrugged at her as if to say, *Yes, that.*

She was *not* going to cry. She was not.

Putting an arm around Rosetta's little shoulders, she said, "I'm not going anywhere. Except into that shed."

"Mika, that might not be wise," said Ken, his brow creased with concern. "He's strong, angry, and likely to lash out in his panic."

"He's not a mythical monster or an angry mob with pitchforks," said Mika. "He's just a man. And considering he just saw a skeleton prancing around in a dead woman's clothes, the very least I can do is spin him a tale that'll stop him from trying to institutionalise the girls."

"Fine," said Jamie curtly. "I'm coming with you, though."

Altamira hugged Mika round the waist. "Be careful. I'm a bit scared of Edward. He was so nice and polite when he first came in the house, and then he got really big and angry and *mean*."

"I promise you, there is no universe in which that man is going to bring any harm to you," Mika said fiercely.

She turned on her heel and crossed the garden to the shed, Jamie just a step behind her. She undid the lock on the door, opened it, and stepped inside.

Mika could see at once why Altamira had found Edward Foxhaven intimidating. He was a tallish, broadish white man in his late forties or so, and he probably would have looked perfectly respectable if it wasn't for the way he swivelled to face them when they walked in, red-faced and sneering. Then there was the fact that the shed was nigh on destroyed, tools flung at the walls, the wood chipped.

Edward's mouth twisted at the sight of Jamie. "There you are. I wondered where you'd got to. Busy hiding a different corpse?" He tossed Mika a brief, dismissive look. "Who's that? The new maid?"

Jamie made a sudden movement, his eyes blazing, but Mika slipped quickly between him and Edward. Around them, clouds of gold dust swirled angrily.

She tried to be understanding. Edward had to be afraid, after all. He'd been accosted by a skeleton, then locked in a shed.

"You probably have a lot of questions," she said gently. "Why don't you come back into the house and we can talk about it properly? Maybe if you understood what's really going on here—"

"I understand perfectly," Edward interrupted her, scoffing. "I've been kidnapped and imprisoned by three mostly feral children. My phone has been taken from me to prevent me from calling for help or reporting any of the crimes I've been witness to. And someone has killed an innocent woman, no doubt for her money. I warned her. I told her none of you could be trusted. What a pity she didn't listen."

"No one *killed* her," Jamie snapped. "It's ridiculously irresponsible to throw around accusations like that."

"Well, it'll be up to the police to determine that one way or another."

"Edward, if you'd just listen—"

"I think not." His eyes sparked spitefully. "*You*, on the other hand, are going to listen because I feel I need to be very, very clear about what's going to happen next. You will release me from this shed. You will return my phone to me. I will call the police. And by the end of the day, ideally, you will all be paying through the nose to get someone like me to defend you from the accusations I am going to rain down on your wicked, unnatural heads."

There was a ringing silence after this speech. Mika could feel Jamie's rage humming through his body behind her. She couldn't move. She couldn't breathe. For a moment, she was rooted in place by the cruelty of the words, the spite in his voice. She was afraid, as she'd always been afraid, of somehow making it worse.

Then the gold dust curled around Mika's ankles like a friendly cat, the dreadful moment passed, and she laughed.

She was done being afraid. She was done letting people like this make her feel small and strange and wrong. She was standing on the cold, damp earth of her own home, and Edward Foxhaven was no match for her.

Mika twitched just a single finger. Slowly, panic wiped the malice from Edward's face. Mika watched, her head tilted with interest, as vines grew out of the dirt below their feet, wrapping around his ankles, coiling around his arms, binding him.

"Absolutely none of those things you just mentioned are going to happen," Mika said, stepping so close to Edward that she could see the size of his terrified, blown pupils. "You're not the only one with power, and in this particular battle, I'll take my chances against you. I'll let the vines swallow you up before I let you hurt any of these people. Do you understand me?"

He nodded, sweat beading on his pale forehead, his muscles jerking against the vines. "What *are* you?"

Mika smiled. "The monster under your bed."

Outside, the door shut and locked once more, Mika released the spell. Inside, the vines would be dropping away, coiling back into the ground.

"You okay?" Jamie asked her quietly. He threaded the fingers of one hand through hers.

Mika was more shaken than she wanted to admit. It wasn't Edward, specifically, but rather the notion that she had no idea how many others like him were out there in the world. She had no doubt that most of the people who had met Edward thought him a perfectly nice man. *Lillian* had. He had never let *her* see the ugly, cruel parts of him.

Danger rarely wore a monstrous face and a wielded a pitch-fork. No, danger came most often in the form of people like Edward, the nice people whose niceness only went so deep, who saved their niceness for people exactly like them, who believed they were more deserving of power and respect than anyone who was a little bit different. And she would never know how many other nice, ordinary people out there were as ugly as Edward underneath.

And yet, even as this thought flashed through her mind, another followed it: Edward was outnumbered. There were people right here with her who were not necessarily nice, but they were all without exception *kind*, which was far more important. They had raised three unusual children with more love than Mika had seen in her entire lifetime. They loved them wholly, without exception. *Because* of everything they were, not *in spite* of some things. It didn't matter to them one bit that Mika and the girls were different. Was it not possible, then, that out there all the Edwards of the world were also outnumbered by all the Jamies, Ians, Kens, and Lucies?

"I *am* okay, actually," she said out loud. "At least, as okay as any of us can be right now."

They went back to the other side of the front garden, to where the others were waiting out of earshot of the shed.

"Did you kill him?" Terracotta asked eagerly.

"Did you turn him into a toad?" Altamira wanted to know.

"No, and no," said Jamie. "But he *is* absolutely petrified of Mika now, so maybe that'll convince him not to say anything about any of this for a little while."

Even if that were to happen, Edward's knowledge would always hover above them like the blade of a guillotine, and they'd never know when it would fall.

"So we're just supposed to let him out?" Ian demanded. "Send him on his way and let the chips fall where they may?"

"Well, we can't actually kill him, Ian, and we can't keep him locked up in there forever, either. And as far as I know, we don't know how to turn back time and make him forget everything he's seen today." Jamie's voice was low, his rage rigidly contained. "So yes, it does seem like the only thing we can do is let him out and send him on his way."

"Or we could give ourselves an hour or two to come up with a way out of this. This is our family, James. We have to fight for it."

Mika stopped listening, stuck once more on the hamster wheel of her thoughts, only this time it was just a few of the words Jamie had said, turning over and over and over.

Turn back time and make him forget everything.

There *was* a way out of this, but it was one that was akin to summoning a gorgon to defeat a gargoyle. The gorgon would certainly defeat the gargoyle, but when the battle was over, who would defeat the gorgon?

"One battle at a time, Mika," she said under her breath.

"What was that?" Ken asked her.

"There's only one way to fix this," she said. "You won't like it, but it's all we've got."

She explained and they listened. They *didn't* like it, and neither did she, but not one person hesitated, either. Better this, better *anything*, than setting Edward loose with all their secrets in his pockets.

So Mika took her phone out of the pocket of her jeans and pressed the green CALL button beside one particular name. And when a voice on the other end answered, she said, "I need your help."

It was like a little girl had once said. Sometimes you had to do whatever was necessary to protect the people you loved.

CHAPTER TWENTY-EIGHT

Mika was sitting cross-legged on her former bed in the attic, plucking absently at the loose threads at the end of her yellow jumper and staring into the middle distance, when Jamie came to find her. He sat down on the edge of the bed, drawing one knee up to nudge hers, and there was so much compassion and so little judgement in his eyes that she leaned on his shoulder and traced distracted lines along his palm.

"Is this a terrible idea?"

"You didn't think so an hour ago," Jamie said reasonably. "You thought this was our only way out of this mess."

"Altamira's very cross with me."

"Speaking from experience, she won't be by the end of the day." He tugged his palm out from under her trailing finger and laced their fingers together. "For what it's worth, I think you did the right thing."

Mika made a face, torn between dread at the thought of what was coming and humour at the absurdity of the situation. "If someone had told me a few weeks ago that I'd turn to Primrose for help—"

"If someone had told *me* a few weeks ago that I wouldn't shudder at the sound of her name—"

They both laughed.

"It's nice to be home," Mika said softly. "I missed this attic."

"Are you willing to share it?"

She smiled. "Only if you bring pink gin."

"As much as you want."

Her phone rang, interrupting the too-brief peace of the moment. "It's her."

"That was quick."

"*She's* where I got my speed spell," Mika said ruefully, and answered the call. "Hi."

"Mika, I'm afraid I cannot find this house you spoke of," came Primrose's crisp, precise voice, sounding slightly aggravated. "The satnav informs me that I'm in the right place, but I see no house."

"Oh, give me a minute and I'll come find you," Mika said. "It's very easy to miss the gates because of the wards."

She hung up and clambered off the bed. Jamie gave her a questioning look. "You want me to go with you?"

"No, I should talk to her alone first. Keep the girls inside as well, okay?"

It took more than a minute for her to get downstairs, put her shoes on, and jog all the way down the drive to the gates, but Mika's phone didn't ring again, so she assumed Primrose had discovered how to be patient in her old age. She stepped out between the gates, looking left and right along the narrow country lane, and spotted Primrose's sleek black car about twenty yards farther down the road, parked on the verge, hazards flashing.

Mika waved to get her attention and stepped aside to let the car pass. Primrose cut the engine the instant she was within the gates, abandoning the car on the drive and getting out with a look of intense curiosity on her face. "These wards are very powerful. Who cast them?"

"I'll get to that part."

Primrose snorted. She inclined her head at the house. "So this is where you've been since you left Brighton. And that story about the class reunion at UEA?"

"Sorry."

"I can't imagine what I've done to make you feel like you have to lie to me," Primrose said, frosty and rigid, like she might be genuinely upset and trying to hide it. "Never mind. What about the unlikely tale you told me over the phone? About three young witches and a solicitor who knows too much?"

"That was all true," said Mika, as they started walking in the direction of the house. "The solicitor's in the garden shed."

"I was under the impression you didn't approve of tampering with memories."

"I'm starting to see that some things aren't quite as black and white as I thought they were."

"Well, I am more than willing to remove all memories of magic from the solicitor's mind. It is, after all, in all of our best interests." Primrose studied the main house up ahead, her eyes tracing the graceful, rustic lines. "Where are these young witches you speak of?"

"They're inside. Out of curiosity," Mika went on, "could *you* re-create these wards if you had to?"

"Not by myself. I could approximate something close, perhaps." Primrose pursed her lips as if it pained her to admit she couldn't do something. "My sister was the one with the talent for protective enchantments. You could have probably benefited from *her* help, were she still alive. Why do you ask? Where's the witch who cast these wards?"

"Well, the thing is, Lillian's dead." Mika grimaced, and failed to notice the way Primrose jerked to a stop like she'd been electrocuted. "There's a lot I'll need to explain that I didn't get into on the phone. These wards will break in the spring. She cast them every year while she was alive."

"Mika," Primrose said urgently, and there was a look on her face that Mika had never seen before. "What did you just say?"

But before Mika could answer her or ask what had made her look suddenly like she might faint, they were interrupted by the sound of the house's front door opening. There was no sign of the children, but Jamie, Ian, Ken, and Lucie came out of the house in a rush, their eyes on Primrose, their faces every bit as ashen as hers.

Mika was bewildered. "What in the—"

And then, a croak from Ian: "Lillian?"

Lillian?

Primrose had gone completely still. "You knew Lillian."

"*You* knew Lillian?" Mika demanded.

"You're *not* Lillian?" Jamie asked.

"Why *would* she be Lillian?" Mika wanted to know. "How could I possibly have gone to fetch Primrose and come back with Lillian?"

"*This* is Primrose?" Lucie asked, wide-eyed.

Christ on a bike, this was downright farcical. What the hell was going on? Why would anyone think—

Mika sucked in a sharp breath. "Oh, God."

Everyone stood frozen as the penny dropped, as the outrageous unfairness of this new reality hit them one by one.

"You told me Lillian's sister's name was Peony!" Mika protested.

"Peony?" Primrose whipped back around to face her. "*My* name was Peony."

Mika was aghast. How had this happened? How had she called Primrose for help, only to summon the one person besides Edward they absolutely did *not* want to find out about Lillian's death?

Ian let out a quiet groan. After a moment, with a sigh, like the weight of the world's grief had suddenly fallen upon her, Primrose reached for the silver chain around her neck. Mika saw now that there was a familiar-looking locket at the end of the necklace, only this one was engraved with the letter *P*.

"Jesus fucking Christ," said *Lucie*, of all people, which was almost as shocking as anything else that had happened today.

Primrose put the locket away. "Lillian was my sister. My twin sister. We were identical. We were born Peony and Lily Smith, but we changed our names when we left our aunt and uncle's home at the age of twenty. We never wanted them to find us, you see."

"Wait," Mika said slowly, conscious of something odd. "You said your sister was dead. You already knew Lillian was dead?"

"We hadn't seen each other in about fifteen years, but I felt it the moment she was gone." Primrose's eyes searched the grounds, tracing the gables and chimneys of the house rather wistfully. "So this was her home. We lived apart after we left home, but it was only in the last thirty years or so that she became secretive about where she was living. We had a difficult relationship."

Mika looked at Jamie and found him looking back at her. There was no blame on his face, but she felt furious with herself anyway. No, there was no way she could have known Primrose had once had a different name, or what that name was, but even so, she couldn't believe what she'd done.

Primrose knew Lillian was dead. Primrose was Lillian's sister, which made her the girls' guardian. And Primrose had very fixed ideas about how young witches should be raised *and* a cast-iron will giving her the authority to do exactly what she wanted with these three particular young witches. The only reason she hadn't turned up to take the girls sooner was because she hadn't known they existed, or where to find them, and Mika had just told her both of those things.

Mika took a breath of cold sea air. One thing at a time. First the gargoyle, then the gorgon.

If only she'd known that the gorgon was a whole lot more powerful than she'd suspected.

"Minerva Hawthorn!" Primrose suddenly exclaimed, and Ian looked startled. "You're Minerva Hawthorn's son! My word, I haven't seen you since you were knee-high."

Ian gave her a weak smile. "I'm afraid I don't remember that."

"No, I suppose you wouldn't." Primrose's eyes drifted back to the house, like she was searching for some trace of Lillian in it. "Was she happy in the end? Lillian?"

Mika saw the others glance at each other. "In her own way, she was," Lucie said cautiously. "She was often away. She was an archaeologist."

Primrose smiled. "No, she wasn't. Or rather, she *was*, but that was just an excuse to get her to places all over the world."

"An excuse?" Jamie's eyebrows drew together. "An excuse for what?"

"My sister and I had a difficult childhood," Primrose explained.

"I'll spare you the worst of it, but in short, our aunt and uncle discovered very early on that we were witches and did their utmost to stamp it out of us. On one memorable occasion, there was an attempted exorcism that almost killed us both. We reacted to this upbringing in vastly different ways. Lillian became reckless while I became cautious and mistrustful. She wanted witches to live out in the open while I wanted the safety of secrecy. That's what she was doing, using the cover of her work as an archaeologist. She was obsessed with the possibility that somewhere out there, there might be a place where witches live openly, without fear, without prejudice. The last time I saw her, fifteen years ago, we had a towering row about it."

There was a pause after this, and Mika felt a surge of pity for the absent Lillian. She had made choices Mika would never understand, but this? *This* she understood.

"Reckless or not, I still can't fathom what she was thinking when she brought three witches here to live together," Primrose went on, sounding genuinely aghast. Mika tensed. "That surge of power Mika took the blame for, was that the children?"

"I *was* the cause," Mika said firmly.

Primrose nodded, frosty and imperious as ever. "Well, we can talk about all that in a bit. First, the solicitor. You need me to extract all of his memories of the events that took place today, correct?"

Mika led Primrose to the garden shed, made sure she had Edward spelled and docile, and then left her to it. She knew, from scattered memories across her childhood, that Primrose's memory magic was delicate, difficult, and took a long time.

While Primrose worked, Mika went into the house to check on the children, who were working on a jigsaw puzzle in Altamira's bedroom (*the* jigsaw puzzle, the one that had caused so much trouble) and pretending they weren't dying to know what was going on outside. Mika told them the truth, briefly. They were more riveted than troubled by the news that Primrose was the mysterious Peony, but Mika suspected that was because they hadn't considered the possibility that they might *actually* be taken from their home and family. They were still certain the grown-ups would fix everything.

By the time she went back outside, armed with a tray laden with cups of sea holly tea for everyone, the sun had dipped below the horizon. Mika put the tray down on a table of knotted vines and sought shelter from the cold beside Jamie, leaning her head into his chest and breathing in the scent of pine needles and the ocean, which never failed to make her feel better. He tightened his arm around her, playing absently with a lock of her hair.

"What will happen when she comes out?" Ken asked quietly.

"We'll decide where we want Edward to wake from the spell, so to speak, and put him there," said Mika. "The driver's seat of his car makes the most sense. Then Primrose will wake him up and he won't remember a single thing he discovered today. In a way, we *do* get to turn back time."

"And start this fiasco all over again," said Ian gloomily.

But Mika suddenly laughed. "No, because when Edward wakes up, he'll see *Primrose*. Who needs a glamour spell when you have an identical twin?"

Some time later, Primrose exited the shed with her usual straight-backed grace, leaving the door open behind her. She looked old and frail, the way she always did after using so much of her power, but she also looked satisfied.

Ian peered into the shed with the liveliest interest, noting that Edward was lying prone on the floor. "Is he dead?"

Primrose gave him a scathing look, like she'd expected better from Minerva Hawthorn's only offspring. "Of course not. He'll have a bit of a headache, but he'll be fine. I have removed all of his memories of today's events. I cannot do anything about the suspicion with which he seems to view you all."

"Well, the thing is," said Mika, "it's in all of our best interests if we remove Edward from our lives for good. And I think there's a way."

Primrose listened to Mika's idea in silence and, by the end, looked almost amused (if it were in fact possible for Primrose to be amused by anything). She waited, sitting on a stool and daintily sipping from her cup of sea holly tea ("This is very nice, poppet. One of yours?"), while Jamie, Lucie, and Ken moved Edward from the shed to the driver's seat of his car.

Primrose stood and moved to stand a few feet away from the car, pinning a charming, if chilly, smile to her face as she woke him up.

Everyone watched, breaths held, as Edward yawned, opened his eyes, and glanced around him as if he was slightly confused by how late in the day it was. He opened the car door and clambered out, adjusting his cuffs.

Then he saw Primrose and his face was an absolute *picture*. "L-Lillian?"

"How are you, Edward?" Primrose said, all grace and poise. "As you can see, I am alive, well, and thoroughly exasperated. While

I commend you for your diligence, I'm afraid you've wasted rather a lot of my time and I don't appreciate being ordered to present myself on your say-so." She sniffed. "Your work has been excellent in the past, so I will not make a formal complaint to your superiors, but let me be plain when I say that I will no longer be requiring your services or that of your firm."

"What? But—"

"I'll send a letter to the firm, of course. And you'll forward all the paperwork to the house, naturally."

Primrose's manner of steamrolling someone was so polite and so utterly unfightable that Mika was not surprised to see even Ian eyeing her with respect bordering on awe.

It didn't take long for her to usher Edward back into his car, press a pair of Ian's snowman-shaped cookies into his hands, and speed him along with a queenly wave.

Even Mika, who had seen Primrose run roughshod over the most formidable of nannies, the most truculent of tutors, and the most opinionated of witches in just such a sweet, merciless way, was impressed.

"We cannot let Lillian linger in limbo forever," Primrose announced, as they watched Edward's car vanish through the gates. "I propose we give it two or three months, and then we'll report that she had an accident abroad. I have a handful of acquaintances in other countries who would be happy to corroborate our story, and if Lillian's remains have to be examined, we can use magic to mask their true age."

"And her will?" asked Jamie, narrowing his eyes. "We can't exactly enact it if we haven't reported her death."

"But we know what it says," said Primrose. "At least, I have a very good idea of what it says and I'm sure there's a copy in the house I can peruse." She patted him gently on the shoulder. "Whether or not we report her death, I am legally responsible for the children in that house."

"You could refuse to be," said Mika. "If you did that, the kids' guardianship will go to Jamie, which is where it should have gone in the first place."

Primrose sighed. "Don't make this difficult, Mika. You know they can't live here together."

But Mika knew no such thing.

The gorgon had fought the gargoyle, but Mika was going to fight the gorgon and, what was more, she was going to win.

CHAPTER TWENTY-NINE

"Let me make something perfectly plain, Primrose," Mika said calmly, even as her body locked up with nerves. "Those kids are staying right here, together, in their home, with their family."

Primrose gave her a look of tired disappointment. "Mika, you know the Rules. That you've been breaking them for weeks is something I have no choice but to overlook at the moment, but you *know* why it's important to keep those children apart. I don't like to do this," she said to the others in a voice that was sincere and almost kind, "and if it would make you feel better, I would of course be happy for one of you to stay with each of the children, but—"

"Like hell we—"

"Primrose, you're not listening to me." Mika cut Ian's explosive outburst off. She took Primrose firmly by the elbow and yanked her some distance away.

Primrose, disapproving of anything so uncouth as *dragging* someone, tightened her lips in annoyance. They were now standing in the shelter of one of the house's gables with a warm, lit window beside them. Fairy lights twinkled above them and the gathering dusk had turned the air even colder. Mika's breath frosted white.

"Don't force me to kick up a fuss and upset those children more than they're already going to be," Primrose said. "I shouldn't have to remind you of how this works. Alone is how—"

"—is how we survive, yes, you've said," said Mika. "I can't say whether that's true or not, but one thing I do know, Primrose, is that alone is not how we *live*."

Primrose's brow wrinkled. She was taken aback, and annoyed about it.

"What would I have done today if I hadn't been able to ask you for help?" Mika went on. "I know you're afraid to maintain anything but the most rigid control over everything, but if you extended the same rules to yourself that you extend to the rest of us, you wouldn't be here right now. I wouldn't even have been able to reach you. How can we possibly exist alone in this world when you know how much we need each other?"

"That is different," said Primrose crisply. "As I've said before, a short meeting like this, or a brief gathering of adult witches in one place, poses very little risk. Three young, untrained witches living *together*, on the other hand, is a disaster and I cannot fathom why you seem unable to see that."

"I do see it," Mika said, laughing as she recalled the last few weeks. "As a matter of fact, I've seen quite a few disasters. I've also had a glimpse into a happier kind of life than anything I've known before."

"I suppose you would argue that that happiness is worth any risk," Primrose said contemptuously, but Mika knew her too well and beneath that contempt, she could hear an old pain.

"Why didn't you raise me yourself?" Mika asked.

This seemed to throw Primrose, who blinked. "I beg your pardon?"

"Why the nannies, and the tutors? All those non-witches, who had to be replaced so often, when you could have simply raised and taught me yourself?" Mika kept her voice gentle, though it was hard because her heart was pounding and she was fiercely, furiously determined to make sure Primrose did *not* get her way. "I know it wasn't because you were afraid of what would happen if two witches of such different ages lived together because I know for a fact that an adult witch is perfectly capable of keeping one child's power in check. So why?"

"Mika, the irrelevance of these questions is beginning to strain my patience," Primrose said icily, but Mika was unmoved.

"You were kind to me," she said. "Not especially *nice*, but kind. Tiny kindnesses that no one would have given a second thought to. When I went back to that house in York, I remembered some of those kindnesses. I also remembered some of the less kind things that happened in that house. Like the caretakers who made me feel small and unworthy. That trauma stuck with me for a long time, Primrose. And I'm wondering now if the reason you kept me at arm's length, if the reason you cling so tightly to control, is because of a trauma of your own." Mika watched as Primrose's face went white. "Your aunt and uncle, I assume? They taught you to believe that you're unlovable? That you'll ruin anything you touch?"

Primrose's angry eyes were ablaze and the air felt heavy with power and electricity, like a thunderstorm was on its way. Mika stood her ground, refusing to break eye contact.

And, for the first time in Mika's lifetime, Primrose looked away first.

"Primrose," Mika said softly. "*Please*. Don't let what they did to you make you afraid to take a chance on something more than the Rules."

"I cannot only consider myself, or you," Primrose said. "I have *all* the witches in our group to watch over. I have to consider all our safety, the consequences to all of us if those children, through no fault of their own, expose our power to the world. Happiness cannot be worth the risk."

"But it is," Mika said passionately. "I know you did what you thought was best, but the way you chose to raise me did far more harm to me than you could have ever done to me yourself. I *know* there are risks when too much power gathers in one place. I *know* it's risky to share who we are with other people and allow them to glimpse our power and trust them with the enormousness of our secret. But I've come to believe—really, *truly* believe—that if we can just be brave enough, we're strong enough to take those risks. We can protect ourselves and each other. We can cast wards and smooth over mistakes. We can grow together instead of apart."

"Romantic twaddle," Primrose muttered under her breath.

"Maybe, but we deserve better than this. All of us." Mika looked at the house beside them, where the fairy lights were warm and welcoming. "I know these kids. They're not just surviving together. They're *thriving*. Don't take that away from them."

"My sister wanted them to be raised by a witch."

Mika smiled. "They will be."

Primrose was quiet for a long, long time, searching Mika's

eyes like she was searching her soul. Mika did not look away. Instead, she reached out and took Primrose's soft, wrinkled hand, holding it tightly.

"I shall need to be kept abreast of any and all developments," Primrose said at last, each syllable crisply enunciated. Her voice hid apprehension and anxiety and other old, complicated feelings that would not be shaken off easily, but she was trying.

Mika let out a trembling breath, but only said, "You could visit and see how things are going for yourself."

At that, Primrose's face softened slightly. "That would be acceptable."

Before Mika could say another word, or turn to tell the others, the front door burst open and three girls tumbled out, closely followed by a dog. Primrose raised delicate eyebrows at the sudden onslaught of noise, which reached its crescendo when Altamira, running up to Jamie and the others, yelled: "Mika did it! Primrose isn't going to try to separate us! She's not so scary after all!"

"They eavesdrop," Mika said sheepishly.

"You told them I was scary?" Primrose demanded, affronted.

"Well, I—"

"Stand aside, Mika," Primrose said. "Let me make the acquaintance of these children, so that they may see for themselves that I am not the terrifying Medusa you have painted me out to be."

Altamira tugged Jamie's sleeve to get his attention. "I thought Medusa was a fish," she whispered, confused.

Mika, who had won her battle and felt both exhausted and exhilarated, practically collapsed into Jamie's arms.

"Thank you," he whispered in her ear, and it was very difficult not to kiss him. (But she didn't, because while she might be a full thirty-one years of age, she would *never* be old enough to allow Primrose to see her kissing someone!)

Primrose and the girls, it turned out, got on like a house on fire. By the time they'd stopped telling her every detail of their lives, night had fallen.

"Oh!" Mika gasped. "It's snowing!"

Her car keys glinting in her hand, Primrose prepared to set off. She allowed the girls to give her a hug, then turned back to Mika. "What about you? Should I expect you to use the house in York?"

"No, you absolutely should *not*," said Terracotta at once, stomping to stand in front of Mika and directing the full and mighty power of her belligerence on Primrose. "You can't have her. She's ours."

Jamie had said it was a leap of faith to love people and to let yourself be loved. It was closing your eyes and stepping off a ledge into nothing and trusting that you'd fly instead of plummet to your tragic and poetic demise.

So Mika stepped off the ledge at last, into nothing, and wouldn't you know it? She flew.

CHAPTER THIRTY

The Very Secret Society of Witches met on the third Thursday
of every third month, but that was just about the only thing
that never changed. They never met in the same place twice; the
last meeting, for instance, had been in Primrose Everly's firelit
drawing-room (yes, she called it a drawing-room), and the one
before that had taken place on a cold, wet pier in the Outer Hebrides. *This* meeting, on the other hand, was on a fine April morning
in a quiet, beautiful corner of Norfolk.

And there were a lot more than twenty-one people in atten-
dance.

It had taken Mika a long time to convince Primrose and Jamie, both quite intractable in their own ways, to consent to what
Primrose had roundly declared a harebrained scheme. Frankly,
Mika was amazed it had only taken a few months to get here,
considering she had been expecting to have to battle the pair of
them on this for *years*.

Of course, the wards had helped. They'd needed to be recast,
and Mika couldn't do it alone, so she'd pointed out that she
needed the other witches here.

For his part, Jamie's objection was not to the idea itself but to the invasion, as he put it, of strangers into the territory he guarded in the most curmudgeonly of ways. "Why can't you do it somewhere else?" had been the refrain. "Cast the wards, then take the kids and *definitely* take Ian, but just, for the love of God, do it somewhere else."

In the end, it had not been Mika's reasoned arguments, impassioned pleas, or shameless sexual favours that had swayed him. "I'll agree to this," Jamie had said, his eyes twinkling wickedly, "if *you* stop making excuses and just open your magical tea and potion shop."

So Mika had (heroically, she felt) overcome her terror of catastrophic failure. She and Ian had converted the barn into a beautiful, whimsical, olde-worldy kind of potion shop, and she had created a website full of artsy pictures of tea leaves and herbs, and Primrose had immediately sent all the witches in the Society the link and address.

Mika had sold all of her first batch in less than a week.

Which meant Jamie had to agree to them hosting the next meeting of the Very Secret Society of Witches, a meeting that, after much arguing with Primrose, would be *quite* unprecedented.

Because *everyone* was invited. Every witch in the Society was welcome, of course, but so was every person who had raised them, grown up with them, or loved them (as long as they were still trusted, and wanted to, of course). Primrose resisted and protested and had an infinite number of very sensible reasons to reject this idea out of hand, but even she was unable to withstand the force of Mika in the full, passionate throes of determination.

So on that spring morning, with a fat, golden sun in the sky, the sea holly in bloom on the dunes, the ocean an endless blue, and bluebells growing wild in the woods, the front garden of Nowhere House had been transformed into something that Ian said was perilously like a *party*.

All the witches had come, of course, and a fair few had accepted Mika's invitation to bring others. Belinda Nkala brought her older brother, a slightly bewildered and bashful Black man in his forties, who came with a lemon cheesecake he'd made himself and which made him an instant favourite; Hilda had brought the two loving Korean aunts who had raised her, her five boisterous cousins, an ill-tempered cat, and her fiancée Kira ("Who is now my *wife*, not my fiancée, and she knows everything!"); and Agatha Jones, to everyone's shock, brought a *boyfriend* who was somehow even more ancient than she was.

It felt like something out of a dream to Mika, standing at the edge of the garden and watching this strange (one might even use the word *irregular*) assortment of people drinking tea, eating cheesecake, and showing off their spells and spellbooks with pride.

Lucie and Ian had taken charge of the buffet table. Circe, deeply suspicious of the ill-tempered cat, was following the creature around as if to make sure no perfidy occurred on her watch. Ken had been deep in conversation with Belinda's brother for half an hour now, the two of them enthusiastically discussing football, and Altamira, rather pleased to find herself much fussed over by so many adults, was solemnly listing every single swear word she knew.

Elsewhere, Rosetta was with Belinda, gazing up at her with a look of total adoration, like she couldn't quite believe she existed. Mika didn't know what it must feel like to be ten years old and to discover the existence of a beautiful Black witch like Belinda—

who had purple streaks in her thick, black coils of hair, a Scottish accent, and a kind, sensible way of dealing with any nonsense— but she imagined it was quite possibly one of the top three experiences of Rosetta's life. Meanwhile, Terracotta was showing off her mastery of the animation spell.

"You've got to come visit me in Wrexham," Sophie Clarke was saying to Hilda and Kira as Mika passed them, her blond curls bouncing enthusiastically. "And you, too, of course, Mika! I *have* to hear more about your librarian!"

"If I can get him to overcome his chronic aversion to social interaction," Mika called back, "you might actually get to meet him!"

But before Mika could make her way indoors to the library where Jamie had cloistered himself, she was waylaid by Primrose, who, a saucer of cheesecake in one hand and a fork in the other, actually seemed to be enjoying herself.

"We *won't* be making a habit of this, of course," she said, because she was Primrose, "but, for what it's worth, dear, you've pulled off something very special."

"I appreciate you saying so," Mika said, absurdly pleased with this compliment. "I know the world won't transform overnight, and I know you still have your doubts, but thank you for trying."

"Hmm," said Primrose, her cheeks pinking slightly as she moved on.

Mika went inside.

Jamie was in an armchair in a corner of the library, behind several bookshelves, obviously hiding lest one of the children try to browbeat him into coming outside. He gave her a wary look as he glanced up from the enormous book sitting open on his lap.

"No," he said.

Mika put the book on the floor with great care and took its place on Jamie's lap. His wary, implacable expression softened and he nuzzled her cheek. "I know you hate people, so I won't pester you to come outside," she said. "I'll just say, once, that I would love it if you did."

"I don't *hate* people!"

"You do," Mika said lovingly. "You have the soul of a cantankerous old man who yells at little kids to get off his lawn."

Jamie obviously felt this was unjust. "Kids are the only people I like!"

"I think it's going well," said Mika, watching his hand idly trace circles on her knee.

"I'm not surprised. It was a good idea, even if a part of me still wishes it was a good idea you'd executed far, far away." He pulled a face. "If nothing else, I refuse to come outside and have Primrose observe me like a specimen beneath her microscope. She does it every single time. I don't think she's completely sure how I feel about you."

"Out of interest, how *do* you feel about me?"

He rolled his eyes. "You know exactly how I feel about you."

"You have to *say* it!" Mika said indignantly. "You read books! You know Swoony Words must be said! Words like *You pierce my soul. I am half agony, half hope.* Or like *My feelings will not be repressed. You must allow me to tell you how ardently I admire and—*"

Jamie looked amused. "Do you know any romantic declarations that weren't written by Jane Austen?"

"Well, they've been on my mind. You can thank Rosetta's Captain Wentworth obsession for that. She's about to move on to Mr. Knightley."

"Is *thank* the right word? Or would *blame* be more appropriate?"

Mika sighed. Truly, this was tragic.

"Oh, well," she said, cheering up. "You're going to be stuck with me for a long, long time. I'll get you to say it sooner or later."

The corner of his mouth lifted in a smile, the smile he only ever gave her, the one that crept slowly into his eyes and lit them up like the sun. Her heart kicked in her chest. She'd never seen him look at anyone the way he looked at her. Who needed words?

She hopped off his lap and left him to his book, but before she reached the door, there was a thump as he closed the book and stood.

"If I loved you less," he said quietly, the words no less true for the laugh that threaded through his voice, *"I might be able to talk about it more."*

Mika spun around, cannoning into his arms. "I love you, too."

"I know you do."

"Does this mean you'll come outside and meet everybody?"

"Reluctantly," said Jamie wryly, "and with tremendous ill grace, but yes. I will."

Mika smiled happily up at him, then leaned up on her toes to kiss him, slow and deep. "I'll make it up to you later."

"I'll hold you to that."

So they went outside together, and Primrose did indeed scrutinize Jamie critically, and Hilda decided they were going to be the best of friends, and Altamira insisted on swinging off his arm, and Mika felt that the day was at last perfectly, wholly complete.

So, for that matter, was she.

Maybe, somewhere out there, there was a witch who would uncover all their secrets, a witch who would build a lasting bridge between witches and non-witches. A witch who would, in short, transform the world. It was a lovely idea, a vision of a golden future, but Mika was content with the knowledge that the witch who conjured it would not be her.

She, Mika Moon, would not be the witch who transformed the world, but she was making it a little better, day by day. She had once believed witches would never have friendship, community, and each other, but here they were. She had once believed she would never have a family, but here they were, too. She, who had once believed she would never leave a mark on anybody, knew now that the marks she had left were unerasable, as much a part of forever as the sea.

And, really, who could ask for more than that?

ACKNOWLEDGMENTS

When I started writing this book, we were eight months into the pandemic and all I wanted to work on was a warm, cozy, romantic story about magic and family. A story that was, above all things, about love and human connection.

And it was love and human connection that got me to the end of a first draft, through edits, and all the way to the moment where the book becomes a *book*. It wouldn't have been possible to write this story alone, so this is where I want to thank some of the wonderful people who contributed to it.

First, to my husband, Steve, who makes it possible for me to write books at all. Thank you for the endless cups of tea, the time and space, the love, and the past thirteen years of relentless cheerleading.

To my agent, Penny Moore, a superstar in every possible way. Thank you for your support, your brilliance, your friendship, and, above all, for looking at my weird, half-baked ideas and saying, "Yes, do it!"

To my editor, Jessica Wade, without whom I shudder to think of what this book might have become! A million thank-yous for your passion, your sharp eye, your incredibly smart ideas, and your guidance every step of the way.

To Katie Anderson and Lisa Perrin, for an absolute *dream* of a cover.

To the rest of the fantastic team at Berkley and Penguin Random House: Miranda Hill, Megan Elmore, Megan Gerrity, Alexis Nixon, Stephanie Felty, Elisha Katz, and Tawanna Sullivan. Thank you all for bringing so much talent to Mika's story.

To the wonderful, extraordinary team at Hodder UK, otherwise known as the Very UnSecret Mika Moon Fan Club: editorial director Molly Powell and assistant editor Natasha Qureshi for your incredible support and enthusiasm; publicity and marketing dream team Kate Keehan and Callie Robertson; and Lydia Blagden, Irene Neyman and Juliette Winter for designing, illustrating and producing such a stunning, magical book. I can't thank you all enough.

To the Berkletes and all the other authors who welcomed me so enthusiastically to the world of writing for adults. And, of course, to the author friends with whom I've shared the ups and downs of publishing over the years.

To my family, kids, and friends, who remind me to stay connected to other people even when I'm buried in deadlines.

And to you, dear reader. Thank you for following Mika to the very end.

The

VERY SECRET SOCIETY

of

IRREGULAR WITCHES

SANGU MANDANNA

QUESTIONS FOR DISCUSSION

1. What three words would you use to describe Mika as a character? What made her an engaging heroine?

2. Prior to coming to Nowhere House, Mika lived a lifestyle that meant she never stayed in one place long. Why do you think she chose to live her life like that, and how do you think that changes over the course of the book?

3. Mika and Jamie have very different personalities but find themselves drawn to each other. Why do you think that is? What parts of their personalities would complicate or complement each other in a relationship?

4. After meeting his mother and brothers again, Jamie states that "some kinds of trauma can't be revisited—and some *need* to be." What do you think he means by this, and how does this impact Mika's own journey in the novel?

5. Edward and Primrose are both viewed as antagonists. How do you think they differ from each other, and how do these differences affect the way Mika deals with them?

6. Did the plot twists in the book surprise you? Why or why not?

7. If you had the opportunity to adapt the novel into a film or TV show, who would your ideal cast be?